BLOODBATH

BLOODBATH

A Novel

Ray Rao

Book Cover Design by Anna Fong
Interior Layout by Derek Vasconi
Printed in the United States of America

ACKNOWLEDGMENT

I would like to acknowledge all the people who have helped make Bloodbath a reality.

First is my editor, Derek Vasconi, of Sakura Publishing, whose skill and commitment have made the words of a first-time author look so good. Derek, in particular, taught me that it isn't just about having a great story and knowing how and what to write. It means knowing what *not* to write—details I thought were integral to the story but were clearly getting in its way. He earned my trust by becoming so vested in Bloodbath that he has come to know the story and characters (almost) as well as I do.

Along with him is my Senior Graphic Designer, Anna Wong, whose craft and creativity are behind the spectacular cover design.

I must also thank Girish Chavan for introducing me to Derek. He and his wife, Ketaki Desai, emboldened me to publish a story I wrote for a lark, never imagining it would actually see the light of day as a book. Nor did I imagine I might actually experience something that underpins Bloodbath—that it is possible to share a deep filial affection without participating in upbringing. Or be viewed as a parent without sharing genes!

Most of all, I want to thank my wife, Kanchan, and two daughters, Divya and Anjali. They are my three biggest cheerleaders. Writing a book while pursuing a full-time academic career as a physician has been a challenge—maybe much more so for Kanchan than me! To write without jeopardizing the precious bonds of family has meant many late nights and weekend evenings in seclusion. It is a measure of Kanchan's strength and love that her commitment to me and my writing never flagged.

As for my daughters, they not only taught me what it means to be a father, they, along with their mother, helped me meet the biggest challenge any man can face: trying to realistically portray a woman's thoughts and feelings. Their insights, and their patience in dealing with my cluelessness in trying to figure it all out, are the reason so much of Bloodbath, to my mind, feels authentic.

Lastly, I must acknowledge the late Peter O'Donnell, creator of Modesty Blaise, for taking time to read an early draft version of Bloodbath that I sent to him unsolicited. His compliment of "you have a talent for writing" has stayed with me. In updating and contemporizing Bloodbath to its current form, I have attempted to live up to his fulsome praise.

DEDICATION

To my wife and two daughters.
Three wonderful women who make my life.
They are strong yet gentle. Smart yet modest.
Resilient yet unyielding in adversity.
And beautiful—inside even more than out.
They are my template for Alexis.

CONTENTS

PROLOGUE

BLOOD SACRIFICE

They brought the girl to the temple at the stroke of midnight. Even in the gloom, it was clear she was little more than a child. Only in her pubescent breasts was there any hint of the first buds of a womanhood waiting to flower. She seemed completely oblivious of her surroundings, as if the world around her had ceased to make sense, making no effort to shield her nakedness from the watchers assembled in the temple. Her arms dangled at different angles, like a helpless marionette, because of the height difference of the two men holding her by the shoulders—one a veritable giant, almost seven feet tall, the other squat and bull-necked, like a gorilla. She whimpered as they dragged her across the courtyard, her rubbery feet leaving smears of blood on the rough-hewn stone.

A sob escaped her lips as they dumped her on an altar set in front of the inner sanctum. The uneven surface ground into her scrawny buttocks, and she cringed, but her captors neither noticed nor cared. A sharp blow to her chest sent her sprawling, eliciting another barely audible cry. After that, she lay with her eyes closed while they shackled her limbs to four iron rings sunk into the corners of the altar. She had been living this obscene moment for a week, and she was past all caring now, waiting only for the release that death would bring.

A groan pierced the silence, jolting the girl out of her stupor. She turned her head towards the temple sanctum a few feet from her. The doors guarding its entrance swung open to reveal the figure of a man silhouetted in the doorway. He was naked except for a loincloth, and so short and slightly built that he appeared to be no more than a boy. His head was down, and he was holding aloft a sickle of burnished gold.

Backlit by the dancing flames of dozens of oil lamps burning inside the sanctum, he cast a shadow that pranced at his feet like some ghoul from Hell. The girl stared at the apparition on the ground, transfixed. Then the man moved, and the shadow went into a manic frenzy. Seeing it lurch towards her, she mewled like a kitten in agony.

The apparition never reached her. At the last instant, it vanished, subsumed under the feet of the man as he stepped over the threshold.

The interior of the sanctum was now visible through the open doorway behind him. In the center stood a towering idol made from black marble. The form was human, with feminine contours, but the face was hideous, with large eyes and a blood-red tongue protruding from its mouth all the way down its chest. A garland of human skulls stood out against its bare-breasted torso. It had four arms, one brandishing a broad-bladed scimitar, another wielding a trident, and a third holding a loop of cord. From the fourth, a severed head dangled by its hair.

The girl fainted.

Mercifully, she neither heard the bestial scream that rent the air, nor felt the sickle slice through her neck. Blood gushed over the hands of her executioner as he crouched over her body for several minutes, mouthing forbidden Sanskrit mantras. It poured over the edges of the altar into a gutter skirting its base to run down a channel leading to the sanctum, and wash over the feet of the idol.

PART ONE

FIRST BLOOD

CHAPTER 1

Fear hit Jason Wolff like an ice-cold hammer in the gut when the door opened. He knew he was in trouble.

Everything had been following a well-rehearsed script, familiar to anyone who entered the corrupt back-alleys of bureaucratic India. The script involved a stranded *firangi*—a white-skinned foreigner—desperate for a ticket on a sold-out train, an off-duty railway clerk with a whispered offer of help, and a stroll through bustling alleyways of the old walled city of Delhi to meet a man who could make the impossible happen. The script should have ended with an exchange of money, the discovery of an open seat, and smiles all around.

He could forget that ending. The script was in tatters.

Jason hesitated in the doorway, sweaty hands balling into fists. Then, two years of reclusive peace fell away like a shed skin. He was, once again, Major Jason Wolff of the Alpha Tau Brigade, the elite anti-terrorist commando unit in the South African Defence Forces. He relaxed, and his combat instinct sprang back to life, sending him into threat-assessment mode.

There were three men in the windowless room, not counting the scrawny Indian Railways clerk accompanying him—a non-combatant, safely disregarded.

One seated at a desk at the far end, so slightly built that only his head and shoulders were showing. His eyes, glittering like a cobra's just before it strikes, screamed "Boss-man"! Too deadly to disregard, but another non-combatant.

Two others standing on either side behind him. The lethal weapons!

3

On the left, a Gurkha. Head shaved clean as a billiard ball. Built like a gorilla, with immense shoulders and a squat torso perched on legs resembling tree-trunks. Hanging at his left hip, a sheathed *kukri*, the machete-like weapon of his race.

On the right, a bearded Sikh, wearing a turban. A full head taller than Jason. Unarmed. But hands like blunt axes!

With every detail fed into the combat computer in his brain, Jason sauntered up to the desk with a disarming smile. Dropping his backpack on the floor, he said, "I hope you can get me a ticket to Dehra Dun tonight, Sir."

The reply was devoid of all emotion. "You ask for the impossible. That train is sold out."

"But miracles are routine in India, aren't they?" Jason said. "That's why I'm here."

"Miracles, as you say, are routine. What you want is a fantasy."

His impeccable Indian 'public school' accent and mastery of English idiom were startling, but they were reassuring. "Fantasies can become reality in India, even for a firangi like me, with the help of the right magic from someone like you."

"That depends, Mr...?"

"Wolff. Jason Wolff."

"It depends on the price you are willing to pay for—what did you call it?—my magic, Mr. Wolff."

Jason was pleased to negotiate. "Name your price, Sir."

The Indian stared at him for a couple of seconds, then his thin lips twitched into a wintry smile. "Everything you have—passport, wallet, and backpack—in return for safe conduct out of this room. With your ticket, of course."

The clerk behind him sniggered. Jason knew the Indian was playing some sick game of cat-and-mouse. A feathery hand

4

caressed his spine, triggering a spurt of adrenaline that sent his combat instinct into overdrive. He knew he stood no chance in a direct confrontation—not with both bodyguards poised on a hair trigger. So...!

"What...what the hell do you mean? It's...that's criminal! I'm going straight to the police!" Jason spluttered.

The Indian's voice remained soft. "By rejecting my first offer you have only one option. Agree now and you can leave with only half the bones in your body broken." He held up his hand to forestall Jason's retort and continued. "Think carefully before you speak, Mr. Wolff. My next offer will be even less generous."

Jason pretended to bluster. "How dare you threaten me, you little creep!"

The Indian slammed his hand down on the desk and hissed, "You will not live to regret that remark, you white-skinned ape."

Without taking his eyes off Jason, he said in Hindi, "Jarnail! I have always wanted to hear the squeal of a white pig being slaughtered. Make this firangi pig squeal for me by breaking every bone in his body. Then break his neck."

Jason understood Hindi. He saw the Sikh nod.

Allowing his shoulders to slump, he begged, "I am very sorry for insulting you, Sir. Take my backpack. Even my passport and wallet. Just don't hurt me."

He let his knees and hips buckle, as if from terror, and placed the palm of his left hand flat on the desk for support. With the other, he pulled out his wallet from his hip pocket and thrust it forward, pleading "Take all my money! Just don't hurt me, I beg you, please."

Seeing their eyes drawn to the wallet, he exploded into action.

Using his planted left hand as the pivot, he catapulted up and over the desk into a side-on vault, like a gymnast mounting a pommel-horse. As he came across, he lashed his legs into a two-footed leaping side-kick that struck the Sikh in the throat. At the same time, his clenched right fist hit the Gurkha under his nose, with the knuckle of the middle finger protruding.

The twin strikes, powered by two hundred pounds of airborne momentum, were devastating. His steel-capped boots smashed into the Sikh's throat and jaw, lifting the giant off his feet and hurling him backwards. The *ippon-ken* fist-strike, delivered with a corkscrew twist, shattered the Gurkha's facial bones. He went down, arms flung outwards like a rag doll.

Jason arched his body over the seated man to land behind the chair, perfectly balanced on his feet. Before the man could get up, Jason's right elbow stabbed down into the root of his neck in a paralyzing *empi* strike to the brachial nerve plexus, pinning him to the chair. In the same instant, he whipped his forearm across the man's throat to grip the crook of the striking elbow, while his right hand snaked around the back of the man's head and forced it down.

It was an unscripted combination of vital-point strike, choke hold, and head lock that paralyzed the victim's right arm and rendered him helpless.

"If you make a sound," Jason whispered in English, "the last thing you'll hear is the snap of your scrawny neck, you vicious little bastard. Do you understand?"

Jason saw a frantic wiggle of the left hand, and shifted his attention to the clerk. "Lie down on your stomach with your arms and legs spread out, or your boss dies."

The clerk obeyed. Jason released his hold and delivered a *shuto* strike below and behind the seated man's ear. Jason left him slumped over the desk and walked over to kneel down beside the clerk. "I'm not going to kill you, understand? Don't struggle."

The terrified clerk nodded. Jason felt for the carotid pulses in his neck and squeezed down. He went limp in seconds.

Jason maintained the sleeper hold long enough to ensure the clerk remained unconscious for a while. Then, he took a deep breath and went to check on the bodyguards.

Both were out cold. The Sikh's jaw was broken and there was an ominous rattle in his throat with each breath. The Gurkha had his face stove in, and nose and upper lip mangled into pulp. But neither appeared in danger of dying, other than from drowning in their own blood, so Jason left them lying face down.

He took another deep breath as he tried to make sense of what just happened. Graft was integral to life in India, even for a firangi like him. Why had this transaction deteriorated into lethal extortion? He knew none of the four men, and no idea who or what he was facing—the scrawny man's papers identified him as an Indian Railways reservation clerk Karim Chand, but none of the other three carried IDs.

One thing was certain, though. The cobra-eyed psychopath must be a very powerful underworld don to operate with such impunity in Delhi. Which left Jason in a very precarious situation, in a derelict building in the old walled-city of Delhi, a place where no firangi ever dared venture alone. Without the clerk to accompany him, he had no hope of getting back to the station without someone accosting him or alerting the police. Then the corrupt Indian judicial system would deliver him into the hands of the very forces he was trying to elude.

As he grappled with the problem of getting away, his roving gaze fell on the Sikh. And inspiration struck!

His shoulders shaking with silent laughter, he stripped all four men of their clothes, leaving them completely naked. He set aside the Sikh's garments, and tore the rest into strips, which he used to tie all four men and gag the two who weren't injured.

Next, he dressed himself in the Sikh's *kudtha-pajama*, the traditional garb of the North Indian male, consisting of a loose-fitting knee-length shirt and shapeless trousers. He rolled up the sleeves of the kudtha, tucked the pajama up under the drawstring, and tied the Sikh's turban around his own head in a different style, learned from an expatriate *Pathan* from Pakistan. With his build, fair skin, and light brown eyes, he could pass for a Pathan himself. Or so he hoped.

He stuffed his own clothes and the kukri into his backpack and walked out, shutting the door behind him. No one cast a second glance at him as he made his way back to the railway station.

CHAPTER 2

Tears of rage and shame filled Karim Chand's eyes.

This day began with such hope.

The man he worshipped had dropped in to inspect this tiny outpost of his far-flung empire. He did not ask for much, just a little fun, and Karim Chand was delighted to oblige, recognizing an opportunity to catch the eye of the don of dons in the Indian underworld. With the Sikh and Gurkha there to provide muscle, it should have been a cakewalk. Instead, that deceitful firangi devil had inflicted a devastating defeat on two men Karim Chand thought invincible.

He craned his neck to look at them. Both lay on their stomachs, bleeding from the mouth. A horrific bruise covered the Sikh's swollen jaw, face and neck, and his throat rattled with each breath. The Gurkha's features were totally mangled.

The sour taste of vomit flooded his mouth. He almost choked on it behind the gag, but he didn't care. He would rather die than witness his master's degradation when help arrived and he was found naked and helpless. The public humiliation would destroy his master's dread aura and emasculate him forever.

Karim Chand knew he was responsible. He wanted to die—!

Suddenly, a light shone in his brain, and he saw what he must do. It would cost him his job, and he'd never be able to show his face in this part of town—the *mohalla* where he'd lived all his life. It would mean his social death, but what did that matter, as long as it preserved the dignity and power of the man he worshipped?

He put every ounce of strength into a violent effort to break free, and felt a flash of searing pain unlike anything he ever felt as

9

the skin on his wrists ripped open like tissue paper. He screamed into the gag, feeling something warm and sticky on his palms.

Sobbing in pain, Karim Chand bit down on the gag and thought only about preserving his master's dignity. He began to twist and untwist his hands again, and again, and again.

* * * * * * * * * * *

Getting away was the easy part, thought Jason, as he made his way back to the train station. *Staying alive is going to be the challenge.*

He knew that the man with the cobra eyes would come after him with a single-minded obsession, verging on the psychotic. The man would find him too—a firangi would leave a trail wide enough for the blind to follow. To stay alive, he had to obliterate that trail.

Going to Dehra Dun was out. Fortunately, it wasn't the only way to get to his destination, a remote ashram, hundred miles north of Dehra Dun. An alternative was to go to Shimla, instead, and cut east on foot through the hilly terrain of the Shivalik range. In that vast hinterland, he would simply disappear.

The problem was getting to Shimla without being noticed. His disguise might work for a casual glance from a passerby, but not for an interaction with a ticket clerk at the station. The clerk would remember Jason and his destination, so the gang would have no trouble finding him.

He exited the inner-city bazaar, still preoccupied with his dilemma, and stepped off the curb to cross the main road without looking. And the solution almost ran smack into him!

Jason leapt back just in time to avoid being run over by a bus headed for the 'Inter State Bus Terminus'. As it lumbered past, he jumped on the running board and bought a ticket from the surprised conductor before sitting down.

Bloodbath

It was 8 p.m. An overnight bus would get him to Shimla by morning. Problem solved.

He was just beginning to relax when, without warning, he felt as if he was suffocating, and he knew that Alexis was having one of her night terrors.

CHAPTER 3

Alexis is dreaming. It is a very familiar dream. And it begins so happily.

She is waving goodbye to her parents at the farm where she grew up in South Africa. She's leaving for America, and will go trekking across the veldt one last time with Gabe, the wily little bushman who's been childhood companion, guide, and teacher to her and Jason.

Just like old times. Except Jay isn't around. Why? Doesn't he always come along?

Of course! He's a commando now. Can't waste time on frivolous things like reliving childhood memories with his twin sister.

That's okay. She likes being with Gabe. She always learns something new from him.

The dreamscape shifts abruptly, like a kaleidoscope.

She is sleeping on the veldt, and a familiar voice is calling to her with desperate urgency, "Lek-see, Lek-see!" Terror grips her…she can't let Gabe wake her in her dream…something terrible will happen if she allows him to wake her. But she is powerless to resist the dream.

Now Gabe is leaning over her, the 'S'-shaped black ruby dangling from his neck, glittering in the moonlight. "Wake up Lek-see," he says. "We go! Now!"

He is very worried. It's that sixth sense of his. Always warning him something bad will happen. It usually turns out to be something like a scorpion, or a snake. This time is very different. She has never seen him like this before. Almost distraught!

Bloodbath

They are running through the night. He is remote and withdrawn...in a terrible hurry...will not stop to rest. Good thing she's in the best shape of her life.

Suddenly, she is at the hill above the farm. Tendrils of smoke are rising from burnt buildings...the stench of charred flesh is unforgettable...she can taste the bile in her throat.

The dreamscape shifts again, and she is crying. Someone in a uniform is asking if she could identify the bodies. They can't wait for Jay...something about the heat...the flies...

Then she is screaming...screaming...screaming....

* * * * * * * * * * *

Alexis's eyes snapped open, but she lay unmoving, oblivious of the surroundings, her mind paralyzed by the grip of terror.

The twittering of birds, rising from the trees in alarm penetrated her brain, and her first sentient thought was that she had screamed. Cognition returned, and terror gradually eased its grip. On her mind. Not on her racing heart or ragged breathing, or the rivers of sweat.

And worse was to come. The aftermath.

She braced for it with escalating panic. It started at the base of her spine as the merest shiver, and gathered strength and ferocity as it spread, becoming a convulsive flailing of her limbs. Her only recourse was to wrap her arms around her knees, hug them to her chest, and curl up in a fetal position to limit its violence.

When the paroxysm abated, she sat up, her mind floundering in the turmoil raging inside her. Images flashed of the mutilated remains of her parents, butchered in a guerilla atrocity in South Africa, and she felt like she was suffocating...unable to breathe—!

All of a sudden, a long-forgotten memory bubbled up out of the turmoil. *Pranayama.* A mystical *yogic* breathing technique she learned from the *lamas* in Ladakh. Why it should surface now, for the first time ever, was inexplicable, but she seized it like a lifeline.

Closing her eyes, she assumed the lotus pose and started the laborious process of controlling her ragged breathing, one breath at a time. As her breathing steadied, it became slower and deeper, and the trembling and panic receded.

Twenty minutes later, when her breathing had become so slow as to be imperceptible, she found herself at the edge of a reservoir of inner stillness deep in the core of her being. She submerged her mind in it, sinking effortlessly into a state approaching suspended animation.

She remained in that restorative trance, oblivious of her surroundings, as darkness retreated and the forest awakened. When sunlight found its way through the forest canopy to her face, she surfaced to instant alertness and inhaled the crisp air of the mountains.

Right then, she felt Jason reaching out, as if to touch her.

CHAPTER 4

J ason relaxed for the first time in hours. He was on a bus, speeding through the outskirts of Delhi, heading for Shimla. In a week, with any luck, he'd be at the ashram, where the cobra-eyed Indian would never find him.

His pulse quickened at the thought of the ashram and the serene beauty of the Himalayas. They represented sanctuary from both the outside world and his inner demons.

The specter of uncontrollable rage had stalked him since the brutal massacre of his mother and stepfather in South Africa. Fearing he might kill someone while in its grip, he abandoned his homeland for India, seeking respite, but the specter went with him.

In the past year, though, he had started to believe he would find the respite he sought in the practice of yoga. His guru said he would slay the demon when he found something called *aatmabodha*, which translated loosely to self-awareness.

Jason had no idea what it really meant. But today, for the first time ever, his rage did not surface under extreme provocation. So, even if the specter was not yet defeated, at least it had been stayed.

He started to rejoice. Then he remembered the suffocating sensation from earlier, and an old, familiar sadness resurfaced.

In his pocket was a letter he collected earlier today from the American Express office—the first from Alexis since they parted at a Buddhist lamasery in Ladakh a year ago. It was the reason he came to Delhi as fast as he could without reserving his return.

It was strangely impersonal. She was in an ancient *Yamabushi* monastery in the mountains of Japan and doing well. She hoped he was well and looked forward to meeting him soon. That was all.

Why Japan, for God's sake, and why the Yamabushi sect? They were Buddhists, like the lamas, and celibates, but any similarity ended there. They practiced the most rigorous asceticism, and were adept at the most mystical forms of martial art. And they didn't welcome women or foreigners. Nothing short of divine intervention could have broken down those barriers. Maybe the head of the Ladakh lamasery had worked the miracle on her behalf.

It saddened him that her search for peace took her in a direction so different from his—*ninjutsu* for her, yoga for him. Could there be two paths more different? Yet, the spiritual compass, Buddhist for her, Hindu for him, and emphasis on the inner self, were almost identical, even if the tools and techniques were very different.

"Very different, yet almost identical!" His stepfather's words echoed in his head. They couldn't be more spot on!

He and Alexis couldn't be more different in appearance. Brown hair and eyes for him, red tresses and dazzling green eyes for her. And mirror opposites in temperament, too. His calm exterior hid a violent temper, whereas her exuberant demeanor hid a serene resilience bordering on stubbornness.

Those outward differences, however, were transcended by their shared values, sense of humor, and outlook on life. And a psychic bond that no one, not even they, could explain. It wasn't like they could read each other's minds. It was more a 'connection' that allowed one to sense some powerful emotion in the other, regardless of the distance separating them.

Like when he sensed she was having her night terror and was now back in control. And that curious period of—could it be serenity? As if she had found sanctuary from her turmoil for the first time ever! He hoped desperately she had. Then she might, in time, even conquer her demons and return to the world. To him!

He sighed. He missed her. It was the one lack in his life. Other than that he was content. He laid his head back and dozed.

CHAPTER 5

At that moment, back in New Delhi, the Principal Private Secretary to the Prime Minister of India had just returned to his desk, having just ushered a wheelchair-bound American into the PM's presence.

It was a measure of the American's clout that he could request—and get!—a private audience with the PM so late at night, without the PM asking why. Few had the first privilege, but the secretary could count those who had the second on one hand.

Of course, this firangi was no ordinary man.

At first glance, you wouldn't think it. He looked like a misshapen troll, with his over-developed shoulders and arms and withered legs. When you looked in his eyes, though, his aura of power hit you like a physical force. Then you forgot his disability.

The secretary tried to imagine what it was like to be one of the richest men in the world. Then, realizing he was being stupid to even try, he got back to work.

* * * * * * * * * *

Jonathan Wolff reveled in the fact that few Indians would recognize his name, let alone know he was the reclusive founder of the worldwide business conglomerate called Lone Wolf Corporation, with investments in India worth over a billion dollars.

The few who were privy to that knowledge existed only at the highest levels of government, guaranteeing him access to the corridors of power. Even so, a private audience with the prime minister went far beyond access. It was an extraordinary favor.

He lost no time acknowledging it. "Thank you, Prime Minister, for seeing me. I know how difficult it must be for you to find the time to meet me at such short notice."

The prime minister sounded petulant. "You left me no choice, Mr. Wolff. You called to say you were coming to Delhi on a matter of utmost urgency, with grave implications for India. When a good friend of India uses such words, I get worried. I have to listen."

"Thank you, Prime Minister. I have just heard that there will be an attempt on your life in the near future. I do not know where or when, as yet, but I take it very seriously."

The prime minister laughed. "Is that all? Mr. Wolff, every minister hears ten whispers like that each day. If we launched full-scale investigations each time, the government would cease to function. Of course, some might say that nobody would notice the difference!"

"This is no laughing matter, Prime Minister. Please believe me. I wouldn't have flown here from New York if it was."

"I appreciate that, Mr. Wolff, but I must have something more than hearsay. Some concrete proof." The prime minister grimaced. "In a democracy with an independent judiciary, not even I can order an arrest on hearsay alone. Our experiment with that form of totalitarian rule was thankfully short-lived."

Jonathan recognized the allusion to the infamous "Emergency" declared in the mid-seventies by the autocratic Indira Gandhi. He let it pass. "To get concrete proof, Prime Minister, I need resources that I myself do not have in India. It will require coordination between my experts and yours in counter-intelligence. I leave the choice to you, but I suggest you pick only someone you can literally trust with your life."

"That would be the chief of my security detail."

Jonathan thought it wise not to bring up the touchy subject of Prime Minister Indira Gandhi's assassination by members of her own security detail. "I know he is above suspicion, Prime

Minister," he said, "but I was thinking more on the lines of someone in the intelligence apparatus who you trust implicitly."

"Why are you being so paranoid, Mr. Wolff?"

"Does the name Kalidas mean anything to you, Sir?"

The prime minister's head snapped back as if struck. He stared back at Jason through narrowed eyes. "Kalidas? You can't be serious, Mr. Wolff!"

"I was never more serious in my life, Sir."

"I find it hard to believe."

"Believe it, Prime Minister. Your life and the future of India rest on it."

"Come now, Mr. Wolff! Dispense with dramatics. How are you so sure of it, when we have not even heard a whisper? Kalidas is known as an arms dealer and a drug baron, interested in profits, not politics."

"You are right that profit drives him. But he plans to use political assassination to get it."

"Without proof, that is just speculation, Mr. Wolff."

"Not speculation, Prime Minister. We are certain of it. My sources—"

The prime minister interrupted him. "Your sources? Since when have you become so interested in Kalidas?"

"Since last year, Sir, when an executive from our Indian subsidiary was kidnapped and executed by Kashmiri militants. We heard that Kalidas was the brains behind it."

The prime minister was irritated. "Hearsay and half-baked rumors again! I'm fed up with them! My so-called experts tell me that Kalidas is the principal supplier to every major insurgent group in India. But when I demand proof, I get none."

"I understand your frustration, Sir. I am only trying to explain how we came to be interested in Kalidas. You need proof and you

19

need to know where to find him. We have information that might help you get the proof and find the man. I'm willing to share it with someone you trust."

"I appreciate that, Mr. Wolff. But you still haven't told me what Kalidas has to gain by assassinating me."

"My experts believe, Prime Minister, that Kalidas sees an opportunity to expand his market beyond Kashmir and the North-East, and may have decided to play for very high stakes by assassinating you."

"How would he profit from that? In a democracy, a leader dies and another steps in to take his place. The country goes on. Nobody is indispensable. That is the strength of democracies, as our own history proves—and America's, too, I might add. So what would he gain by killing me?"

"Quite a lot, Sir, if he picks the right assassin. You just referred to your history. The carnage after the assassination of Prime Minister Indira Gandhi by her Sikh guards would seem like a garden party if the Hindu-Muslim riots of Partition played out on a nationwide stage. With Kalidas only too ready to supply sophisticated weapons to the participants, it could mean a civil war unmatched in scale by any in history—which, of course, is the outcome he wants."

"Okay, I admit it's plausible. I'll have IB handle it."

Jonathan Wolff winced inwardly at the mention of the Intelligence Bureau. The domestic intelligence agency was so hopelessly politicized that secrecy would be the first casualty in its internecine wars. He chose his next words carefully. "That, Sir, is a political risk that you may not want to take."

"What do you mean?"

"You were kind enough, Sir, to call me a friend of India. There are others, including some in your Cabinet, who don't agree with that view of my motives. If they found out you gave your blessing to something in which I was mixed up—and you know they will if

20

you bring the IB into it—can you imagine their delight? They would smear you with the infamous 'foreign hand in India' and you would have to resign."

"I see. That leaves us with only one option then."

The PM picked up the phone. "Find Mr. Ravi Iyer, please."

After a pause, he snapped, "Now!"

Another pause. Then, "Get me a number where he can be reached."

He hung up and said, "Ravi Iyer is the foremost counter-terror intel expert in India, responsible for averting several terrorist attacks with roots in expatriate communities."

Jonathan said patiently, "We are talking about an arms supplier to home-grown Indian terrorists, not expatriates, Prime Minister."

"Mr. Wolff, you asked for someone I would trust with my life. Iyer is that person. He is apolitical and incorruptible. To find either in India is rare. The combination is priceless."

A knock on the door saved Jonathan from having to respond. The PM's secretary handed the prime minister a note, which he read and passed to Jonathan, saying, "As you can see from this, Mr. Wolff, Iyer is at present in New York on government business. You can contact him there. He has been told to expect a call from one of your people."

"That will be Sol Steinberg, the India expert in my security department."

"I will make sure Iyer knows. Thank you Mr. Wolff."

"Thank you, Prime Minister, for your time and patience."

He shook hands with the PM and wheeled himself out.

CHAPTER 6

An incident occurred a few months later during the Prime Minister's visit to New York to address the United Nations General Assembly. It received extensive media coverage in India.

The facts reported were straightforward. A "harmless intruder" strayed into a supposedly secure area of the New York hotel in which the prime minister was staying. It was a grievous lapse of security. Even worse, the intruder got away unscathed.

The editorials delighted in pointing out that it was true to the standards of bumbling inefficiency set by the prime minister's security detail. Its members also came in for scathing criticism in Parliament. They were spared from official censure only because the prime minister refused to authorize it. He insisted he was not even in the hotel when the so-called "incident" occurred.

Of these so-called facts, only one was accurate. The prime minister was, indeed, not in the hotel at the time of the incident. The rest were so far from the truth as to be laughable.

For one thing, the intruder was a professional assassin. For another, those responsible for the prime minister's security, far from being the bumbling buffoons portrayed in the media, acted in an exemplary manner—with one notable exception.

For a third, there was no doubt the attempt would have succeeded but for a phone call taken by the prime minister two hours earlier. Only he and his private secretary knew the identity of the caller but, shortly after receiving it, the prime minister left the hotel via the service entrance and was whisked away in a limousine belonging to the Lone Wolf Corporation. With him were his secretary and the chief of his security detail. Since none of the three was dressed in the traditional Indian garb the prime minister always wore, his departure went unnoticed.

A short time later, the prime minister's security guards killed the assassin, an expatriate Kashmiri Muslim with ties to Pakistani jihadi groups. Also killed in the encounter was the Chief of Security at the Indian Consulate in New York, who was in charge of local security during the prime minister's visit. No one heard the shots from the silenced weapons and the bodies vanished, courtesy of an FBI clean-up team acting under orders from the Director himself.

All that appeared in the news media was an official press release lamenting the death of the Head of Security at the New York Consulate from a self-inflicted gunshot wound to the chest. The official report blamed profound depression, compounded by the stress and heavy workload from the prime minister's visit. The body was badly decomposed when found, so it was cremated and the ashes flown back to India at government expense. The prime minister offered his condolences to the family, with his appreciation of the man's years of faithful service.

The media knew nothing about a letter Jonathan Wolff received from the prime minister, thanking him for helping to foil the assassination plot, and for providing a dossier compiled by Lone Wolf on the activities of Kalidas, the man behind the assassination attempt. The letter concluded with the prime minister's regret that the service had to remain a secret.

Only two copies of the letter existed. The recipient made sure no other eyes ever saw his copy. The other was marked "TOP SECRET! P.M.O. HIGHEST SECURITY CLEARANCE ONLY!", and filed in a vault in the basement of the Prime Minister's Office Building. It meant that the only people with access to it were the PM, the Cabinet Secretary, and the Secretary and Additional Secretary in the P.M.O.—all career bureaucrats, akin to a chief of staff, and deputy and assistant chiefs of staff in a presidential system.

When the prime minister returned to India, a covert manhunt was launched for Kalidas. Despite the high quality of intelligence behind it, the manhunt was a total waste of time and money. The quarry had an uncanny knack of anticipating his hunters' moves, slipping through their fingers just when they seemed to have him trapped. After twelve weeks of relentless pursuit, the quarry vanished, leaving behind only rumors of high-level informants in local and state government.

For a year, nothing more was heard of Kalidas. Then, whispers began to spread of a giant Sikh with the voice of a ghoul, and a Gurkha with a face to match, who appeared only in the night to kill in Kalidas's name, and vanished without a trace. People said they were demons from hell, recruited by Kalidas from the grave to do his bidding.

Suddenly, every unexplained murder and disappearance became their doing. First, it was a series of brutal slayings of prostitutes in widely separated regions of the country, associated with unconfirmed sightings of one or the other of the "ghouls". Then, a fear took hold that they were kidnapping young girls for sale in the Gulf.

Just as suddenly, the prostitute killings and the kidnappings stopped, even though the sightings continued, keeping Kalidas's name alive in the public's memory. Few dared speak his name, however, and those who did, whispered it, and always with a glance over their shoulder to see if they were overheard.

Kalidas, the man, disappeared.

PART TWO

BLOOD TIES

CHAPTER 1

Today was not a day to look back. It was to look ahead.

To vengeance.

Against India, the country. For inflicting his only defeat.

And against a man. For his utter humiliation.

He was obsessed with vengeance. And consumed by hatred. Together, they formed his lifeblood, pulsing through his veins, eating into the very fiber of his being.

Four years later, both remained undying and undiminished, surrounded as he was by constant reminders of his humiliation.

His hair, once jet-black, turned snow-white from shock. The puckered scars on Karim Chand's mutilated wrists. The hideous opening that served as Gurung's mouth. The raspy whisper that was Jarnail Singh's voice.

Each was a running sore in his psyche that would never heal without vengeance.

He would have his vengeance against the country. It couldn't hide from him. Not the man, though. He had vanished without a trace. But their paths would cross again, of that he was absolutely sure. His vengeance was guaranteed by his devotion to the one Supreme Being who ruled his universe.

Mother Kali, baleful goddess of Hinduism's dark side.

Omnipotent. Omnipresent. Omniscient.

And he was her foremost servant—he had even changed his name to Kalidas, meaning 'Servant of Kali.'

No one dared to call him by name, anyway, since the only form of address he countenanced was "Huzoor", the honorific reserved for kings in the old days. However, no sovereign of India, ancient or modern—not even Asoka, the greatest of them all!—ever held sway over an empire to match his.

From its epicenter in Myanmar—what the British called Burma—his power extended east to Indo-China and west, across the Indian subcontinent, to Iran.

Myanmar was his base of operations, but it wasn't by choice. Four years ago, when he was on the run, being hunted like an animal, he found sanctuary here. A place to lick his wounds and lie low, without fear of discovery or betrayal. The perfect hideaway, closed to the world, and ruled with an iron fist by a military junta.

He bought the patronage of the ruling generals and, in return, got the security he needed for his resurgence as overlord of the most powerful criminal organization in Southeast Asia.

His camp was in the Patkai Hills in Myanmar's inaccessible north, under the official designation of a 'geological survey operation'. The Indian border lay just a hundred miles away, but the intervening terrain included some of the densest and most impenetrable jungle on the planet. The Indians had no idea he was hiding under their noses.

It needed to stay that way for another year. Then it wouldn't matter. India would be too preoccupied with its survival to think about him.

Today, he would take the first step to achieving the greatest triumph of his life.

Time to summon Randhawa.

* * * * * * * * * * *

Randhawa exited the helicopter and saw Karim Chand waiting at the helipad. Randhawa waved, and the man waved back, his mutilated wrists glistening pink in the sunlight.

Bloodbath

Randhawa wondered for the thousandth time how they got that way. Not that he would dare to ask. The only man who ever asked died instantly, his neck broken by the Sikh at the same instant the Gurkha disemboweled him. Randhawa was there when it happened and it was something he would never forget.

Shaking off the gut-churning memory, he followed Karim Chand and was ushered into Kalidas's presence. Keeping his eyes downcast, he asked, "You wanted to see me, Huzoor?"

Kalidas's voice was soft. "Yes, Randhawa. You are to deliver a sample of heroin to Bindra's man in New York."

"As you command, Huzoor."

"Bindra is expanding his drug network from Canada to the US, and is looking for a big-time supplier. If the sample meets his expectations, he will require bulk supplies, and that is what I need to fund Bloodbath. Everything depends on it. Including your life, if you fail."

Randhawa's voice quavered as he said, "I will not fail, Huzoor."

"Make sure you don't. Karim Chand has arranged your itinerary from Bangkok to New York, through London. Now go!"

Randhawa left the room as quickly as he could.

CHAPTER 2

The email from the Amex Office in New Delhi arrived while Jason was mid-flight from Chicago to Honolulu. So, the first he knew of it was when he checked his phone while waiting at Baggage Claim.

The instant he saw there was an attachment, his hands began to shake. He had kept the Amex channel open through the years for exactly this! Not for the New Year and birthday greeting cards, with the usual platitudes. Those were nice, but this meant something much, much more.

His hopes soared as he read the first line of her handwritten letter—the first since the one he got in Delhi, four years ago! It said she was leaving Japan for good, and would wait in Tokyo for four days to hear from him. If she hadn't heard by then, she would leave for London and stay there until he contacted her. She had included her flight itinerary from Tokyo to London, hotel names and dates of stay in both cities.

His hopes came crashing down to earth when he read the itinerary. Her flight left Tokyo just four hours ago.

Why it took four days for Amex to forward the letter to him was inexplicable, but it meant he now had to fly halfway around the world to meet her in London, instead of the relatively short hop from Honolulu to Tokyo.

He collected his bag and headed straight to Ticketing to book a seat on the first available flight out of Honolulu. He didn't care which airline, class, or direction—eastbound or westbound, it would take the same time to get from Honolulu to London.

CHAPTER 3

Twenty-four hours in a cramped seat—forty, including the chopper trip to Yangon and a jeep ride across the border into Thailand—had put Randhawa in a very irritable mood.

Never one to sleep on a flight, he expected to pass the time in idle chitchat with seatmates. To his bad luck, the elderly Thai couple next to him on the flight from Bangkok to Heathrow spoke no English. London to New York was no better. The woman in the window seat, a gorgeous redhead with a great figure, slept through most of the flight.

Randhawa tried to strike up a conversation when she woke up for lunch, but she clearly she didn't want to talk, replying with curt, one-word answers. All he got from it was that she was meeting her brother and staying in Manhattan at some hotel he'd never heard of. He couldn't place her accent—he wasn't very good at accents, but it sounded kind of British. Australian, maybe? And rich, going by her Gucci carryon, shoulder bag and exclusive luggage tags.

Before he could ask, though, she put on her headset, turned her face to the window, and went to sleep.

At least the flight was nearing its end. In just twenty minutes, they'd land at JFK, and he would breeze through Customs. Interpol had nothing on him. Nor would there be any hassle with Immigration—his documents were impeccable. But, with so many flights arriving at this time of day, it could mean waiting more than two hours in line. Better to visit the lavatory now.

The signs showed every toilet in the rear was occupied, so he headed for the middle cluster next to the galley. It was an accident of fate, but it saved his skin.

Because he was there, he overheard a flight attendant's excited whisper on the other side of the partition. "I just found out that the feds have asked the captain for a visual on 49C!"

Randhawa was jolted alert. That was his seat number!

"No!" a second voice hissed.

"It's true. I heard Ron give the captain his description."

"My God! A terrorist! Is he going to blow up the plane?"

"Silly! The flight marshals would have grabbed him then."

The voices faded and Randhawa slumped down on the toilet.

There must have been a leak at Bindra's end! Kalidas would have to deal with that, but it didn't help Randhawa. His only way out was to dump the stuff and abort the mission. Kalidas would be furious, but he had no choice.

He returned to his seat just as the warning bell rang and the "Fasten Seat Belts" sign came on. He retrieved his briefcase from the overhead bin, extracted a package, and tucked it under his jacket. As he replaced the briefcase, he heard the announcement for all passengers to return to their seats in preparation for landing.

Randhawa shut the bin and turned to go to the restroom, but a flight attendant barred his way, advising him firmly to sit down. His nametag said 'Ron'—the one who got his description! One glance at his face told Randhawa he'd better obey. The last thing he needed was an altercation with that package tucked in his armpit.

He sat down in a panic. He had to get rid of the stuff. But how? He couldn't leave it on the plane—his fingerprints were all over the bag in the stuffed elephant he bought in Yangon. So, he'd have to dump it in the toilet after the plane landed.

His decision made, he relaxed.

Ten minutes later, the wheels hit the tarmac and the landing announcement began, "Ladies and gentlemen! British Airways welcomes you to New York's John F. Kennedy International Airport. The time is…"

He tuned out the flight attendant's voice, imagining how he would duck into the lavatory, rip open the elephant, take out the bag, and flush the heroin down the toilet. Even if they arrested—!

The attendant's voice exploded in his ears like a thunderclap.

"Security at Kennedy Airport has asked for our cooperation. When we arrive at the terminal, officers will be boarding the plane to conduct a routine drill. So, once the plane comes to a halt, the seat belt sign will stay on. Please do not to stand up or obstruct the aisles. I repeat, this is a routine drill, so please don't be alarmed. Remain seated until they complete their drill and the captain announces it is okay to leave the plane. Thank you."

Randhawa panicked. He had to dump the elephant on some unsuspecting idiot who had no idea it was dumped on them. Someone the feds would never suspect—!

All of a sudden, he had his answer. The woman sleeping in the window seat! Her shoulder bag was right there on the floor between them, its mouth half-open.

He reached down unobtrusively, shoved in the elephant, and straightened up, taking a casual glance around. No one was looking his way—his spur-of-the-moment move had gone unnoticed!

He breathed a sigh of relief. It didn't matter now what the feds suspected. They'd have to let him go. The woman would take the elephant through Customs, unchallenged. Even if she found it later, she wouldn't throw away a harmless toy. He could get it back. He knew where she was staying. Something about the monsoons.

No—Seasons! That was it. The Four Seasons in Manhattan.

And he even knew her name from her luggage tag. Alexis Wolff.

CHAPTER 4

Alexis woke up with a start, and looked around, perplexed. No one was getting up, even though the plane was at the terminal, the engines had powered down and the airplane door was open.

Then she saw uniformed security personnel heading down the aisle towards her. She felt momentary alarm, but it wasn't her they were interested in, but the bearded Sikh in the aisle seat. They asked him to accompany them, but he refused, wanting to know what he was supposed to have done. Their response was implacable. "Sir, we advise you to cooperate, or you will be forcibly removed."

Casting a rueful glance in her direction, he shrugged and left with the officers. His briefcase went with them.

Alexis heard a collective sigh of relief, followed by a smattering of applause when the captain announced it was okay to get up. She walked off the plane, wondering how often there was an arrest on an aircraft. Maybe the world had changed a lot more in five years than she realized. The more she thought about it, the more she hoped and prayed Jason would be there to meet her.

He called her from Honolulu to say how sorry he was that her message reached him too late to meet her in Tokyo, and it made the most sense to meet in New York. He had booked their flights, timing their arrivals so he would get there before her.

She exited the Arrivals Hall, but didn't see him in the crowd outside. She lingered for several minutes, wondering with mounting panic what she should do. Then she heard the P.A. announcer ask British Airways' Passenger Alexis Wolff to pick up a courtesy phone for a message, and was overwhelmed by relief.

Bloodbath

It had to be Jason!

She hurried to a phone and identified herself, but her heart sank when she heard the message. It was from Jason, all right, but it wasn't what she wanted to hear. His flight had developed engine trouble an hour out of Honolulu, forcing it to return. No seats were available for the next twenty-four hours, but he was on standby and would send her a message at the Four Seasons as soon as he got on a flight. Until then, she should enjoy her stay in New York. He had reserved a rental car at the airport in her name.

She hung up the phone, frustrated and angry. Frustrated by yet another delay in his arrival—first Tokyo, then London, and now New York. And angry that he was forcing her to drive. Didn't he know she wasn't ready for it, and would much rather take a cab?

Even as she asked the question, she saw the truth staring at her. She was afraid of the world to which she was returning! It was the reason she hadn't left her hotel room in London or Tokyo. Jason was sending her a gentle signal that she had to take the plunge sometime, somewhere, so why not here and now?

She went to the car rental counter with new-found confidence.

Thirty minutes later, she was on the Van Wyck Expressway, her confidence growing with each passing mile, until she was flying along at almost seventy miles per hour.

Then she hit her first pothole.

The suspension bottomed out with a bone-jarring crunch, but the car seemed fine. She thought she heard something in the trunk hit the lid quite hard. It didn't really matter—there was nothing fragile in her luggage. Still, she reduced speed to sixty, paying closer attention to the road.

* * * * * * * * * * *

Randhawa survived the relentless barrage of questions from the narcotics agents. The strip search, X-rays and scans, and cavity examinations left him feeling violated, but his nerve held. His cover was foolproof—Kalidas's arrangements always were—so, with no evidence he was carrying drugs, they had to let him go.

Knowing they would be watching his every move, he checked into a seedy hotel in the Asian part of Newark, far from his pre-arranged rendezvous with Bindra's man. He was hungry and tired, but food and rest could wait. His first priority was to locate the woman. The advantage of a seedy hotel was that it had an old-fashioned payphone in the lobby for its seedy clientele!

* * * * * * * * * * *

The phone rang just as Alexis came out of the shower. She grabbed it, asking eagerly, "Jason?"

A man with an Indian accent answered. "Miss Vulff?"

"Who is this?"

"I am so sorry to bother you, Miss Vulff. I sat next to you on the airplane and I am calling to ask for your assistance."

The accent was from Punjab, but the tone was peremptory, very unlike the Indian tradition of humility when seeking a favor. It set her on edge right away.

"What is it?" she responded curtly.

"I know you saw me taken off the plane by Customs, and must be wondering why I am calling you." His tone suddenly became servile. It made Alexis even more suspicious.

"So why are you calling me?"

"It was a big misunderstanding. Someone on the plane thought I looked like a Sikh terrorist, and the police couldn't ignore

36

it. They had to escort me from the plane. But I am a businessman, and my papers were in perfect order. When they realized their mistake, they had to let me go, with an apology."

"Why you are calling me? And how do you know my name, and where to call me?"

She heard a forced laugh. "You told me yourself, remember?"

Had she? She couldn't remember, but she must have. How else did he track her down?

He continued. "It's very silly. I bought a small toy in Heathrow for my niece. I took it out while rearranging my briefcase, and must have left it out on the seat between us, because I can't find it now. It must have rolled off the seat and into your bag. Look for it."

The peremptory tone reappeared in the demand, making her bristle. "I know it isn't there," she asserted tersely.

"You are wrong!" he said, with an ugly snap in his voice. "Look again!"

"Don't tell me what to do," she snapped back. "I know what I unpacked. There's nothing in any of my bags that even remotely resembles a toy."

"I tell you to look once more!" he shouted. "I know it's there."

"I have no intention of looking again. I know it isn't there. And don't you dare use that threatening tone to me!"

After several seconds of silence, she heard him take a deep breath and say in a sibilant whisper, "So, that's how you want it. I ask for your help, but you refuse. I won't forget this."

The threat shocked her, but he hung up before she could think of a retort. She slammed the phone down, fuming with rage, and waited, willing him to call back, but it stayed silent. Just as she was about to turn away the phone rang.

She snatched it and barked, "How dare you call me again!"

There was a moment of silence, then a hesitant "Miss Wolff? This is the front desk."

"I…I'm so sorry! I just got a nuisance call from someone, and thought he called again."

"I'm very sorry to hear that, Ma'am. Would you like us to screen your calls?"

"Oh, no! Please don't bother. I'm terribly sorry I was so rude."

"No problem, Ma'am. I called to tell you that we received a fax for you from Honolulu."

Her heart lurched. "Please send it up, right away," she said.

The message was from Jason, all right, but it was not what she wanted to hear. He was reaching Los Angeles tonight and was booked on the redeye to New York. He expected to see her at the airport tomorrow morning.

Alexis was surprised that she wasn't resentful, like she was in the morning. She was excited about spending the day in New York!

Then it dawned on her that the unhealthy cocoon in which she had wrapped herself for five years might be unraveling.

* * * * * * * * * *

Randhawa slammed down the payphone, swearing obscenities in Punjabi. If that was how the bitch wanted it, so be it! She had spurned his polite request. Now she'd get what she deserved.

He couldn't do it himself. Not with the feds on his tail. But Dhindsa, Kalidas's local agent in New York, could. He was ideal for the job. He owned a limo service. He was extremely skilled at teaching bitches like Alexis Wolff a lesson. And he took great delight in it. By the time Dhindsa was done with her, she'd be begging to not just give him the elephant, but even fuck a real one!

He dialed Dhindsa.

There was the minor problem of identifying her to Dhindsa, but he knew a way to get around that. While he waited for Dhindsa to answer, he searched for a florist on his cell phone.

CHAPTER 5

N ew York!

It was dirty, smelly, and loud…but vibrant with life! And Alexis found it exhilarating—the ideal antidote to five years of seclusion.

She wandered through Manhattan, drinking in the sights, the sounds, and even the smells of the city, like a thirsty wayfarer at an oasis in the desert. The approach of dusk, however, forced her to call a reluctant halt to her burgeoning love affair with the city and return to her hotel, humming under her breath.

On entering the hotel, she saw a turbaned Sikh sitting in the foyer, looking resplendent in tux and bowtie, with a bouquet that seemed jarringly over-the-top. Memories of roaming across India with Jason came flooding back, and she had a sudden craving for Indian food. She made a beeline to the concierge's desk for a recommendation, and introduced herself to the young man behind it, "I'm Alexis Wolff, from Room 1138—"

The concierge interrupted her. "Oh, yes! Miss Wolff! I'm glad you stopped by. Someone's been waiting all day to see you."

He beckoned to someone behind her, and she turned to see the tuxedo-clad Sikh walk up to her, bouquet in hand. He bowed, lifting a hand to his turban in a deferential *salaam*, and handed her the bouquet. "The gentleman on the plane wants to apologize for his rudeness this morning. He hopes you will forgive him."

The card was signed 'Your Fellow Traveler', and reading it made her strangely queasy. But she could hardly return the flowers now. She gave an uncertain laugh. "I'd forgotten about it. But what's his name?"

Bloodbath

The Sikh said, "I don't know, Madam. I'm just a limo driver. My instructions were to hand the flowers to you in person, not leave them at the desk, and to tell you he has paid for the limo, so I'm at your service all day, today and tomorrow, unlimited miles."

"But—but—," she stammered, "I don't need a limo."

"The customer will be upset with me if you refuse, Madam."

She felt herself getting irritated. "I don't give a damn if he's upset," she said sharply. "I don't want a limo. I prefer to walk."

She knew he was just a driver, and had nothing to do with the "apology", but something about him—and the nauseatingly ostentatious bouquet!—had triggered her ninja instinct, warning her to be wary. She turned away with angry finality.

"Is there something I can help you with, Madam?" the concierge asked.

She stared at him, nonplussed, then remembered. "Can you recommend an Indian restaurant nearby?"

"I'd be happy to, Madam." He took out a street map of Manhattan and marked the location of an Indian restaurant called Dawat, which he touted as the best in the city. It was just a few blocks away, within walking distance.

She thanked him and turned to leave, only to find the limo driver right behind her, holding out a clipboard as he said, "Can Madam please sign this receipt for the flowers?"

She hesitated, feeling her unease return. Then, realizing how unreasonable it was, she scrawled her initials where he pointed and walked away. When she got off the elevator, she threw the bouquet into a garbage bin, took a deep breath, and forgot about it.

* * * * * * * * * * *

41

Dhindsa removed his turban and gave his fake beard a thoughtful scratch as he drove away.

It was a pity she didn't fall for the free limo offer. It would have made things so much easier. At least, he knew where she was going tonight. She liked walking too. It would be simple to hustle her into a car, take her some place quiet, and persuade her to tell him what she had done with the stuffed elephant.

After seeing her, he understood why Randhawa said that getting this gorgeous woman to sing would be reward enough for Dhindsa—worth a thousand times more than the money Dhindsa would get for recovering the elephant!

Dhindsa had to agree. Come to think of it, he would've been willing to do it for free, that was how much he was looking forward to it after seeing her! He wouldn't tell Randhawa that, of course.

He wondered how long she would last. She looked like a model, which meant she was vain. He expected she would plead for mercy at the first threat, and give him anything he wanted just to save her looks. That was too bad, because it was more fun when they fought back. Still, there were ways of prolonging the fun. He was going to enjoy persuading her!

Dhindsa began to whistle as he drove.

CHAPTER 6

Ravi Iyer knew it was time to go. It was past eleven, his check was paid, and the restaurant was empty, except for the striking young woman sitting a few tables away, absentmindedly fingering a strand of pearls as she drank her tea.

He hadn't been able to take his eyes off her all evening. Her beauty was reason enough, but there was an air of vulnerability about her that captivated him. He wished she would stand up so he could see the bodylines only hinted at while she was seated.

Too bad, he'd never see them. He couldn't wait any longer. She hadn't noticed him staring at her as yet. But he had to leave before she became aware of his attention. There was also the small matter of catching an early flight to Toronto.

He got up with a sigh of regret, and walked out.

Outside, he paused to get his bearings, then began walking to his car, parked a couple of blocks away. He had no doubts about his ability to handle himself, but it was late and the city's history demanded he stay vigilant. Of course, current reality was far removed from the city's reputation in India, as he well knew from past trips. New York, like London, Toronto, Chicago, LA and Vancouver, was an essential stop on his annual tour of expatriate Indian communities, where naive ideals could blur into fanaticism.

The Air India disaster of 1987 was the perfect case in point. Over three hundred lives were lost on a flight from Toronto to New Delhi because of a bomb placed in the luggage by Sikh terrorists demanding an independent homeland in Punjab.

Canada—Vancouver, to be precise!—was the birthplace of that catastrophe, but the seeds of similar acts of insane violence existed everywhere. There was no foolproof way of preventing every seed from sprouting, but Ravi was proud that his advance intelligence had prevented at least five major catastrophes, including the attempted assassination of the PM a few years back.

As he walked, lost in thought, he heard a man hiss from behind him, "How much longer is the red-headed whore going to take? Is she screwing someone in there?"

Ordinarily, it wouldn't have registered. But it did. Because it was spoken in Punjabi!

He glanced over his shoulder to see the speaker, just as a car chanced to pass by. In its headlights, he saw the faces of two men sitting in a car parked a few feet behind him.

A fleeting glance—that was all it took for him to recognize the face that had haunted him for eighteen years. The shock was so savage that it was all he could do to stop from stumbling.

He did not need a second glance to confirm it was Gurdeep Singh Dhindsa, the self-styled 'Killer Khalsa'. Nor did it make a difference that the man was without a beard or turban. He knew that face better than his own. In all its mutations and disguises.

For eighteen long years, he had been clinging to the hope that one day he would see those features as justice demanded. In grotesque caricature, suffused and swollen, at the end of the hangman's rope. The souls of more than two thousand five hundred victims who died in a train wreck near Ambala officially "credited" to the Killer Khalsa cried out for it.

He heard every one of those voices. But the anguished cries of two were seared in his memory. A twenty-four year-old woman and her two-year-old daughter.

They were the instigators of his single-minded dedication to transforming himself from run-of-the-mill police officer to foremost expert on counter-terrorism in India. And the twin forces driving his craving for vengeance even more than justice.

Bloodbath

All the grief, bitterness, and pain pent up over eighteen years erupted in a single volcanic explosion, blinding him to reality. Just as he was about to whirl around to accost the man, reality, more bitter and hurtful than the all the pain and grief in his heart, hit like a sledgehammer.

He had no jurisdiction in New York, so what was he thinking to do? Arrest Dhindsa?

To call the police was even more ludicrous. What police officer would arrest a blameless citizen, doing nothing more than sitting in a car, on the say-so of a foreigner who claimed, without any proof, that the man was a terrorist wanted in another country?

There wasn't time, anyway. Dhindsa was lying in wait for the red-head in the restaurant and she must be getting ready to leave. Dhindsa would do whatever he was planning to do and be gone long before Iyer was able to locate help, let alone someone to believe him.

Frustration burned like acid. Then his analytical brain took over.

He had no idea why Dhindsa was targeting the woman in the restaurant. He knew Dhindsa, though. The Killer Khalsa had only one purpose. To kill.

For one split-second, Iyer considered going back to warn her...only to think better of it. An attractive woman would take it for a perverted variant of a pick-up line. Even if she hadn't noticed his interest, which he did precious little to hide.

Torn by indecision, his footsteps faltered as he entered a temporary passageway through a maze of scaffolding that had been erected to renovate a building. He remembered coming through it on his way to the restaurant.

All of a sudden, he knew what he had to do.

This had nothing to do with the redhead. This was for him.

CHAPTER 7

A lexis Wolff had no illusions about her effect on men. Unlike many attractive women, though, she neither dwelt on it nor tried to exploit it. So, she was more amused than flattered or offended by the surreptitious attention from the Indian.

She felt her nerves tingle, as they had all evening whenever she felt his eyes on her. She knew why. She had been celibate for so long that her mind had become her worst enemy, letting forbidden thoughts prance around inside her head.

Like wondering whether he was going to proposition her!

It made her blush, and she lowered her head, stealing a sidelong glance in his direction, only to see him walking out without even looking at her.

So much for that, you silly woman, she scolded herself, and checked her watch. It was well past eleven. *Time to go,* she thought. *But not just yet. Can't give him the wrong impression!*

Her check was paid, but she didn't want him to think she was following him. So she waited a few minutes before leaving.

The street was deserted as she began walking towards Madison Avenue a hundred yards away, still teeming with cars and people. Inevitably, her mind darted back to her ridiculous fantasy about the Indian trying to pick her up. Would it have offended or flattered her? A bit of both, she decided, and felt her nerves tingle again.

Distracted by the reawakening of long-dormant emotions, she never saw the man in the shadows until it was too late. She froze.

He stepped in front of her, and she knew it was the limo driver who delivered the bouquet, even without his turban and beard! The next instant, she felt something hard jab her in the back, and she knew she had missed not one, but two men.

46

Bloodbath

There was a hoarse whisper from behind in an Indian accent. "Don't do anything stupid, like trying to run or scream. This is a silenced gun."

Limo Man jammed his gun into her chin, saying, "Tell me where the elephant is, or I will have to force you to tell me?"

"What elephant?" she gasped.

"Don't pretend, bitch!" he snarled, grinding the gun barrel into her chin to force it up. "Tell me where it is."

Before she could answer, she heard footsteps on the temporary sidewalk under the scaffolding. "Someone's coming," the man behind her hissed.

Limo Man went to join him, whispering, "Make a sound and you die." The pressure from the gun barrel in her back vanished, and she stole a quick glance over her shoulder to see if they had left her an opening. They were too far from her and each other to take them both out together.

A figure emerged from the temporary passageway and she did a double take. It was the Indian from the restaurant! But he looked nothing like the guy she fantasized over. This was a disheveled drunk, reeling on unsteady feet as he staggered towards her.

For an instant, she thought it was a set-up engineered by him, but he stumbled past without even glancing at her. All of a sudden, he noticed her captors and stopped alongside them. Teetering back and forth with his hands on his hips, he asked with insouciant belligerence, "Who the hell are you?"

Limo Man was closest to him. He stepped towards him to push him away, but the drunk lost his balance and fell into him, sending him stumbling backwards. He would have fallen had he not grabbed on to the drunk.

Out of nowhere, the 'drunk' drove a lightning-fast elbow strike into Limo Man's solar plexus. There was a strangled grunt, and Alexis saw her other captor snatch his gun from his pocket and step towards his comrade to intervene. Then instinct took over.

She twisted and bent forward at the right hip until her head was almost touching her right knee, at the same time sweeping her left leg backwards to cock it at the hip in one smooth movement. Then, looking up from under her left shoulder, she lashed her left leg into extension with all the strength she could muster.

The *ushiro-geri* back kick, delivered while fully bent, required extraordinary flexibility, athleticism, and precision. The ball of her right foot struck her captor's jaw under his right ear as he was rushing forward, further amplifying its force at impact.

His head snapped back as if struck by a bullet.

She felt something snap, like a dry twig and there was a muffled cough from the silenced gun being fired in a reflexive death spasm.

She spun out of her kick and landed facing the other two, who were locked in embrace, except that the 'drunk's' right arm was now clamped around Limo Man's neck in a crushing *hadaka-jime* arm lock. She sprang forward, hand flashing back to strike, but before she could, the Indian let go of Limo Man, letting him fall. He dropped to his knees an instant later.

Alexis panicked, thinking the bullet had found him. Then she saw him feel for a pulse in the man's neck, and relaxed, turning her ninja focus on making sure no other threats lurked in the shadows.

Reassured there were none, she looked with renewed interest at the Indian, as he bent down to make sure the man she had kicked was dead, and wondered who he was, and why he went to such lengths to help her.

"Come on! Snap out of it!" he hissed. "We don't have time to waste, daydreaming. Help me hide the bodies in the walkway."

The sharp tone surprised her, but it made sense. She nodded and helped him carry the bodies into the covered walkway. As they dumped the second body next to it, it struck her they could easily hide the truth behind how the two men died by—!

"What's wrong?" the Indian asked impatiently, interrupting her train of thought.

"Nothing," she replied, "but wouldn't it be better to make it look like they killed each other?"

He gave her a startled look, then nodded with a quizzical expression on his face. After they positioned the bodies to look like they killed each other in a fight, she scuffed the knuckles of the man who was shot and smeared a drop of his blood on the other's jaw.

When she stood up, she saw new-found respect in her rescuer's eyes. They walked in silence through the scaffolding to the far end of the walkway, and were about to exit it when she heard laughter.

A group of pedestrians was almost upon them! No point trying to hide. They had been spotted. In a matter of seconds, the group would walk past and discover the two dead men.

"Quick! Kiss me!" the Indian hissed.

His sheer brazenness left her speechless. As she stood gaping at him, he reached out impatiently and pulled her into his arms, clearly intending to kiss her.

Her instinctive reaction was to try and pull away. Then she understood his purpose. He was counting on the fact that most people would find it distasteful to try squeezing through the narrow entrance with a kissing couple blocking it.

She stopped resisting and felt his lips meet hers. She heard the footsteps pause, and there was a derisive snigger, followed by a whisper of "Hooker! Better walk on the street", and the footsteps receded. Then there was only a roaring in her head, as her universe narrowed to the feel and taste of his mouth on hers.

She hung on to him for several second, then pulled away, mortified by her hungry reaction to his kiss.

"I'm sorry about that, but it was the only way to get us out of that jam," he said.

Too embarrassed to think, let alone speak, she said nothing.

He went on without waiting for her response. "It wouldn't be good to be linked to these two bodies. I happen to know who and what they are. Let's get out of here."

She still said nothing, avoiding his eyes as she struggled to regain her composure, and the pounding in her head wasn't helping!

He tried again. "Of course, if you prefer, we can wait till someone else comes along and perform an encore."

"I'm sorry!" she blurted out, "but I must get back to the Four Seasons."

"What a coincidence. That's where I'm staying. Can I drive you there?"

"Yes, please!"

She felt awkward and gauche as they walked to his car, like a teenager on a first date. He held the door for her as she got in and she noticed that he was tall and broad-shouldered, rangy rather than big-made. Not particularly handsome, but very virile.

She felt a rush of panic and tried to think of something to stop her mind from going there. "What were you doing at the Dawat?" she asked as he started the car.

"Dining, as I recall. The concierge recommended it."

She kept her mouth shut, then, rather than risk saying something foolish again.

He seemed not to notice. "My name is Ravi Iyer."

"I'm Alexis," she replied. "And sorry for being so abrupt. I'm glad you decided to dine at the Dawat. I haven't even thanked you for saving my life or for your quick thinking in the tunnel."

"Your idea to set it up like a brawl, and to remember to scuff the guy's knuckles was even better thinking. And, judging from your ushiro-geri and that guy's neck, my help was hardly needed."

She sensed he was teasing her to make her relax. "Your help was just what I needed. Judging from what your hadaka-jime did to the other guy's neck," she teased back.

"I had to do it." The intensity in his voice was startling.

Unsettled by it, she responded sharply, "You took one hell of a risk, though! Against two armed goons! What were you thinking?

To commit suicide? For all you knew, I could've been a helpless female and then where would you have been?"

"Probably dead in the alley, like that helpless female." He laughed. "I wasn't thinking clearly, so I forgot where I was."

"Still, it was very brave of you. What made you do it? If I didn't know there were two dead bodies back there, I might suspect it was an elaborate ploy to pick me up."

He grimaced, as if her words made him uncomfortable. "I owe you an explanation about that. I recognized one of the men. The one I killed was a very, very dangerous man. A terrorist wanted in India for killing thousands of innocent civilians."

"Are you a policeman?"

"I was. In India, I mean. Old habits die hard."

"So, what are you doing in New York, Mr. Iyer?"

"Please call me Ravi. I think that's reasonable, under the circumstances, don't you?"

"Under the circumstances, I couldn't agree more. But only if you call me Alexis."

"All right, Alexis. But why were those two scumbags after you? Do you know them?"

"I recognized the man you killed as the limo driver who delivered a bouquet of flowers to me at the hotel earlier today."

"Why in hell did a terrorist from India send you flowers?"

"They weren't from him. They were ostensibly on behalf of a passenger on my flight, apologizing for being rude to me earlier. Other than that, I have no idea who they are, or why they should think I had an elephant they'd lost."

"It's a little difficult to carry something that big around! Where did they think you'd hidden it?" He was looking at her from head to foot, making no effort to hide his appreciation.

For some reason, it made her bristle. "I don't think they meant a real elephant," she snapped.

51

"I'm sorry. That was very insensitive of me. Please don't take offense."

He seemed so contrite she was mollified. "Sorry I snapped at you. It's hardly the way a damsel in distress should treat her *otokodate*!"

She saw his face break into a smile and knew he understood the compliment in Japanese. "I've been called many things in my life, but never a knight errant!"

"There's always a first time," she said, smiling back.

They were at the entrance to the Four Seasons.

"Do you want to join me for a drink at the bar?" Alexis asked. "I know I need one."

"I'd like that."

The tingling she felt in the restaurant returned. All of a sudden, she felt light-headed.

CHAPTER 8

When Jason saw Alexis, he felt as if his chest would explode from anxiety. Then their eyes met and he saw her wave to him and smile. Five years vanished by magic and he was back at the lamasery in Ladakh, watching her wave goodbye to him with that same smile.

An instant later, she was giving him a bear hug, and his heart was bursting from joy. He held her at arm's length and, wonder of wonders, he saw none of the pain and torment that always lurked there. Instead, there was a radiance he hadn't seen for years.

It was so stunning that he had to look away. And his eyes fell on the tall Indian standing a few feet away, with a copy of Newsweek in his hand, trying not to intrude on their reunion. He knew then, without having to ask, that he was the reason the old Alexis had returned, and he smiled with gratitude at the man.

Alexis introduced him to Ravi Iyer, and Jason took an instant liking to the man. There was no time to get to know him, however, because Ravi had a plane to catch for Toronto.

Jason shook hands and turned away to let Alexis say her goodbyes, his head spinning from conflicting emotions. Happiness at seeing her after so many years. And anxiety that she might be taken away from him so soon after she came back into his life.

He felt her tap him on his elbow with the magazine, and turned around. "Not to worry, Jay," she said, smiling. "No commitments, either way. Neither of us needs it in our lives."

He felt a weight lift from his mind. In its place was delight, hearing her call him "Jay", the nickname she coined for him, after he started calling her "Red" in childhood. It was as if nothing had changed, and everything was back the way it always was.

"Welcome back, Red. Five long years I've waited to say that!"

"Five long years for me too, Jay! It's great to be back."

She stuck the magazine in her pocket and linked her arm with his as they walked to Baggage Claim, content to let the silence rest between them, light and comfortable like always.

They collected Jason's bag and headed to the parking garage in silence. It was natural. Silence never felt uncomfortable with her.

She looked exactly like he remembered. But everything about her was different. Maybe, those dreadful nightmares were gone, too—he hadn't "felt" her having one for a while. He shivered, feeling a shadow reach out from the past. Then, she spoke, and the shadow retreated, driven back by the serenity in her voice.

"I haven't felt this good for some time, Jay. Can't say for sure yet, but just maybe I've put the past behind me, and can move on."

"I'm so glad to hear that, Red. I worried you'd be mad because I rented you a car."

"I *was* mad at you, but not for that. For sending that fax instead of calling me."

"Can you blame me? You sounded so cold in London that I was afraid to call you again."

"Don't blame me, Jay. And I wasn't cold. I was terrified. First, you don't show up in Tokyo. Then you stand me up in London with some lame excuse that it was Amex's fault. What did you expect? Cartwheels and cheers? I thought you were avoiding me."

"Good God! Me avoid you? How could you think that? You're the only family I have."

"Works both ways, Jay. How could you think I'd be cold to the only family I have?"

"Touché!" Jason replied, squeezing her arm, and they walked on in companionable silence.

Bloodbath

She tossed him the keys when they reached the car, and he unlocked the trunk. As he put in his bag, he spied something wedged in a recess at the back, almost hidden from view. He reached in to extract a small package wrapped in plain brown paper, and squeezed it out of curiosity. It felt like a stuffed toy.

Before he could ask Alexis about it, she picked up the conversation right where they left it moments ago. "Speaking of the only family we have, Ravi asked me a strange question about some man called Jonathon Wolff, wondering if he was related to me. I told him that was the name of my biological father, but he was dead, along with all his first degree relatives. So it had to be either a very distant relative, or a coincidence. It felt spooky, though, to hear his name."

He heard her and his mind went blank. He had lived in dread of this moment when she discovered the truth about the man named Jonathan Wolff, praying only that it came after her demons were gone forever. But he was so unprepared for it that he felt the world spin and had to grab on to the car to keep his balance. The package fell from his hand and rolled under the car.

Then he heard a strangled sob from Alexis, saw her stagger and fall against the car, and everything else in the world ceased to exist.

He ran to grab her before she fell, yanked open the passenger-side door to lower her into the seat, and knelt down beside her.

Her face was grey from shock, with huge, unfocused orbs for eyes. A face remembered from the worst time in his life. Slack, as if paralyzed. Devoid of all expression. Blank eyes staring at nothingness. What the doctors termed catatonia.

He looked down at her hands, clawed like talons around the page of a magazine, and he pried it from her grasp. He saw the headline "The Reclusive Wolf who is Taming the Asian Tigers", with the picture of a man in a wheelchair underneath, and felt sick to the stomach. The recluse had chosen this of all weeks to give his first public interview in decades.

Then he smoothed out the page crumpled by her clawed hand, and saw the inset panel titled 'From Rags to Riches on Wheels'', with the picture of a young Marine. And his blood ran cold.

It was the picture their mother had treasured. Of a man she believed dead.

He heard Alexis let out a heart-rending cry, and all he could do was put his arms around her and hold her close, whispering he was there and would never leave her.

CHAPTER 9

Randhawa was getting desperate. There had been no news from Dhindsa for twelve hours.

He didn't dare call Dhindsa's office or his cell phone, in case he was under arrest.

By two o'clock, anxiety turned to panic, forcing Randhawa to do something expressly forbidden by Kalidas. He called Dhindsa at home.

A woman's voice answered and he introduced himself, asking for Dhindsa.

The response was a barrage of sobs and wails, mingled with incomprehensible words. He held the phone away from his ear for several seconds, and was about to disconnect when a male voice, coherent and controlled, came on the line. And he heard what happened.

Dhindsa and Kalra were both dead, Dhindsa from a single gunshot from Kalra's gun and Kalra from a blow that broke his neck and jaw. There were no witnesses, but the deaths were simultaneous. The police believed they fought and killed each other.

Randhawa mouthed a meaningless condolence, then hung up, swearing to himself.

The mother-fuckers! What were they doing, brawling like hoodlums? Damn them! Damn the whore, too! Even if she had the elephant, he couldn't do a fucking thing to get it back. Not with the feds watching his every move.

He remembered Kalidas's warning and was terrified. It wasn't his fault that the sample was lost, but that made no difference. Kalidas would carry out his threat.

He saw himself standing with arms upraised, handcuffed to a pair of rings under the cross bar of the soccer goal in the camp, and Gurung with his whip…and almost pissed in his pants.

* * * * * * * * * * *

Kalidas had never felt affection for any human being. The closest he came to it might be his kinship with the three men sitting across from him—a bond steeped in the blood of those who dared to stand in his way.

Gurung and Jarnail Singh were his sword arms, to wield as and when he chose, for the single purpose of meting out death.

And Karim Chand, who attended to the day-to-day running of his criminal enterprise, was even more indispensable. Skinny, short, and bespectacled, the man had an uncanny ability to anticipate Kalidas's needs and thoughts. And a fanatical devotion to the service of his master. Which meant Kalidas's devotion to the Mother became Karim Chand's purpose as well. And the need to offer a blood sacrifice to Kali at regular intervals became his need, too. That was why he prized the man above the other two.

But affection? That was reserved for the Mother. No one else. Not even Karim Chand.

Kalidas watched his secretary finish decoding the message from Randhawa and waited for him to speak, but Karim Chand just sat with his head bowed, saying nothing.

"What are you waiting for?" Kalidas snapped.

As always, he spoke in Hindi, the only language that all four had in common, even though it was mother tongue only to Karim Chand.

His secretary lifted his head. Kalidas took one look at his face, grey with shock, and leaned over to snatch the message from his fingers. He read the first three lines and it was as though someone kicked him in his stomach. "Who is this Alexis Wolff?" he shouted. "Is she related to the bastard who humiliated us?"

Karim Chand cringed. "We never found him, Huzoor, so I can't say."

"Then find out," Kalidas said.

"But he disappeared, Huzoor!"

"You idiot! Much has changed since then. We now have high-level sources like Chittale in the External Affairs Ministry and Baruah in the Prime Minister's Office. I want them to search all records under the name of J. Wolff. Old visa records will be most helpful. I want a detailed report within a week. Do I make myself clear?"

"Yes, Huzoor. It will be done."

"This is priority number one, but I will not tolerate it as an excuse for delays or glitches in our grand plan for the next year. It's on a very tight schedule, which Randhawa's carelessness has made even tighter. We don't have time to look for another buyer. We stay with Bindra, but he must find and eliminate the leak in his organization before we can proceed."

Karim Chand nodded. "I will tell him, Huzoor."

"Tell him also that I, not he, will decide how to get the sample to him."

"I will, Huzoor."

"One last thing. Tell Randhawa to report here for punishment. Gurung, you will see to it."

He saw the Gurkha's eyes light up.

CHAPTER 10

Jack Reynolds, Chief of Security for Lone Wolf Corporation, watched the man known behind his back as "Ole Jaws" and braced for the storm he knew was coming.

To his surprise, Jonathan Wolff's response was muted. "When did you find out about this, Jack?" he asked mildly.

"She called yesterday, Jonathan, but I wanted to wait until we could confirm it was a hoax, before bringing it to your attention."

"Why, pray tell, are you unable to confirm it is a hoax?"

Reynolds felt his stomach muscles tighten. Underneath Jonathan Wolff's voice was something like the rumble in a tiger's throat. He chose his words with great care, knowing he was entering very dangerous territory.

"We have verified that a female of that name was born in Miami on the date she gave. We have also verified that a woman named Alexis Wolff spent the first twenty-odd years of her life in South Africa. We have no more than that to go on right now."

"Then get more!" The rumble was now the snarl of an enraged tiger. "I want to know everything about this bitch. Everything! Do you hear? Every detail. How many times she takes a crap. The name of every man she ever screwed. If she ever missed a period or had a toenail cut, I want to know it.

"When you have all that, start again and find out everything even she doesn't know. Like every man her mother fucked. Like the sewer out of which her father crawled. Do you understand?"

Even though he had braced for it, the Jekyll-to-Hyde switch was so stunning that it was all Reynolds could do to nod.

Wolff continued in a more normal voice, "Then, my friend, we're going to nail her hide to the wall, just like all the others."

Bloodbath

Reynolds was so rattled that he couldn't stop from blurting out, "Jonathan, is there any chance she might be the real thing?"

No sooner were the words out of his mouth than he knew he had made a dreadful mistake. He saw Wolff's face blanch and waited for another explosion.

Wolff just stared at him for several second. Then he said, in a barely audible whisper, "If anyone but you had asked me that…"

The unspoken threat hung in the air. Then he said, in a normal voice, "I will answer only because of our twenty-year friendship. The answer has been, and always will be, 'No!' You, of all people, should know why she is an out-and-out fraud. A gold-digger!"

"I'm sorry, Jonathan. I should never have asked."

Wolff gave a thin smile. "You were only doing your job."

"She said she would call back in one week. She wanted to give you enough time to check out her background."

"Cocky bitch!"

"I know. We'll have all we need by then. The staff are on it."

Wolff nodded and Reynolds left the room. Outside, he leaned against the wall and wiped his sweaty hands on his thighs, waiting for the hammering in his head to subside.

* * * * * * * * * * *

Alexis's upcoming meeting with Jonathan Wolff was becoming a full-fledged obsession. She played it in her mind again, and again, trying to imagine how he might react to her.

In one imagining he was cold and contemptuous, and she felt utter contempt for him. In another, he was defiant and angry, and she felt anger explode. However, when she imagined him faking regret for abandoning her mother, hatred lashed her soul, leaving her shaking like a leaf.

On its heels came a deep sorrow for her mother, a gentle woman who preserved the memory of her betrayer for the sake of her children, never suspecting he was alive. Then the tears would start, hour after hour, without as much as a sob.

She knew Jason was very worried. He tried his best to stop her from going through with it, saying that the man in the magazine was not the one in the photo their mother kept of their father. She confounded him when she produced the photo, showing they were the same man.

He changed tactics then, reminding her how fragile she was. The shrinks called it post-traumatic stress disorder. The night terrors that came with it were not as frequent as they once were, but their ferocity was undiminished. So, he said, why risk her sanity to revive something that had been dead for so long that the man might as well be dead? She should bury it, just as he did when he discovered the truth.

Deep inside, she knew Jason was right. She was rushing headlong into an emotional minefield. Once entered, there would be no leaving it. Yet, she was helpless to resist.

Like a moth to a flame.

* * * * * * * * * * *

Jonathan Wolff stared at the ceiling of his bedroom, unable to sleep. The shadows were taunting him again.

Poor little rich man, they sneered. So rich, you could buy anything you wanted in the world! So how come you're so lonely, rich man? Can't buy your way out of that, can you rich man?

He heard the shadows and knew they were right. They knew what the rest of the world did not. This was his greatest handicap. Not the withered legs and wheelchair the world saw.

The shadows knew better. They saw his loneliness and mocked his weakness.

For years, he had kept it a secret from the world. The "Lone Wolf," they called him—a cliché, but not one he resented. His corporate logo, after all, was the head of a timber wolf, howling at the moon.

He identified with the image. The wolf was a predator without peer. A survivor in life's harshest environment. Without a pack and no mate, though, the lone wolf was destined to roam the wilderness alone until he died.

Jonathan Wolff knew it for his own destiny. The Lone Wolf could never take a mate. Nor could he sire any cubs.

This was his Achilles heel, the one place where his resolve could not protect him. It compelled him to destroy charlatans like the woman who called herself Alexis Wolff. He was going to crucify her.

The thought gave him momentary solace.

Then the shadows began to laugh again.

CHAPTER 11

The reports from Chittale and Baruah both arrived on the morning the master's one-week deadline was set to expire. Karim Chand knew what they contained because he decoded them.

The one from Chittale, in the Ministry of External Affairs, was a rehash of what they already knew, except for one nugget of new information. The bombshell was in Baruah's report from the P.M.O. He was dreading the moment when Kalidas read it.

Karim Chand watched as Kalidas read Chittale's report at the daily morning briefing and put it down with a smile of satisfaction "So! It is as I suspected. They are brother and sister. No wonder we could not find him then. He was hiding like a jackal in a remote ashram. I want our agents in the U.K., the U.S., and South Africa to find out everything about them. When the time comes, we will arrange something very painful and unpleasant to happen to them."

He tossed the reports across the table to Karim Chand, and said, "Congratulate Chittale and Baruah for a job well done, and make sure they get a substantial bonus."

Karim Chand pushed the reports back towards Kalidas. "I think you should read Baruah's report too, Huzoor," he said. "There is something in it that is important."

Kalidas frowned and picked up Baruah's report. As he read it, his face turned black with rage, and the veins in his neck distending almost to the point of rupture. When he was done, he crushed the message in his fist and slammed it down on the table, letting out a scream that had Jarnail and Gurung jumping up, thinking the master was suffering some sort of seizure.

Kalidas waved them back down. Still unable to articulate, he gestured to Karim Chand. He rushed to explain. "Do you remember when we were on the run, how the Indians seemed to know exactly where we were headed?"

"You don't have to remind us," Gurung said angrily. "What does that have to do with this brother and sister?"

"Baruah discovered that an American company gave the Indians a dossier about Huzoor that dossier was so good and so detailed that they knew everything about us when they launched their manhunt. The owner of that company is named Wolff."

Both Jarnail and Gurung jumped out of their chairs. "You mean the sister-fucker who humiliated us?" Gurung shouted.

"No. Not Jason Wolff," answered Karim Chand. "This one is Jonathan Wolff."

"I do not believe this," said Gurung. "The same last name, yet again? Is this some kind of ridiculous joke? I will kill Baruah for reporting such garbage."

"It isn't garbage. Baruah found it by accident, when he searched for files cross-referenced under the name of 'J. Wolff'. Two were identical to what Chittale found, about the sister and the ashram where Jason Wolff stayed. The third had all the stuff on Jonathan, not Jason Wolff, and was marked Top Secret, but Baruah had access as the Additional Secretary in the P.M.O."

"Another Wolff!" his master snarled. "It is not a common name. I am sure they are related. I want to know everything there is to know about this Wolff family. Assign our American contacts to work full-time on finding out about them."

Karim Chand relished the chance to show he had anticipated his master's needs. "I have the information you need right here, Huzoor. Jonathan Wolff just gave his first-ever interview to an American news magazine."

He held up last week's issue of Newsweek and waved it triumphantly. "It says here that Jonathan Wolff is a reclusive billionaire with no living relatives, and no family of his own. He is an orphan and he never married."

"You fool," Kalidas said. "That means nothing. Have you not heard of illegitimate children?"

"Huzoor! There is no way Jonathan Wolff can be their father. It says here that he suffered an injury as a Marine that left him paralyzed at the age of twenty. That injury also castrated him."

Karim Chand flipped the magazine open and pointed to a photograph of a man in a wheelchair. "Jonathan Wolff is an impotent cripple—a miserable eunuch confined to a wheelchair for nearly thirty years."

CHAPTER 12

The phone went dead, but the contempt in the voice of the woman named Alexis Wolff stayed with him, like a coating of filth.

Jonathan Wolff sat frozen in his wheelchair, feeling the constant, debilitating pain in his groin rise to the surface, gnawing at his bones with all its old intensity. He tried to suppress it, but the contempt in that voice had sapped his resolve.

He looked down at his withered legs and, for the first time in decades, he felt revulsion for the physical and emotional cripple he had become. It was the legacy of the Al-Husseini missile strike on the Dhahran military barracks during the First Gulf War, in which 44 Pennsylvania Army Reservist were killed. He happened to be visiting a friend from school when the missile hit. It killed his friend. He wasn't so lucky. He survived—at a terrible price.

A piece of shrapnel tore into his groin, emasculating him. Another severed his spinal cord, leaving him paralyzed from the waist down. After multiple surgeries and months of rehabilitation, he got his discharge. With a wheelchair and a Purple Heart. He kept the first. He threw away the other. The last thing he needed was another piece of metal to remind him of the metal still in him.

Afterwards, he sank into an abyss of drugs and despair. For three long years, he wallowed in that hellhole, somehow surviving through the worst of his self-destructive urges. When he emerged, miraculously whole, he discovered he was the inheritor of three hundred thousand dollars left to him by his grandfather!

It was an unbelievable sum for that time, and it started him on a journey that would make him one of the richest men in the world.

But it was a journey made alone.

The old man was his only family. He took the place of both the father who died in Vietnam, and the mother who didn't survive his birth. He got the news that the old man had died while he was convalescing from his second major surgery, so the old man was buried with no one to cry over him. That night Jonathan cried for the first and last time in his adult life. After that, he had no one left to cry for. And no one left to cry for him.

Or so he thought.

He looked at the folder on his desk. The words 'Alexis Wolff' sprang out at him and he flinched.

The biographical details in the folder were straightforward.

Twenty-six years old. A doctor. Born in Miami, Florida. Grows up in South Africa. World-class markswoman with a rifle. Second *dan* black belt in karate. U.S. citizen by birthright. Selected for the Olympics in shooting. Withdraws because parents are victims of a presumed guerrilla atrocity on their farm in South Africa. Twin brother, Jason, ex-commando, a major in the Alpha-Tau brigade, the elite and highly secret anti-terrorism unit in South Africa. Both millionaires, thanks to a reward from DeBeers for recovering the single biggest haul of smuggled diamonds ever—half-a-billion dollars' worth. Details sketchy.

The accompanying psychological profile assembled by the team was anything *but* straightforward:

MAJOR TRAUMA:

Parents butchered. She identified the horribly mutilated bodies.

GUILT:

She escaped because she was off on a trip in the bush.

ABERRANT BEHAVIOR:

Short-term: Catatonic withdrawal.

Medium term: Joins extreme right wing organization called the Self Defence League, dedicated to re-establishing white supremacy in South Africa through violent overthrow.

Long term: Lives as a recluse for five years at a ninja monastery in Japan.

ASSESSMENT/DIAGNOSIS:

Post-Traumatic Stress Disorder.

PROGNOSIS:

Emotionally unstable, potentially dangerous.

Even worse was the supplementary information about her mother, and the accompanying questions to which the investigating team could find no answers.

Mother, Mary O'Reilly, from Export, PA, just outside Pittsburgh, home town of JAW. She claims that Jonathan Alexander Wolff is the father of her children. *Why?*

Mary O'Reilly migrates to South Africa at seventeen to join her only living relative, an uncle, after her entire family dies in a car crash. She is the only one not in the car. *Why?*

Mary O'Reilly comes to the US to give birth to her twin children, claims JAW is their father, yet she does not try to contact JAW. *Why?*

His mind screamed out the answers. *I KNOW WHY!*

She was the last woman I slept with, nine months almost to the day of their birth. She knew I was their father. That's why she listed Jonathan Alexander Wolff as their father. That's why she named them Jason and Alexis.

The night her family died was the night she conceived, just before I left for the Middle East. That's why she wasn't in that car.

After the bombing, even if she tried to find out what happened to me, the Marines would have told her nothing, because she wasn't a relative. I never tried to contact her and she couldn't contact me even if she tried because, for the next three years, I was dead as far as the world was concerned, anyway. So, for all she knew, I was dead.

He buried his face in his hands and sat without moving.

He had never cared if she even existed!

He could not recall if he ever considered Mary O'Reilly anything more than a conquest. A once-in-a-lifetime experience that was too hurtful to remember. So, he locked it away behind a door in his memory, never to be touched again.

Now he couldn't even remember the color of her hair or eyes.

He leaned forward and flicked open the folder. Taped inside the cover was the picture of a seventeen-year-old girl, the most recent one of Alexis Wolff they could find at such short notice.

It transfixed him. Not just her beauty. The. Or the eyes. It was her face that captivated him! With its mix of serenity and passion, of vulnerability and strength. A rare mix that would be striking even in someone much older.

And that flaming red hair hinted at a temper in sharp contrast to the humor and mischief sparkling in those crystalline green eyes.

It was because he was staring into those eyes that the door in his memory crashed open, and it was as if he had stepped through a time-warp. All of a sudden, he was looking at the face of that other seventeen-year-old girl from decades ago.

He heard her voice in his head and spectral fingers caressed the nape of his neck. For a moment, he thought he was looking at a ghost arisen from his long-dead past.

He slammed the folder shut, thrusting her picture away from him. Then his rational brain took over and his lips twisted into a sardonic smile. After all, what was there to fear from any ghost in his past, when he had danced with Death, himself, and won?

The thought comforted him for a few seconds, but then came a disturbing realization. He knew now that the one thing he yearned for all his life could have been his for the asking had he only thought to search for it.

Until his dying day, that regret would haunt him. Now there would be no escaping the shadows. Their taunts were far more malevolent than anything he had to fear from the vengeful ghost of Mary O'Reilly, resurrected in the flesh of her daughter.

Then, without thinking, he corrected himself. *No! My daughter.*

The words barely popped into his head when their significance hit him. From far away, he heard a whisper of "My daughter!" and felt anguish that he never dreamed even existed. Compared to it, all the physical pain he endured was nothing.

Then the tears came, for the first time since the day he got the news that the old man was dead. He had cried then for what he lost and could never have again. He wept now for something that would never be his to lose.

CHAPTER 13

A lexis's hands were trembling as she stepped toward the closed door. She had been anticipating this moment with dread ever since that phone call a week ago. Now that it was upon her, there was no going back. She steadied her nerve and knocked.

She heard a voice say, "Please come in."

She opened the door, entering his office, calm and composed on the outside but fighting to control the panic inside her.

No sooner did the door close behind her, his wheelchair drifted towards her and he extended his hand in greeting.

She took a step forward and then stopped dead in her tracks, caught off-guard by his powerful aura. For a moment, she felt something she never expected. Was it…could it be…pride?

Guilt exploded inside her. She was there to confront the charlatan, not to admire him, for God's sake!

She ignored his outstretched hand and looked into his eyes instead.

She received her second shock.

There was no anger or contempt in his eyes. No faked regret. Not even cold indifference. Just uncertain anxiety.

He withdrew his hand and turned his wheelchair sideways to usher her into the room. "Miss Wolff. How nice of you to come to see me. What can I do for you?"

Alexis was bitter. "I'm glad that at least you will not deny me my name, Mr. Wolff," she said, anger in her voice. "It certainly breaks a pattern you set with my mother."

She saw a desperate hurt in his eyes and was pleased by it. She continued. "I hope you haven't spent a great deal of money researching my background."

She pointed to the folder lying on the table in plain view, but his eyes never left her face. She refused to back down now, not when she knew she could wound him.

"In case you're worried I am some gold-digger, trying to milk you of your fortune, let me reassure you. You and everything you have are worthless to me because you denied my mother the right to either. So, why would I want anything to do with you, let alone your fortune?"

She paused to lick her dry lips and steady the tremor that crept into her voice. He just sat unmoving in his wheelchair, his eyes never leaving hers. She might as well be talking to a statue carved from stone.

"As long as I live, I will pray that it will dawn on you one day that you willfully threw away something you can never buy with all your money. I just hope you get some small comfort from knowing your daughter will hate you every day of her life, because it is all you will have to comfort you on your deathbed. Goodbye, Mr. Wolff."

At last, she had her wish.

The veil slipped from his eyes and she was gazing into the agony in his soul, stark and raw, like a wound. Something she said had struck an almost mortal blow to his psyche. She had achieved her purpose but she felt no triumph, only the numbness of defeat.

She saw a flicker of surprise in his eyes, and looked away, furious at herself for revealing her own torment.

Then, she heard him say, "I have listened to all that you had to say. And say it you did, because you are so sure you're right. Surely you can't be so self-righteous as to refuse to even countenance the possibility that an alternative explanation might exist for what happened all those years ago?"

She opened her mouth to retort, but the words died, unsaid.

He said gently, "I ask you to just hear what I have to say. Then, if you still feel my actions were unjustified, you are free to leave."

A voice in her head warned her to leave now—that there might be a very malevolent purpose behind his stunning transformation. From desperate hurt to assertive confidence in that one instant when she revealed the hurt in her own soul.

She ignored the voice.

Maybe she needed a reason to hate him. Maybe it was the same moth-to-flame attraction that brought her here. Whatever it was, she knew only that she was in too deep to pull back.

Taking a deep breath, she walked towards the sofa. She sat down, fighting to control her emotions, and waited with fearful anticipation for him to start speaking.

PART THREE

BLOOD SHED

CHAPTER 1

Alexis awakened to the screech of a bald eagle. Through the canopy of Douglas firs, she could see the blue sky. Dawn had broken.

She was camped in the Canadian Rockies about a mile from an Inuit village near the border between Nunavut and the Yukon. The wilderness was so integral to her existence that she seized any opportunity to escape into it, even if it was just for one night in the midst of a grueling two-week trip across Northwest Canada. It was a spiritual lifeline that had its roots in the open veldts of her homeland in South Africa, extended to the mountains of Hokkaido in Japan, and had found its current home in the Rockies.

She broke camp and began the hike back to the village, marveling at how her life had changed in the year since that fateful first meeting with Jonathan. Thanks to him, she was working as a physician, delivering basic health care to remote Native Canadian villages in the inaccessible interior of western Canada. Her unique combination of skills as a physician and helicopter pilot made her ideal for it, but it still took some doing on Jonathan's part for the Canadian authorities to grant her a license.

They got a potent inducement from the Lone Wolf Foundation, Jonathan's philanthropic arm. A generous donation of two helicopters, funds for their maintenance, ancillary support staff, and all medical supplies needed for the purpose. In perpetuity! With only one precondition: Alexis had to be the Physician Director. It took almost a year to cut through the red tape but, thanks to Jonathan, her life now had purpose.

As wonderful as that was, it still paled in significance compared to something else Jonathan brought into her life. Peace.

The awkwardness of their first meeting and her bitter hatred for his perceived betrayal and abandonment were now a distant memory. She knew now that his ruthlessly driven exterior was a cloak for his vulnerability, and that what she thought was his 'betrayal' was the product of circumstance, not malice.

Acceptance did not come overnight, and there were many missteps along the way, but the last few months had seen the blossoming of something special for him as much as for her.

For her, it sprang from a need to fill the void left in her life by the death of the stepfather who doted on her. For Jonathan, it was a longing for the family he never had.

It was a perfect match. Sensing her need, he became openly paternal. And his need for family became the foundation of her psychological rebirth. Even the dreaded night terrors had vanished. She hadn't had one for a year.

Jonathan's presence in her life was the source of her inner peace. It was Jason, though, to whom she owed her sanity. He was the one constant she relied on to maintain some semblance of normalcy in her life. Every cliché she could think of applied to him. Bedrock. Sheet anchor. Lifeline.

It was part of a pattern set years earlier. She could not remember a time when he was not there for her to lean on. During the days after the massacre, when she had her breakdown, he stood by her, forgetting his own pain to heal hers. Even afterwards, when hate drove her to join the Self Defence League, he refused to criticize her obsession with the weapons drills, the military exercises, and flight instruction to become a chopper pilot.

He waited for the hate to work its way out of her system, trusting her to wake up one day to the realization that she would not find inner peace by participating in a race war in South Africa. When that day dawned, and she decided to flee to India in search of that elusive inner peace, Jason went with her, without her even having to ask.

Bloodbath

His support never wavered even after she abandoned him, thinking she could escape her demons by hiding from the world. He waited patiently for her to come to her senses, never judging or resenting her for abandoning him. And, the instant she returned to the world, he was right there for her to lean on, yet again.

Because of Jason, she learned to live again.

Because of Jonathan, she found peace, and her purpose in life.

The two men were developing a camaraderie of their own, contributing to her sense of—dare she say it?—family. She loved that she was the reason for their burgeoning relationship. Jason had to overcome his own antipathy towards Jonathan, but he did, sensing how much it meant to her. When Jonathan realized how important Jason was to her, he reached out to Jason himself. That mutual outreach led to Jonathan's discovery that Jason possessed an analytical mind that made him perfectly suited to the role of a trusted advisor.

Even if it stayed that way without evolving any further, she wouldn't care. It was enough for her that the three of them were now a unit and she was the glue that held it together.

Jonathan was going to make it official, with a statement to the press. Knowing the furor it would cause, she and Jason were far away, counting on the famously short attention span of the paparazzi and public to be diverted by the time they returned.

Jonathan's public acknowledgement of their relationship held much more than symbolic significance for her. It would be a perfect foundation on which to finish rebuilding her psyche.

CHAPTER 2

K alidas's icy demeanor did not change as he read the message from Randhawa saying that the fifth and last consignment had gone through without a hitch.

His initial failure a year ago aside, Randhawa had been nothing short of perfect, successfully overseeing the transfer of one-and-a-quarter metric tons of pure heroin to Bindra in the past year—a wholesale value of almost two hundred million dollars. All that remained was for Bindra to transfer the final payment to his bank in Macao for the total in his account to top half-a-billion dollars!

It was an extraordinary amount, even for his criminal enterprise—the cumulative profits from his drug and arms deals over the past four years. The deal just concluded with Bindra was the big killing, the one he needed to get to that magical number.

Who would have thought that the near-disaster of a year ago would result in such success? The Wolff woman's interference had forced Bindra to deal with the leak in his organization. Even more importantly, it forced Kalidas to devise a foolproof method for shipping heroin in bulk quantities without risk of discovery.

It required a mid-ocean transfer between his cargo ships plying the Bangkok-LA route and a deep-sea fishing trawler belonging to Bindra. The key was to bring the two vessels together in the vastness of the Pacific Ocean at a precise location and time, without breaking radio silence or using the GPS system. One of his lieutenants, an electronics whiz named Grewal, solved the problem.

Using old-fashioned navigational skill, both ships had to reach a pre-selected sector. Then, a low-frequency radio signal, transmitted by a continuously varying random frequency generator and matching transponder on each ship, drew them together. After transferring the cargo, the cargo ship went on to dock at L.A., and the trawler made its way back to British Columbia with the cases of heroin buried under the tons of catch in its hold. It had worked flawlessly six times, once to send the sample for Bindra's approval, and for five shipments of heroin, weighing two-hundred and fifty kilograms each.

It was a satisfying conclusion to the operation.

It was also the beginning of Bloodbath.

"Bloodbath!" he said, rolling the word over his tongue.

He said it aloud again, and then again, like a parent repeating the name of a favorite child. That was exactly how he viewed it. As his brain child.

Its official code-name in Hindi was "Khoon ka Snaan", but the phrase did not trip off the tongue like the English word "Bloodbath", its literal translation. He named it in recognition of his ritual bloodbath in Kali's honor. The name represented his intent to cause a bloodbath on a scale never seen in the world. The entire population of India—over a billion human beings!—would be involved in a cataclysm of terror that would make every other civil war in history look like a backyard skirmish.

It was breathtaking in concept, and its launch was just weeks away. It needed just one more ingredient to succeed, which was the most critical of all.

The grace of Kali.

He had no concerns about that, though. The date for the launch of Bloodbath coincided with *amaavasya*, the darkest night of the lunar month, when the power of Kali and all those who served her was at its zenith. He would harness that power with a ritual timed for the very night of the launch of Bloodbath.

It would be the perfect counterpoint for a defining event in the history of the world. Nine of the most violent terrorist organizations in India would participate in a 'summit' he was organizing to launch it. The two major militant rebel factions in Kashmir were coming in order to further their jihad in Kashmir.

81

Even though they received funding from Pakistan, that bankrupt nation could not do what he could do for them.

The three militant groups still engaged in a hopeless fight for a Sikh homeland in Punjab were sending their top men. The return of peace had made their quest futile, but Bloodbath would change that, as it would for four other organizations from different corners of India with an inflated sense of their importance. The National Socialist Council of Nagaland, the Peoples War Group in Andhra Pradesh, the Naxal Bari movement in West Bengal, and the Mizoram National Front. Their much-touted 'successes' never threatened India's survival. The giant simply brushed them off like pinpricks and kept going. Their only hope lay in Bloodbath. That was why they had no choice but to come.

The names of the attendees were a roll call of the most wanted terrorists in India, who agreed to put aside their differences and find common cause at his bidding, even though terrorism was all they had in common.

No one else could have pulled off anything with this scope and sweep. Kalidas did because he recognized that it could not be about joining forces. He coined the slogan "Interdependence without sacrificing independence" to give them a common objective.

That objective was to stretch and weaken India's resources through a strategy of tactical coordination, launching simultaneous offensives at several locations. It would improve everyone's chances of winning their individual battles, because the enemy would not be able to shift his forces from one sector to shore up his defenses in another.

The logic was ruthless. Yet, the obstacles he faced were almost insurmountable, simply because he was dealing with some of the most paranoid and closed groups on the planet.

The first problem was getting them to see they shared a common goal. He solved that through the trust he had earned as their major weapons supplier, coaxing them into accepting that a collective effort would serve everyone's individual interest.

Bloodbath

Once that obstacle was overcome, the next problem was the logistical nightmare of getting them to coordinate their operations. He broke the deadlock by offering his own extensive communications network to coordinate the effort, free of charge.

Last, but not least, he had to make sure that the effort did not lose steam because one group failed to fulfill its end of the bargain due to a shortage of funds. That was where the half-a-billion dollars now sitting in his account in Macao came in. After setting aside fifty million for his operating expenses, he would split the remainder nine ways—a gift of fifty million dollars' worth of weapons and munitions to each group just to get things started.

That was how he would light India's funeral pyre.

Bloodbath would further an even more ambitious agenda of his. After all, not even he could afford to throw away half-a-billion dollars just for personal gratification. Bloodbath was much more than a vehicle for vengeance. It was an investment for the future.

First, a civil war in India would give him a near-inexhaustible market for his wares. Second, he hoped it would lead to a breakdown in the civilian command-and-control that India had in place for its nuclear arsenal. Then he would harvest the nuclear dividend for which he really lusted.

Even if the civilian nuclear safeguards somehow held in democratic India, they would not in Pakistan, a failed nation-state whose very existence depended on a common interest in the destruction of India, and on a shadow military government that controlled everything. With the common enemy gone, thanks to Bloodbath, it would take little more than a nudge for Pakistan to fall apart, and with it its almost non-existent nuclear command-and-control. Then, Pakistan's nuclear weapons, if not India's own arsenal, would be easy pickings.

Either way, the destruction of India was the key to his becoming the most powerful contraband arms dealer in the world.

A knock on the door broke his train of thought.

"Enter!" he said, raising his voice.

His three closest assistants came in and sat down. He looked at Karim Chand with raised eyebrows and received a nod that told him the last installment of money was in. Not that he doubted it, but he never took such things for granted.

He looked around the table at the three men. He stood on the threshold of doing something that would change the world, and he needed their unquestioning loyalty more than ever. Yet, when he began to issue his instructions, his voice was cold and emotionless, as if he was discussing the routine business of the camp.

"Each one of you will be responsible for very specific aspects of the summit. I will start with you, Karim. You are in charge of transport and hospitality."

"As you command, Huzoor," replied Karim Chand.

"For security reasons, I will not allow individual arrivals at this camp. All participants will arrive in Yangon on the day before the summit and be flown to our forward camp in Shan State in our private jets. They will be brought here as one group, under cover of darkness, in the Sikorsky helicopters."

"It will be done, Huzoor!"

"While they are here, the participants will stay in the guest cottages, one to each group. I want the cottages ready for my inspection in two days."

"They will be ready, Huzoor."

"The Lynx helicopter will be on standby at the Shan camp in case Dr. Pramod needs to be brought here at short notice for a medical emergency. Since Bansal was a medical orderly in the Indian army, he can handle minor problems, but he must check our medical inventory here."

"I will see to it, Huzoor."

Kalidas now turned to Gurung. "You are in charge of assembling each participating organizations' wish list."

He handed a file to the Gurkha. "Fifty million dollars buys a lot of ordnance, and no one expects to receive it all at once. So pick a few items on each wish list, about a million dollars' worth, as my parting gift to them."

"As you command, Huzoor," Gurung said.

Kalidas addressed the Sikh last of all. "Jarnail, you will handle security. We cannot be too careful. If there is a breach of security, we must be ready for anything the Indians throw at us. Check the radar equipment and make sure the surface-to-air missile launchers, including those in the armory, are fully charged and operational, and put the missile platoon on full alert starting today."

The Sikh nodded without saying a word.

"There is one last thing!" Kalidas turned his attention back to Karim Chand.

"Have you found a subject for the ritual on the night the summit ends?"

Karim grinned. "I want it to be a surprise, Huzoor. Rest assured she will be everything that you—I mean, the Mother— would desire."

Kalidas smiled. "Okay, Karim. If that is how you want it. Make sure, for your own sake, that she is all you say she is. After all, you have a stake in this, too!"

Kalidas dismissed the three men with a wave of his hand and returned to his daydream when the door closed behind them.

After the launch of Bloodbath, he would turn his attention to two remaining items on his agenda for revenge.

It was curious that both were named Wolff. He still couldn't believe they were unrelated.

CHAPTER 3

Karim Chand rode the elevator down to the bunker in a state of extreme sexual arousal. He knew he was in for a big reward if his selection met the master's expectations.

The elevator doors opened, and the lights in the hallway came on, triggered by motion sensors installed by Grewal.

It was a rare indulgence permitted by Kalidas. Every other electronic gadget in the camp was strictly utilitarian. Like the elevator's hand-print scanner that restricted bunker access to just the master and him. And the programmable electronic lock for the armory, whose code was known only to Jarnail, Gurung, and him.

He walked through the first door on his right into the "Filing Room". Except, the "files" were actually CD's and DVDs containing every piece of information relating to Kalidas's activities, past and present, and every detail of every individual who ever worked for Kalidas. Those disks ensured that death was the only release from his master's embrace.

Karim Chand had eyes only for the one old-fashioned file cabinet in the room. It held the records of the system he developed so his master could fulfill his pledge to offer Kali human blood four times each year.

In the early days, Jarnail and Gurung provided subjects for the ritual blood sacrifice through random kidnappings of young girls. However, the public outcry quickly escalated to the level of hysteria, so it fell to Karim Chand to devise a plan that the master himself called a stroke of genius.

He hit upon the idea of suborning individuals working in orphanages and shelters for the homeless and destitute in India. In return for a handsome annual retainer, they identified potential candidates "suitable for sale as prostitutes". Now, he could get four subjects each year, from different sources, without anyone in his feeder network suspecting his true purpose.

He catalogued every subject with meticulous care, using a star rating to reflect desirability. The upcoming ritual deserved nothing less than five-star rating. And there was only one subject of that standard in his portfolio. She was filed under 'C' for 'Chakraborthy', the warden at the Hostel for Destitute Women in Kolkata, one of his most reliable suppliers.

He opened her file and gazed at the photographs, conscious of an ache in his loins. The photographs were black-and-white, but the face and figure needed no embellishment. Something about the set of her jaw and look in her eyes said she would not go meekly like a lamb to the slaughter. This one would fight and struggle until the very last moment. He imagined her spread-eagled naked on the altar, and the ache in his loins became even stronger.

He scurried to the door, holding the photograph in his hand, and cast a furtive glance at the elevator. It was still at bunker level.

He hesitated for a moment. Then, unable to contain himself, he darted down the corridor towards his bedroom, almost tripping over his feet in his haste.

* * * * * * * * * * *

The 'outside' phone rang at 5:05 a.m., jolting Karim Chand awake. He scrambled out of bed, cursing whoever was calling so early, and ran to the radio in the Communications Room across the hall from his bedroom. The news had better be important or the caller would answer for it!

The radio was the sole conduit for communication between the camp and the outside world, and only a handful of individuals in Kalidas's network had the equipment and contact information to use it. It was equipped with a scrambler, of course, custom-built by Grewal, so calls were impossible to trace or tap.

The call was from Mukherjee, Kalidas's agent in Kolkata, to report Jonathan Wolff's latest press conference. Karim Chand scrawled the information down on the pad where he logged all incoming and outgoing calls. Then, trembling with anxiety, he made his way to his master's bedroom and knocked on the door.

A sleepy voice commanded him to enter and he walked to where his master lay, propped on his elbow. He held out the message, with downcast eyes, and had it snatched from his hands.

He flinched when Kalidas said, "So!" But, miracle of miracles, his master did not berate him!

"You see, Karim," he said, "I was right. The cripple is the father of the two younger jackals. He acknowledged it himself."

Karim Chand sank to his knees and clutched his master's feet. "Y-yes, Huzoor. I misled you. I beg for your forgiveness."

Kalidas bent down and lifted him up. "You are forgiven, Karim. All that happens is Kali's will. Get Jarnail and Gurung. We meet in fifteen minutes."

Karim Chand scuttled out of the room.

* * * * * * * * * * *

Silence was the hallmark of Jarnail Singh's existence, but even he hadn't experienced silence he could actually feel. It lay on the room like an oppressive weight, as they waited for Kalidas to speak. Then Kalidas's voice cracked through the silence like a bolt of static, making him jump.

"Wolff! We know now that all three members of that accursed clan are engaged in a calculated and coordinated assault on me. I knew it in my heart. But Karim Chand was so sure they weren't related…"

Karim Chand ducked his head obsequiously. "You were right, Huzoor!" he said. "I shouldn't have doubted your wisdom. After all, the voice of the Mother speaks through you."

Kalidas smiled at Karim Chand. "Yes, Karim! The Mother has shown me what to do." The smile vanished. Kalidas continued. "This isn't an accident. It's a reminder from Kali that there can be no honor for me until I destroy the vermin who have sullied her glory. If I don't, Bloodbath will fail."

"So what will you do, Huzoor?" asked Gurung.

Kalidas's spoke softly. "Jonathan Wolff spends the summer in Vancouver, with no one but a chauffeur for a companion."

Jarnail Singh was puzzled. "Why is that important, Huzoor?"

"It represents opportunity. I will take revenge against all three Wolffs in one stroke, and in a manner that satisfies all of us."

Jarnail Singh felt a surge of rage. "How will their execution thousands of miles away satisfy me or Gurung? To regain our honor, we must ourselves kill the bastard who humiliated us. And you can't avenge your honor unless the man who humiliated you grovels at your feet."

"All in good time, Jarnail." His eyes shifted to Karim Chand. "Karim, are the men who did the delivery to Bindra in Vancouver?"

"Yes, Huzoor. Reddy, Grewal and Randhawa are in Vancouver, waiting for permission to take a week off in America, now that the money transfer is confirmed."

Kalidas waved his hand in dismissal. "Permission denied. In fact, all leave is cancelled until the Bloodbath summit. And anyone who complains will feel Gurung's whip."

Then Kalidas leaned forward and looked at Jarnail. "You asked me, Jarnail, how we would all get revenge against the Wolffs."

He paused, and Jarnail saw his face break into a smile—the dreadful one that always meant death. "I give you three simple steps. Kill the woman to show we mean business. Kidnap the father for bait. The son comes to us!"

The smile vanished. "This is what I want..."

CHAPTER 4

Grewal knew Reddy was angry. Kalidas had assigned the Wolff woman's execution to Randhawa, because he wanted a horrific, gangland-style murder to evoke rage and cloud reason. Randhawa had made drive-by assassination an art form in the killing fields of Punjab.

Randhawa was the natural choice, but that didn't make it any easier for Reddy to accept. His words said it all. "How much fun is it to kidnap a fucking cripple?" But Reddy would do as ordered. The penalty for disobedience or failure would be terrible.

Grewal couldn't worry about Reddy's problems, though. He had enough to worry about, himself. His assigned task required a level of skill with electronic gadgetry that no one but he possessed.

Simply put, he had to make it possible for Reddy to enter the penthouse of a building with the most sophisticated electronic security money could buy, without being seen by the security guards. Reddy would then have to exit the building unobserved, with the target subdued. All at no more than a moment's notice.

Seen like that, it was impossible. But, with unfettered access to the building for a few hours, Grewal could make the impossible easy. It would have taken forever to find the man Grewal needed to get access to the building where Jonathan Wolff lived—there were over two hundred thousand Sikhs living in British Columbia!

That was precisely why they needed a local contact in Vancouver. He was a Sikh named Surjeet Singh Khullar, who led a small group of Sikh militants—a bunch of hopeless amateurs still clutching onto the long-dead dream of a Sikh homeland in Punjab. It took them just twenty-four hours to find not one, but two Sikhs who worked in the building.

One was a gardener who did not have access to the building. The other was a janitor named Bains. Reddy was going to 'talk' to Bains today about helping them. Grewal had no doubt Bains would 'listen'. Reddy could be very persuasive!

* * * * * * * * * * *

It was past midnight when they drove into the underground garage with Grewal crouched behind the front seat, hidden from the video cameras at the entrance. He heard Bains roll down the window, then the garage door opened, and the car started forward again, made a couple of sharp turns, and came to a stop. Then he heard Bains say, "You can come out now," and sat up.

He got out and was about to saunter into the garage to stretch his legs when Bains gave a panicked squeak. "Noooo! They will see you on the camera. This is the only corner where they cannot. So don't go anywhere, please."

Bains's state of mind was understandable. He bore several marks from Reddy's "request for help". Before the "conversation" went too far, Bains caved in, begging to help, so Reddy didn't have to threaten his wife and children in Vancouver or his family in Punjab. The threat still hung over him, so he would stay caved in.

Suitcase in hand, Grewal followed Bains to the service elevator. Their destination was the penthouse, where the man who owned the building lived. He was not expected for another four days. That was more than enough time for Grewal to disable, bypass, or control every security feature installed in the garage, penthouse and elevators, and override the video cameras in the garage, so Reddy could get in and out in minutes with the target subdued.

Grewal rode the elevator, humming under his breath.

CHAPTER 5

The prospect of an execution thrilled Khullar.

It had been almost thirty years since he last witnessed the work of Randhawa, an old comrade-in-arms from the now-dormant Sikh freedom struggle in Punjab.

He had vivid memories of their time together, conducting hit-and-run raids on police stations and army outposts, planting bombs in busy bazaars and train stations, assassinating locals who dared defy them, and—best of all—hijacking buses and executing every male without a turban to terrorize all non-Sikhs into leaving Punjab.

Those were heady times when nothing seemed impossible. Vast tracts of rural territory fell under their control, and freedom—Khalistan, an independent Sikh nation!—seemed within reach.

Then the tide turned. The Indian security forces stopped playing fair, and met terror with terror. Suddenly, it was not fun anymore. They started losing—first battles, then territory and men, and finally their financial backers. Then came the last straw. The damned Indians held elections and the people, traitors all, turned out to vote in droves! Now, the dream of Khalistan lived on only because true adherents to the cause, like him, would not let it die. But it was on life support. All it would take to rejuvenate the dream was the backing of Kalidas. And Khullar hoped to secure it through two critical contributions to Kalidas's plans to kidnap Jonathan Wolff and execute his daughter.

The first was finding Bains, a janitor in Jonathan Wolff's building. He was the key to pulling off the kidnapping. The second was to force Randhawa to abandon his idiotic plan to wait in a car on the street for as long as it took, and gun the woman down whenever she showed up.

Randhawa had no idea how ridiculous that was. This was Canada, not the Punjab. A pair of Sikhs hanging around a white neighborhood for hours would be arrested for vagrancy. Or worse!

Randhawa pushed back with a profane challenge to come up with a better plan. Khullar knew that bugging the woman's apartment was the key to timing the drive-by. Unfortunately, there was no Sikh like Bains on the service staff to terrorize into helping them. A Sikh family by the name of Siddhu did live in the building, but an exploratory request for a "contribution" to the cause was met with an emphatic counter-threat from Siddhu to report them for extortion. They had to back off.

Grewal solved their problem. He supplied them with a laser device that picked up oscillations generated in window glass by sounds inside a room. A computer then translated those to sound. All that was left was to rent a suite in a vacant office block, two hundred yards away, with an unobstructed sightline of the windows in the woman's apartment.

For the past four days, either Khullar or his second-in-command, Gill, had the headphones on at all times. They had no idea how long it might continue. Discreet enquiries revealed that the woman left town on a trip to the Yukon ten days ago, but no one knew when she would return.

He wondered for the hundredth time what the two targets, father and daughter, had done to piss off Kalidas.

CHAPTER 6

Alexis brought the Lynx helicopter to a cruising altitude, then handed the controls to her co-pilot. Not only was he a nurse, he was an ex-airman with flight training on helicopters, and an Inuit to boot, so he spoke the local language.

She radioed Vancouver, giving the controller her flight schedule, route, and expected arrival time. After receiving approval, she tuned to the frequency reserved for Jonathan's private use.

"Bush Lady calling Wolf's Lair," she said. Her unique call sign said she was one of three authorized users. "Do you copy? Over."

The response was immediate. "Coming through loud and clear, Bush Lady. Over."

"Have either Mr. Wheels or Argonaut checked in recently? Over." The tongue-in-cheek humor in Jonathan's call sign was obvious, but Jason's was a double take on his name and wanderlust.

"Mr. Wheels is at a board meeting in L.A., and Argonaut is on a company jet somewhere over Alaska right now. I can patch you through, if you wish. Over."

"Yes, please."

"Please stand by."

She heard Jason's voice come through. "Red! Welcome back!"

"Jay! Thanks, but I don't think we have a welcome waiting in Vancouver."

"The worst is over, Red. Jonathan says they are now chasing after the latest Hollywood scandal. So we're off the hook."

"What a relief! Do you feel like going to dinner tonight?"

"I'd love to. But I won't be in until about eight. I'm on my way from Anchorage to Juneau. Something's come up there that Jonathan wants me to take care of on the way home."

"By the way, how was your trek into the Alaskan wilderness?"

"Gorgeous! The wildflowers were in bloom, the salmon were running and the grizzlies were out in force. It made for a perfect escape from the world. You'd love it, Red."

"You can tell me all about it over dinner tonight. Call me when you get home. Then we can fix a time to meet."

"I'll call you around eight."

"All right, Jay. Bush Lady to Argonaut, signing off."

* * * * * * * * * * *

After two weeks in the wilderness, Alexis could think of nothing other than a hot bath and her own bed as she headed for the elevators. As she reached for the call button, the doors opened and a little girl bounced out. The instant she saw Alexis, she shrieked in delight and leapt into her arms.

"Oh Alexis! I'm so glad you're back," the little girl said. "I just have to show you what I got for my birthday. I wanted to invite you for my party, but you were away. We had lots of cake and ice cream and it was fun to watch the grownups pin the tail on the donkey. None of them came even close to the bum!"

She spoke so fast that she was done by the time her mother got off the elevator. She seemed mortified, saying, "I am so sorry, Miss Wolff. I don't know where she got the idea she could call you by your first name." Taking her daughter gently by the shoulder, she scolded, "Pammie! Apologize to Miss Wolff and take back the vulgar word you just used."

The child protested. "Aw, Ma-ji! She told me to call her Alexis. And besides," she added, "Where else does the tail of the donkey go, except on the bum?"

Alexis tried to play peacemaker. "Pammie's right on both counts, Mrs. Siddhu. I did ask her to call me Alexis and, as far as anatomy goes, she's correct. I'm not offended at all."

"That's very kind of you, Miss Wolff. Pammie seems to think you're her age and you want to hear everything that's happened to her. We try to control it, but it makes no difference!"

"Please don't, Mrs. Siddhu. Pammie is a delightful child and I really do enjoy her exuberance and her company."

It was true. She felt a curious bond of friendship with the happy, talkative little Sikh girl.

Alexis bent down and said to Pammie ("Short for Parminder," she was told), "Let's get together tomorrow so I can find out what I've missed."

Pammie looked crestfallen. "We'll have to wait until after the weekend. We're leaving for our cottage in the mountains as soon as Daddy gets back from work tonight. But I'll make sure to come up to your apartment when we get back Sunday."

"I'll look forward to it," Alexis said.

She kissed Pammie's cheek and said goodbye. Then she got on the elevator, humming under her breath. Some of that joy rubbed off on her every time she talked to Pammie. She even wondered if she felt a maternal instinct towards the child, knowing she had no way to fulfill it for the foreseeable future.

She felt no regret. She would be quite content if motherhood never happened for her. She had no desire for a serious relationship while still trying to shed the emotional strait-jacket in which she had been all her life. All her flings with men in the past year had been short-lived and she was happy with the way things were.

She soaked in a bath for an hour, emerging relaxed and refreshed. She toweled off in front of the mirror checking out her reflection. "Tall and leggy" was how she would describe herself. Not skinny enough to be model material—her breasts were far too generous for it anyway. Not that anyone had complained.

She didn't have an ounce of extra fat. Her stomach was flat as a board, her thighs and buttocks tightly muscled. All products of a lifetime of athletic conditioning that she still maintained, no matter what.

Satisfied, she turned and walked into the bedroom. She looked at the time, set her internal clock, and lay down. She was asleep ten seconds after her head touched the pillow.

She lay without stirring until her eyes opened again, just before 8 p.m.

She stretched and pulled the phone to her. Preferring to remain in bed without holding the receiver, she switched to speaker mode and dialed Jason's apartment.

He picked up at the second ring. "Hello again, Jay," she said.

"Hello, Red. I was just about to call you. Are you rested from your travels?"

"Yes. I'd almost forgotten what a hot bath felt like."

"If you like hot baths that much, how come you spend so much time in the wilderness?"

He knew he was teasing her, but she replied in all seriousness, "The wilderness is what may be restoring my sanity. I'd give up hot baths before I gave that up."

"Then don't. Thank God—and Jonathan!—for that."

"Speaking of Jonathan, did he say when he'd be back in town?"

"Tomorrow evening."

"Good! Let's get together with him tomorrow."

"Fine with me. So, what about tonight?"

"Let's leave it until after the dinner rush. How does ten o'clock sound?"

"Perfect! I'll pick you up outside. You'll get to see Jonathan's latest acquisition."

Whenever Jonathan was out of town, Jason never failed to drive Jonathan's custom-made Rolls Royce Corniche convertible, its front passenger seat specially adapted for his wheelchair.

"So I get to ride in the Rolls, for a change!" Alexis responded. "I can't wait to see what makes all your girlfriends swoon."

He chuckled. "Liar! But I like that you want to indulge me. Ten sharp, then. Be ready."

"I'll be waiting for you at the curb."

She got out of bed, thinking of her relationship with her twin. He was her best friend in the world. There had never been any sibling rivalry or misunderstanding, except in their teenage years, when he appointed himself her Protector and Guardian against the big, bad world of men.

One night, after he insulted her date, sending him storming out of the house, she snapped. What began as a scream of frustration— the only time that she could remember raising her voice at him in anger—turned into a tongue-lashing of such epic proportions that she could still remember the look on his face as he stared back at her, goggle-eyed.

She couldn't remember what she actually said that day, but it made a deep impression on Jason. He stopped meddling in her affairs. Ever since, their relationship had been problem-free.

Jason was one person who she could both trust implicitly and rely on to return her trust unreservedly. That, more than anything, made their relationship so different from any other.

CHAPTER 7

Randhawa rushed to the suite when Khullar called to say the bitch had returned, only to discover she had gone to sleep by the time he got there. With nothing to do except wait, he took a nap.

A shout from Gill brought him to instant alertness. He checked his watch. It was 8 p.m.

Gill switched the audio feed to the speaker so he and Khullar could also hear the Wolff woman's conversation with her brother. The first thing they heard was that Jonathan Wolff was returning tomorrow. Reddy and Grewal would appreciate the information. The only other thing that interested him was that she would be waiting on the sidewalk at 10 p.m.

Randhawa was calm. He had never failed. The woman would die. It was as simple as that. He needed only a gun and a car. For the first, he preferred an Uzi semi-automatic for its accuracy when he had a single target, and soft-nosed bullets to shred the body to horrifying effect.

As for the car, he had no preference, as long as it was untraceable. He gave Khullar explicit instructions about getting one and went back to sleep.

* * * * * * * * * * *

Khullar waited an hour at a cinema theater until he saw a young couple park their car and hurry away. Then he walked up to the car and opened the door in five seconds with a jimmy. He shorted the ignition and, less than three minutes later, he was driving away.

Bloodbath

It was past 9:15 p.m. when he opened the door to find Randhawa pacing the floor like a caged tiger. The man burst out in a rage. "Where the bloody hell have you been all this time? Did you have to sell your ass to get hold of a car?"

"It isn't easy to find a car that won't be missed for two hours," Khullar replied.

"Fuck you!" Randhawa yelled. He slung his bag over his shoulder, and walked out. They rode down in the elevator and walked to the car in silence. When Randhawa saw the tiny two-door Ford Fit at the curb, he scowled. "When you sold your ass for the car did they base it on the size of your prick?"

Khullar had enough. "You wanted something that wouldn't be missed for a couple of hours. If you don't like it, go sell your own ass."

That shut Randhawa up, at least until he began to swear again as he folded his six-foot frame into the seat.

They drove the short distance to their destination in silence. Khullar knew that parking was forbidden in front of the building for anyone but the residents, so he pulled into a parking space on the street about fifty yards away.

The dashboard clock read 9:33 p.m.

Randhawa was in a foul mood. He poured out one insult after another at the Wolff woman. Khullar knew she had done something that landed Randhawa in serious trouble with Kalidas a year ago. He knew better than to ask what it was, though.

The clock now read 9:44 p.m. A car pulled to the curb in front of the building, drawing Khullar's attention. He was surprised to see the driver wore a turban. This must be Siddhu.

It was a pity there wasn't time to "convert" the man. It was amazing how effective a little pressure could be, particularly if a child was involved. Siddhu had a daughter, he knew, so it was

101

particularly pleasant to think of the opportunities this might provide for Cheema's talents.

Khullar's mind drifted until he saw four figures emerge from the entrance of the building.

Recognizing one of them as the target, he reached for the ignition wires, just as Randhawa hissed, "Quickly, you fool. This is our chance!"

The ignition caught and he put the car into gear. Out of the corner of his eye, Khullar saw Randhawa reach into the bag at his feet and pull out the Uzi.

It was 9:58 p.m.

CHAPTER 8

Alexis took a quick glance at her watch as she rode the elevator. She was glad to see she'd make it with a few minutes to spare. Her twin was punctual to a fault!

The elevator doors opened and she walked through the foyer to the exit. Half-way there, a shriek of "Alexis!" made her spin around to see Pammie Siddhu racing towards her, pigtails dancing in the air. Alexis caught the little girl and swung her around. Even before she set her down, words came tumbling out of Pammie.

"Dad came home late from work, so we're leaving now instead of earlier. I don't mind, though. I get to stay up late, and I can wake up whenever I want tomorrow! No school. Yippee!"

Pammie's parents came up to join them. Her father, who she had only seen wearing formal business attire and a white starched turban, was dressed casually for a change in tee shirt and slacks, with something Pammie called a *patka* on his head, instead of a turban. It was, in reality, nothing more than a square of cloth tied around the head like a skullcap, and outlining a top-knot of hair.

Alexis had not quite figured out how the cloth and hair stayed in place. She could see hairpins at the edges and under the cloth, but was not certain what role they played. She would have to ask Pammie if there was a secret to it.

Alexis walked out with the Siddhus, who headed for a BMW standing at the curb. From the corner of her eye, she saw headlights approaching from the left. She was about to turn that way, when she saw Pammie wave an exuberant goodbye.

Alexis waved back with equal exuberance, then turned to watch the Corniche convertible approaching from two blocks away.

At that moment, Mr. Siddhu called out to offer her a lift, and she looked back over her shoulder to decline…

…Then everything froze!

Mrs. Siddhu was standing a few feet behind, holding Pammie's hand, and Mr. Siddhu was further away to her right, loading bags into the open trunk of the BMW at the curb.

But the only thing that mattered was the car screeching to a halt alongside the BMW, with the distinctive snout of an Uzi poking out of the near window.

Alexis reacted even before the first muzzle flashes.

She whirled around, swinging her right arm out to send Mrs. Siddhu sprawling, and dove towards Pammie to snatch her off her feet just as the Uzi began spewing death. She corkscrewed her body around in midair with the little girl clutched to her chest, feeling a violent jerk as she landed with her right shoulder driving into the sidewalk to cushion the impact. Her momentum took her into a full body roll that ended with her back to the BMW and Pammie underneath her, shielding her from a chance ricochet.

She lay in the shelter of the BMW, hidden from the gunman's view, hearing the metallic thump of the bullets ripping through the body of the car. Then Mrs. Siddhu began to scream.

Alexis realized, all of a sudden, that Pammie hadn't moved or made a sound. Then she felt something warm and sticky on her left forearm and her heart jumped into her mouth.

Oblivious of the bullets hitting the car inches away, she turned Pammie over, saw blood pumping from a wound in her neck, and clamped her hand down on the carotid artery like a vice, compressing it against the vertebral column to stop the blood flow.

Bullets continued to thud into the car. Alexis heard a man cry out. The words were unintelligible, but the triumph in his voice was unmistakable.

Bloodbath

Searing rage swept through Alexis. The rate of fire showed the killer was a professional. So…why didn't he get out of the car to finish the job? She was defenseless against the Uzi.

Then she remembered Jason.

CHAPTER 9

J ason saw Alexis exchange exuberant goodbyes with Pammie Siddhu and felt his heart lift. The bond between Alexis and the irrepressible little Sikh girl made a mockery of their contrasting cultural background and age difference—decorum and dignity be damned!

Preoccupied with happy thoughts, he was only peripherally aware of the car gather speed in the background and come screeching to a halt alongside Alexis. All of a sudden, it became the focal point of his universe. He saw muzzle flashes, heard gunfire, saw her go down, and nothing was left but black despair, knowing he could do nothing to save her. Then he saw the car accelerate towards him, its grisly task done, and murderous rage took over.

He gunned the Rolls toward the oncoming car, watching the gap narrow with implacable detachment.

Just before it went past, he hit the brakes and turned the wheel sharply, sending the Rolls into the path of the oncoming car in a controlled left-hand skid. It left the driver no time to react, let alone the room to swerve around the Rolls.

The oncoming car smashed into the right fender of the Rolls. Its chassis crumpled at impact, and the front axle shattered, snapping the steering tie-rod and launching the steering column backwards like a spear. It impaled the driver, smashing through his sternum and rupturing his heart and lungs.

The engine block tore off its moorings, transforming into a missile. It ripped through the thin sheet-metal enclosing the passenger compartment like tissue paper to strike the front-seat passenger on the knees. He wasn't wearing a seat belt, so his body was catapulting forward when the engine block struck. It jerked

106

him back before his face struck the windshield, leaving it unscathed, and ploughed into the back seat, shearing his body in half.

Jason knew that the collision would be nowhere as devastating for him or the Rolls. The vastly lighter car not only took the worst of it, but the inertia of the Rolls neutralized much of the energy at impact. The remainder was absorbed along the diagonal of the Rolls' massive chassis. Even so, the Roll's front fender crumpled like an eggshell. The crash sent Jason hurtling forward but his seat belt and the car's airbags saved him from serious injury.

Jason fought his way out from behind the deflating airbags and leaped out, oblivious of his bruised face, neck, and shoulder. One glance was all it took to confirm that the occupants of the crushed car were dead, then he ran to Alexis, lying on the sidewalk.

He saw the pool of blood around her and sank to his knees beside her, his legs giving way. Then Alexis rolled over, and the flood of relief was like nothing he had ever known. A split-second later, his heart sank, seeing the body of the little girl, covered with blood, and the stark horror in Alexis's eyes.

"An ambulance, Jay," she croaked in a voice that made his hair stand on end. "Now!"

Jason nodded. He got to his feet just as the concierge came running out, and shouted for an ambulance, then went to check on the man draped half inside the open trunk of the car.

Jason had seen the carnage wrought by semi-automatic weapons fire on the human body and it never failed to make him sick. There was nothing he or anyone could do for the man.

Jason walked over to the woman lying a few feet from Alexis. He could see no injury, and her eyes were open, staring into the heavens. But she was rigid as a board and the blankness in her eyes indicated her mind had shut down to protect itself from madness.

He went back to squat at Alexis's side, hearing the ululating cry of an approaching siren.

CHAPTER 10

Dawn was breaking when the police left Alexis's apartment. But the coming of daylight did not lighten Jason's mood.

Alexis had given the police a comprehensive account of the incident in a low-pitched monotone. After that, she fell silent, leaving Jason to add whatever he could.

He knew how little that was. There was no conceivable explanation for the attack on the Siddhus. The little girl was rushed to hospital, grievously wounded and in a coma. The latest news was that she was in surgery, but there was no word on her prognosis.

Alexis had no injuries. At least in the physical sense. Emotionally, it was a different story. He saw signs of delayed shock in her withdrawal and it worried him. She was sitting completely still, her face slack, and her eyes staring almost without blinking at her hands in her lap. This was how her descent into catatonia began in the aftermath of the massacre.

So why was it happening again?

Where was that inner strength she had built in the past twelve months? Why was she unable to call on it at this moment, when she needed it most? If she did not help herself, all the ground she had clawed back from her demons would be lost. Then, she might withdraw to a place from where there might be no coming back.

Fear clutched at his gut. But he knew he couldn't afford to give in to fear. He had to break the stranglehold of her mental and emotional paralysis.

How, though? He felt helpless, just as he did a year ago at the airport when she discovered Jonathan was alive. The emotional shock then was much worse, but she hadn't collapsed or withdrawn like this. Her fury at Jonathan's perceived "betrayal" wouldn't let her give in to the shock.

And, just like that, Jason had the answer.

He needed her to be angry—not just angry, but enraged, like she was at Jonathan last time.

And it had to be something to do with Pammie, to penetrate the shell she was erecting around herself.

Making his voice as harsh as possible, he said, "The bastards! Why would they want to kill a little girl?"

It worked!

She recoiled, as if struck. The zombie-like blankness faded and her expression hardened into anger.

"I don't know, Jay, but I intend to find out. This is personal. That little kid! She was a friend. That ghastly neck wound… it was just like…." She broke off, unable to go on.

Jason squeezed her forearm, to show her he understood. She smiled and, for the briefest of moments, he saw the remembered pain of past horrors shimmering in her eyes. Then another wave of anger swept over her. "The monsters. I only wish the end hadn't been so quick."

Jason smiled. Thank God for her temper! She had bounced back exactly as he expected.

She started to smile back, then her hand flew to her mouth. "Oh God, Jason! I didn't mean it to come out like that. What you did was incredible. And on the spur of the moment, too! It was every bit as flamboyant as I might have expected from you."

"It was the best I could do," he said lightly. "I'm sorry it had to be at the expense of Jonathan's Rolls, though."

"Trust me! Jonathan will be delighted by that trade-off. And insurance will cover it."

He thought about what was left of the Ford. "The bastards! They deserved every bit of it." He paused. "One of them was a Sikh. Could that have anything to do with it?"

Seeing doubt in her face, he tried again. "They got the father all right."

She shook her head hesitantly.

Something was bothering her, so he persisted. "If not religion, then what? Revenge?"

Her expression became stubborn, almost mulish. She shook her head. "I have a strange feeling there's something wrong—something doesn't fit those scenarios. I can't pin it down."

"What do you mean?"

"I don't know and I wish I could tell you why, but it just doesn't feel right."

Whatever it was must be buried deep in her subconscious. "Leave it, Red. The more you press, the deeper it will sink. It'll come out in good time."

She changed the subject. "What about the police? Do they know who's behind this?"

"The police know as little as we do. The man in charge is an old friend of Jonathan's. He's promised to call us when they have something definite to go on."

"Have you called Jonathan, by the way?"

"No. Because then I'd have to tell him that you'd gone off your rocker."

She knew he was teasing her. "In that case, I can call him myself and tell him I haven't," she said, reaching for the phone.

CHAPTER 11

J onathan Wolff looked at the woman who was his daughter and felt as if his heart would burst. The pain of knowing how close he had come to losing her, especially so soon after she came into his life, was more than he could bear.

Alexis was sitting calmly on the couch with her legs drawn up under her, talking to David Murphy, the inspector in charge of the case, and an old friend of his as well. Her hair was loose about her shoulders, standing out against an emerald green blouse matching the color of her eyes.

"Any leads on the men involved, Inspector?" she asked.

Murphy shook his head. "We have very little to go on, Alexis, other than the identity of the driver. He was a Canadian-born Sikh named Surjeet Singh Khullar, a known adherent to the cause for a Sikh homeland. He's never broken a Canadian law, but he spent a long time in India during the Punjab troubles in the eighties, and was labeled a terrorist by the Indians, mostly on hearsay." Murphy sighed. "You know the deal about one man's terrorist being another's freedom-fighter?"

"What was he doing, then, as the driver for a hit-man?" Alexis asked, surprised.

"We don't know. Nor, apparently, does anyone in the Sikh community. They have nothing but good things to say about Siddhu, of course. But, when we ask why Khullar or anyone else would want to kill him and his family, they just clam up. It's as if a gag order is in place. Not even Inspector Bedi, who is a Sikh, can get them to talk."

"Any link between Khullar and Siddhu?"

"Not that we know."

"What about motive?"

"We're working along the usual lines. The obvious one is a disgruntled Sikh among Siddhu's employees, past and present. Another might be a bit farfetched, but fringe groups in the Sikh freedom movement have used strong-arm tactics to extract donations, although Mrs. Siddhu, who is now coherent, insists Siddhu would've told her of such demands or threats."

"What about the Uzi man?" Jason asked.

"He's a real mystery. No identity papers and no fingerprints on file in Canada. We've circulated his photograph and description among the Indian community in the hope that someone will come forward, and sent his fingerprints to the FBI, Interpol, and the Indians, just in case."

Jason shrugged. "It's worth a try."

Murphy looked at his watch and got up. "I must be going now." He held up his hand to Jonathan. "Don't trouble yourself, Jonathan. I can find my own way out."

Alexis sat lost in thought after the door closed behind Murphy, frowning at the carpet. Jonathan heard her mutter to herself, "There's something not right about this."

Then her head came up and she said to Jason, "Murphy assumed, like you did, that Siddhu was killed because he was a Sikh. I have this feeling that something is fundamentally wrong with that. I don't know why, but I do know this. If Siddhu hadn't called out to me, I'd be dead too. So, I owe it to him and Pammie to find out who's behind this."

Jonathan saw his chance. "I think I might be able to help there. There's someone who works for me by the name of Sol Steinberg. You've met him, Jason. He's an expert on militancy in the expatriate Indian community on this continent. He might have better luck than the police figuring out who Khullar really is and what he was involved in. His contacts might talk to him, even if they won't talk to the police. I called him in New York before coming here and told him to drop everything to work on this. He should have something for us by now."

"That will be a huge help, Jonathan," Jason said.

Jonathan picked up the phone and dialed. When the call went through, he switched to speaker mode. "Jonathan Wolff here. Get me Sol Steinberg, please."

He was kept waiting less than ten seconds. Then Steinberg's voice came on the line. "Steinberg here, Jonathan. Hi."

Dispensing with formalities, Jonathan came straight to the point. "Sol, I have you on speaker phone so Jason and Alexis can hear what you have to say."

Jason and Alexis both said, in unison, "Hi, Sol!"

"Alexis, it's terrible, what happened," Steinberg said, "but I'm glad you're okay. I've been working on it ever since Jonathan called this morning. I have some preliminary stuff on this guy, Khullar, but I'll know more after talking to my contacts in Vancouver. I'm leaving for Vancouver within the hour. I'll brief you when I get there."

"I should've expected nothing else!" Jonathan exclaimed. "We'll see you this evening."

Alexis smiled at Jonathan. "That was really helpful. Thanks so much."

Jonathan felt as if he had done something useful for the first time in his life.

CHAPTER 12

Reddy summoned Gill to the yacht for an early morning conclave to discuss next steps. With Khullar's death, he was now the de facto leader of the Vancouver group.

Reddy addressed him without preamble when he arrived. "Have you heard the news? It's all over radio and TV. The drive-by was a total disaster! The Wolff woman survived—so much for Randhawa, the sure bet! And Khullar—the mother-fucker crashed the car, killing them both. Serves them both bloody right!"

Gill face twisted with grief, appearing on the verge of tears.

Reddy said brutally, "Don't you dare cry, you fat sissy! There's work to be done. We've sent Kalidas a message asking for guidance. Until we hear back, nothing changes. You will continue to monitor the woman's apartment, and we snatch the cripple tonight, unless he says differently."

"Can't you release either Brar or Cheema to help with monitoring?" Gill pleaded tremulously. "You don't need four guys to snatch a cripple with no bodyguards!"

Reddy thought for a moment, then snickered. "You're right. It won't be tough, with everything set up. Okay. You can have Brar. But I'll need Cheema to get us across the border."

"Thank you, Reddy," Gill replied, clearly relieved. "But can you leave us the laser equipment? We can't afford to buy our own."

Reddy saw Grewal nod his approval. "All right. You can keep it if Kalidas authorizes continued monitoring. But let's get back to tonight. Show me the route we're taking."

Gill spread a map on the table showing a highlighted route south from Vancouver to the border. "It's little more than a dirt track through pretty rough country, and it disappears in many places. But it shouldn't be a problem for the Land Rover, and it gets you across the border without being stopped and questioned."

He pointed to a red "X" on the map near Seattle. "This is where you're headed. It's a private airstrip belonging to one of my friends. He'll fly you to L.A. Call me if you run into problems."

"No! There will be no further mobile communications between us until we're across the border and Cheema's heading back. You and Brar are known associates of Khullar, so the police might be monitoring your cell phones. If you call me, I will personally come back and cut off your balls, understand?"

Gill blanched. Reddy knew the fat Sikh wouldn't dare disobey.

It was 6 a.m.—4:30 p.m. in Myanmar. Their message would be making its way up the pipeline to Kalidas, and they should hear back in a few hours. If Kalidas gave them the green light, it should be a cinch to grab the cripple when the right opportunity presented itself. He was returning today, so it wouldn't be too long of a wait.

All that remained were a couple of housekeeping details. Clean out the yacht while they were waiting. And pick up Randhawa's things on the way out of town. The house lay just off the route marked by Gill.

Amazing how everything was falling into place!

CHAPTER 13

Kalidas was dreaming. Something was pounding on the window, trying to break the glass.

He wanted desperately to get away, but there was no way out. The door had vanished and now the walls were beginning to close in on him, and the thing outside was about to smash through.

All of a sudden, he saw it. It was giant wolf with three heads, shrieking his name as it hammered at the window, and he felt mortal dread, knowing he was about to die…

Kalidas's eyes snapped open, and heard insistent knocking and Karim Chand calling to him. His panic subsided. He saw it was 3:30 p.m., and shouted, "Come in!"

Karim Chand entered and the sight of his secretary's ashen face made his gut clench. Something terrible must have happened for Karim Chand to interrupt his afternoon siesta. He gave an impatient flick of his hand and Karim Chand handed him the message, cringing as if he expected to be struck.

It was a message from Reddy. Kalidas read it and leapt out of bed, screaming inarticulately, and began pacing around the room.

The woman had escaped certain death! How could this be?

With Kali's grace to protect him, he had always been invincible. It took the entire might of a nation to inflict the only defeat he ever sustained, when he had to flee to Myanmar. And no man who ever crossed him lived to make that same mistake twice.

Except for the Wolff clan. How could they vanquish him, the Servant of the Supreme Mother, not once, not twice, but four times? And now, one of them had defied a death warrant issued by him in Kali's name!

116

It was inconceivable, unless... unless...

The answer came to him.

He saw the three-headed wolf from his dream and knew it was a message from Kali, warning him that he was fighting a beast from hell—something beyond human mortality.

He felt stupid for not seeing it before. Only something from Hell could have engineered a string of four defeats like these. And the only thing saving him from it—the reason he survived those defeats—was the grace of Kali.

Take Jason Wolff's attempt to destroy his power forever by humiliating him. The grace of Kali saved him, through Karim Chand's act of ultimate self-sacrifice.

Then Jonathan Wolff manipulated the Indians into launching their all-out war against him, driving him into obscurity in Myanmar. By building a temple dedicated to her, though, he didn't just rebuild his power, he increased it a hundred-fold.

With his resurgence came Bloodbath. Enter the daughter, to disrupt his first attempt to negotiate with Bindra. Nothing but a supernatural force could have contrived her presence on that plane. By the grace of Kali, though, that setback also ended in triumph.

Now this! The best drive-by killer in India's history misses Alexis Wolff from ten feet away!

He saw the truth staring him in his face.

The Wolffs were incarnations of the forces opposed to Kali,

He realized, all of a sudden, that it was his sacred duty to annihilate them, and felt a preternatural calm descend. Kali was relying on him, and wouldn't disappoint her.

He stopped his frenetic pacing and walked to where Karim Chand was cowering on his knees, arms wrapped around his head. He bent down and lifted him up, saying, "I should have known, Karim, that these evil beings aren't human. It means they can only be destroyed by harnessing the Mother's power. I must kill them in the temple, in her presence."

His secretary was relieved. "What an amazing idea, Huzoor! How will we achieve that?"

"Reddy says the police believe Siddhu was the target. Let's cement that narrative. Gill's group gets ten thousand dollars to kill someone else who's refused to contribute, and a thousand dollars a day for continuing to monitor the woman's apartment, so we know what the Wolffs are planning."

"I will tell Reddy, Huzoor, but may I ask why?"

"It will keep the Wolffs off balance, not knowing what to believe when the cripple is abducted. If two Sikh's are assassinated, Alexis Wolff surely can't be the drive-by target, right? But if the cripple disappears, doesn't that mean she was? We let them run around like headless chickens trying to figure it out until we are ready. Then, with the old bastard in our hands, we make them come to us, using the cripple as bait, and kill them in Kali's presence."

He rubbed his hands gleefully. "This is working out even better than before."

CHAPTER 14

Pammie Siddhu was on a ventilator, deep in coma.

Alexis spent three of the hardest minutes of her life at her bedside, fighting to keep her emotions under control as she stroked the back of the child's limp hand. Then she returned to the waiting room and sat down to wait with Jason and Jonathan for the trauma surgeon who operated on Pammie.

When Alexis introduced herself to him as a physician, he described Pammie's injuries in graphic detail. The soft-nosed bullet had mushroomed as it tore a jagged path through the left side of her neck, shredding the major blood vessels and the nerves to Pammie's left arm beyond repair. By some miracle, though, it had spared the trachea, esophagus, and vertebral column.

He was much more circumspect about the prospect of permanent brain damage and Pammie's prognosis. Alexis knew that the concussive effects of a bullet passing through the neck could be anything from short-lived to devastating. And, even though she saved Pammie from bleeding to death, stopping blood flow to the brain might well have made the damage worse.

They drove back from the hospital in complete silence.

* * * * * * * * * *

Sol Steinberg arrived just before 7 p.m.

He placed a folder out on the table and got straight to the point. "This was compiled at short notice and a lot of it is off-the-record hearsay from trustworthy contacts in the Sikh community in

Canada. I'll know more after I've spoken to my contacts in Vancouver. Just remember that the police can't know what they tell me, or I'll lose their trust."

Jonathan answered calmly, "We know that, Sol."

"Thanks, Jonathan. Here's what I know. Khullar was a hard-core militant in the bloody insurgency that claimed thousands of lives in the Punjab in the eighties. After its collapse, he returned to Canada, and started this group. With their influence dwindling of late, they've resorted to brazen intimidation to revive the cause. Rumor has it that they targeted Siddhu for a donation and he turned them down, so they made an example of him. That's why everyone is so leery of speaking to the police."

"What about the hit man?" Jason asked.

"His name is Naresh Gupta, a frequent visitor from India, but how he ties into the Siddhu business is a mystery. I've found out some interesting things about him, though. One is that, for the past week, he's been staying in the suburbs of Vancouver in a house owned by a known associate of Khullar's, a tea importer called Gill." He tapped his finger on the folder. "The address is in here."

"Second, his fingerprints match those on file with the FBI of a man named Ranjit Singh Randhawa. Customs at Kennedy detained him a year ago on suspicion of drug smuggling. They found nothing, so they had to let him go. The details are in here.

"Third, this Randhawa matches the description of a high-level operative for a major arms and drug dealer from India named Kalidas. You may remember him, Jonathan."

"Good God, yes!" exclaimed Jonathan. "But why would Kalidas send his henchman all the way to Canada to kill Siddhu?"

"That's actually two questions. Why Canada, and why Siddhu. First, Canada. The biggest market in the world for Kalidas's drugs is only a hundred miles to the south, across the longest unprotected border in the world. We've been hearing whispers for some time that criminal elements in the Sikh community have become involved in drug smuggling from India to resuscitate the moribund insurgency in the Punjab. And there's been a huge influx of high-grade heroin from India into the United States in the past six months. Kalidas is almost certainly behind it."

"And the Americans are content to let it happen?"

"They're not happy about the drugs, obviously. But they've used Kalidas to supply weapons to warlords fighting the Taliban. Many in U.S. intelligence remain loyal to him."

Jonathan was incredulous. "If he's flooding the country with drugs, wouldn't someone realize it's important to go after him?"

"Even if someone did, they'd have to find him first. He disappeared after the Indians chased him out five years ago and rumors place him anywhere from Pakistan to Cambodia. There are even those who say he's dead and that only his name lives on, to serve the organization's purpose. Personally, I believe that he's very much alive, and has rebuilt his network into an even more formidable force. Not everyone agrees with me, though."

"So, why would a guy like Kalidas involve himself in the drive-by shooting of Siddhu?" Jason asked.

Steinberg's answer was decisive. "Not Kalidas. Randhawa. He was Khullar's compatriot in the insurgency, and his specialty was drive-by assassination. So it would make sense for him to lend his old comrade a hand while he was visiting Canada."

Steinberg looked around. "That's it. It isn't much, but it's all I have for now."

"It's a lot more than I expected, Sol," Jonathan said firmly. "You've done a fantastic job. Call us if you learn anything new."

Alexis invited him to stay for dinner but Steinberg declined, mumbling his thanks. After he left, Alexis turned the conversation to other subjects and Jonathan joined Alexis and Jason for dinner.

At ten o'clock, he finally took his leave. He phoned his apartment, waited until Malcolm, his valet-cum-chauffeur, answered. "Malcolm, can you please come and get me?"

Yes sir, Mr. Wolff," answered Malcolm. "I'll be there in fifteen minutes."

CHAPTER 15

J ason knew he couldn't leave Alexis alone in her apartment right after their visit to Pammie. So, he waited until Jonathan left, then said casually while leafing through a magazine, "I don't feel up to driving back to my apartment, Red. Is it okay if I spend the night in the spare bedroom?"

He looked up when he got no response, and saw she was lost in thought, staring blankly at the wall. He said loudly, "A penny for your thoughts, Red?"

She started, then looked at him with exasperation. "Something still doesn't seem right, Jay. I don't know why. But it's as if I should know! That's what's so frustrating." She sighed. "Maybe I'm wrong. Maybe Siddhu was killed by Sikh militants because he pushed back on their demand for a contribution."

Jason reassured her. "Let it go, Red. If it's something else, it'll come out in good time."

She sighed again. "I guess so."

"I don't know what's bothering you, but one thing bothers me." He flipped open Steinberg's folder and pointed to a photograph of the clean-shaven Randhawa/Naresh Gupta. "This guy worked for a big international arms and drug dealer. Why would he risk blowing his cover, getting mixed up in a local fund-raising effort for Khullar?"

Alexis looked down at the photograph, frowning, "I've seen that man before, but I'm not sure where. And, before you ask, I never saw his face in the drive-by."

"The house he stayed at. It's just a half-hour drive from here."

"Are you seriously thinking of going there tonight?"

He looked at her. "Not right now. Maybe around 2 a.m. The house is our only lead. Maybe Randhawa left something that could help us find who or what is behind the attack on the Siddhus."

"Great! I'm going with you." Her voice sounded grim.

He joked to relieve the tension. "Did you think I'd leave you out when I'm about to do some breaking and entering?"

She smiled at him. "So my wonderful brother wants to add B&E to my resume, is it?"

"A simple B&E would be beneath your resume. Or have you forgotten that you were called a natural by the greatest!"

"You mean old Ghasita Ram?" she cried, her face lighting up as she remembered the toothless old locksmith, from Teesrigaon, a remote village in the foothills of the Himalayas.

During their travels in India, they stumbled upon the locksmith late one evening on the banks of a stream, where they planned to camp. He was unconscious from hitting his head after losing his footing on the slippery rocks. Had they not found him, he would surely have died of exposure in the cold winter night.

After Alexis set his broken wrist in the primitive clinic that served as the village health center, Ghasita and his family wouldn't let them leave until his wrist mended, so they reluctantly agreed to stay for a couple of days.

It ended up being almost eight weeks. With wounds of their own to mend, Alexis and Jason found respite in the warmth and kindness of the village folk.

Early in their stay, Ghasita confessed his disappointment that none of his sons wanted to carry on the family tradition, and that all his secrets would die with him. So, Jason asked the old man to teach him his secrets.

Jason quickly discovered that Ghasita had an almost supernatural ability to pick any lock, simply by "feel". But their "training sessions" usually ended with the old man screaming in exasperation, frustrated by Jason's inability to sense what he called the "personality of the lock".

One day, Alexis happened to walk in during one of his rants, and Ghasita begged her to explain to Jason what he was talking about. Before Alexis knew it, she was hooked, When Ghasita realized it came naturally to her, he forgot Jason and switched to teaching her instead.

Jason saw the faraway look in her eyes and knew she was reliving the memories. "Ghasita's testimonial is as good as it gets!"

"Well, I had to find something to do while you were trying to steal the hearts of the pretty village girls," she said, arching her eyebrows.

"A far more difficult task, I remind you, than picking locks," he replied with lofty disdain. "It requires a gift not given to many."

"And, judging by your amazing track record with the girls of Teesrigaon, someone forgot to give you that gift!"

"Don't remind me! Victorian mores are promiscuous compared to those in rural India. If I tried to talk to one of the girls, I was suddenly Jack the Ripper reincarnated. But it was apparently okay for the old goat to flirt with you outrageously."

"Show a little respect. That 'old goat' taught us more about B&E in one day than you learned in all your commando training."

"Okay! Okay!" he grumbled. "But you need to change. A white skirt is a bad choice for a burglary. "

Jason saw her stick out her tongue at him before heading to the bedroom to change, and felt a load lift from his shoulders. He hadn't seen that childish reaction for years—not since before her breakdown! For that relic from happier times to resurface now proved that the nightmare of the morning was over and done.

While he waited for her, he leafed through Steinberg's file. There was a lot of stuff about this man, Kalidas, but he didn't bother to read it. The man's name meant nothing to him.

CHAPTER 16

The penthouse belonging to Jonathan Wolff overlooked a bay where the ultra-rich moored their yachts. But anyone willing to pay the fees could rent an anchorage. Kalidas was footing the bill for Gill's yacht. The location, five hundred yards from the building, was perfect to monitor the penthouse.

When the call ended, they left, Reddy and Grewal in the Land Rover and Cheema in his car. They waited until they saw Wolff's car leave, parked in the garage, and rode the elevator up to the penthouse. There, Grewal used the remote controller to return the elevator to the garage for the chauffeur to find when he returned.

After twenty minutes, they heard the elevator start up and took up their positions, Reddy and Cheema on either side of the elevator with their backs pressed against the wall, and Grewal in the living room, out of sight.

The elevator stopped, a bell sounded, and the doors slid open.

* * * * * * * * * * *

Malcolm was pushing his wheelchair, even though it was motorized, so it was from habit that Jonathan's right hand was resting on the controls as they headed across the foyer to the living room.

They were at the door, when a heavily accented voice shouted from behind them, "Stop or I shoot!"

Jonathan's head spun around. He saw two men by the elevator. Out of the corner of his eye, he also saw Malcolm reach for the shoulder holster under his jacket.

Bloodbath

A gun coughed and Malcolm collapsed on the rug.

The shot galvanized Jonathan. He flicked the control lever under his right hand and the wheelchair shot forward. As it went through the open doorway, he slammed the door shut behind him, hearing the spring lock click into place.

Jonathan grabbed the telephone but a hand clamped down on his mouth from behind. Instinctively, he bit down hard on the flesh between his teeth.

He heard a howl of agony. Then something hard struck him on the back of his head. There was a flash of light, followed by a moment of blinding pain.

He slid down into unconsciousness.

* * * * * * * * * * *

Through the closed door, Reddy heard Grewal swearing up a storm in Punjabi, his tirade punctuated by repeated slaps. Then the door opened and he saw Wolff slumped in his wheelchair, his head snapping from side to side as Grewal kept slapping him again and again.

Reddy saw blood running from Grewal's palm, and let him work out his anger. Afterwards, Reddy said with admiration, "Who thought the crippled old bastard could do that! If you hadn't been in here, he might have got away with it!"

Grewal spat out more curses and raised his hand to hit the unconscious man yet again, but Reddy stepped in. "Enough! He has to survive the trip ahead. If he dies because you beat him, your punishment will be much worse than anything the master has in store for the cripple."

Grewal blanched and lowered his hand.

His point made, Reddy pointed to the dead body in the hallway and said to Cheema, "Wrap the body in the rug. Is there somewhere we can get rid of it and my gun along the way?"

Cheema nodded, saying, "I know just the place to dump it," and went back to the foyer

Grewal then took a pre-filled syringe of phenobarbital from his kit and injected it into Jonathan Wolff. Then he cleaned and dressed his own hand. A chunk of flesh was missing near the base of the thumb. He found it on the floor near the phone and put it in a plastic bag.

After a quick check to make sure they had left no trace of their presence, Reddy nodded to the others and pushed the wheelchair with the unconscious cripple to the elevator. Grewal and Cheema followed, carrying the chauffeur's body, wrapped in the rug.

Kalidas would be pleased. He wanted the old man's disappearance to shock and disorient the son. The shock was achieved. Disorientation would follow when Grewal's monitoring equipment was discovered. And the mystery would only deepen when no ransom note was forthcoming.

CHAPTER 16

The house stood at the end of a row of nondescript homes on a deserted street.

No lights were showing when Alexis and Jason drove past at 2 a.m. Jason pulled over fifty yards beyond the street corner to watch for any sign of life inside or outside.

Fifteen minutes later Jason nodded and they got out of the car. He headed to the front of the house, and Alexis melted into the shadows of the hedge skirting the yard. She ghosted up to the back door, inserted a lock pick into the keyhole, and probed for a couple of seconds. The deadbolt fell back with a snick, and she attacked the spring lock next. She was inside a moment later.

She crouched down to avoid being silhouetted against the window, hearing a soft creak from the front door, followed by a whisper of sound as it closed. She chirped like a cricket, heard an answering chirp, and walked out of the kitchen to meet Jason.

She was in a small hallway about fifteen feet long, extending from the kitchen to the front door. To her left was a living-cum-dining room with a camp cot, a table with four chairs, and piles of clothing scattered across the floor. The wall on her right extended to a staircase landing by the front door, where she could see a stanchion anchoring the banister rail to the floor.

She jabbed a finger upwards and saw Jason shrug his shoulders and point to her, then the staircase.

She nodded and stepped on the lowest stair where it abutted the outside wall. The stair did not creak, so she placed her other foot on the next step, but at the opposite edge of the stair, making sure that it did not creak either.

She went up the stairs like a crab, while Jason waited, knife held by the blade, ready for the throw, and took a quick look around when she got to top floor. The layout was identical to the first level with a bathroom above the kitchen and two bedrooms where the living room was below. After making sure no one was there, she called in a soft voice, "Come on up, Jay."

In the second bedroom, they found an unlocked suitcase. Jason hefted it onto the bed and rummaged through it, giving a low whistle as he held up a leather folder with travel documents.

Right then, Alexis heard a car pull up outside.

Jason reacted instantly. He thrust the folder into his pocket, shut the suitcase, and slid it under the bed. They were halfway down the stairs, when she heard footsteps approach the front door, forcing them retreat up the steps.

She saw Jason point to the open door of the bathroom, and nodded. It was as good a place to hide as any until they got some idea of what they were up against.

It was small, just a sink and toilet on one wall, and a bathtub with a shower curtain on the other. She positioned herself behind the door, while Jason stepped behind the curtain into the tub.

She heard the front door close, then laughter and voices echoing up the stairs. Accented English—Indians!

"So, Grewal, we did it! Thanks to us, Kalidas at least gets half of what he wants." She recognized the accent from South India.

A second voice—a Punjabi—answered, "He'll be very happy. Now he can have the perfect ending to celebrate Bloodbath."

"Careful, Grewal!" said the South Indian. "No one's supposed to call it that."

"Oh! All right!" 'Grewal' grumbled. "Khoon ka Snaan, then."

"That's better," replied 'Reddy'. "Seriously, though, the job you did with the electronic stuff was just incredible. We couldn't

130

have pulled it off without you. And I promise you that will be exactly what I say in my report to Kalidas."

"Thank you, Reddy. You did a great job yourself. It's too bad we won't get the chance to celebrate in L.A. The ship will leave for Kolkata as soon as we get there with our catch."

"I know! Our reward for a job well done is to be fucking baby-sitters, instead of fucking white bitches. I'm sick of those stupid Naga whores in Kalidas's brothel."

"Why don't you take a few hours off to have fun when we get to L.A.? I'll take care of calling Mukherjee in Kolkata to let the master know our schedule."

"I really appreciate that, Grewal. But you should get that hand looked at in L.A."

"Fuck the bastard! I should've just knocked him out at the start." A pause. Then 'Grewal' said, "Where the hell is Cheema?"

Alexis heard the front door open, and a third voice—another Punjabi—joined the conversation. "Don't you think you should get a move on? We can't leave the old bastard out there for long."

"Why, Cheema?" Reddy sounded amused. "Don't tell me you're afraid he might run away? Even if he wakes up, how do you think he's going to run?"

"Stop that, Reddy!" Grewal said, laughing. "But Cheema's right. We should get a move on. I'm going upstairs to take a leak. I'll bring down Randhawa's stuff and we can leave."

"Okay," said Reddy. "I'll get our stuff from the living room."

Footsteps ascended the stairs, then paused when 'Cheema' called out. "Oh! I almost forgot to tell you! Our contributions have gone up quite a bit. Some of the fools who held out have come to their senses after we put the word out that Siddhu and his daughter were shot because he refused to contribute!"

"You guys are going to make out like bandits!"

"Yeah! Isn't it great? If we do another kid like the Siddhu girl, those rich guys will fall over themselves in their rush to contribute."

More laughter, and the footsteps on the stairs resumed.

Rage erupted inside her.

She saw Jason peer out from behind the shower curtain and draw a hand across his throat in a swift slicing motion. Her thoughts exactly!

A man came past the edge of the bathroom door, and she took a half-step forward, hand raised to strike... and froze!

The man was wearing a turban! It covered both vital points for a killing blow, the *dokko* behind the ear and the *keichu* at the nape of the neck.

He went past her to the toilet, oblivious of her presence, and stood with his back to her, looking down while he unzipped his pants. Then Jason's hand flashed down from behind the shower curtain in a killing shuto strike at the keichu, now exposed under the turban.

The man collapsed as if struck by a blunt axe.

Alexis caught his lifeless body just before it hit the floor, but one of his arms flailed out to knock over a glass bottle on the cistern. It fell to the floor with a crash, shattering into pieces.

It took matters out of their hands.

"What's happening, Grewal?" Reddy called out from downstairs. "Did your prick fall off because you shook it too hard?" A vulgar laugh followed.

Jason lifted two fingers and pointed to the stairs. Alexis understood what he meant, and it was so simple and obvious that she did not have to think, just react. Jason grunted unintelligibly, then flushed the toilet, and turned on the taps in the sink to create background noise. Following his lead, Alexis opened the bath tub faucet and ran out of the bathroom, Jason a step behind her.

Bloodbath

She was more than half-way down when she heard Reddy say, "Are you okay, Grewal?" She rounded the corner, taking the last three steps in a single bound. The hallway came into view and her combat instinct kicked in.

A turbaned Sikh in the doorway of the living room. A second man, dark-skinned, clean-shaven, near the kitchen. Both looking towards the staircase with puzzled expressions.

With her hand on the stanchion Alexis used her momentum to catapult her towards the Sikh.

She saw him freeze in mid-step, eyes widening in shock. The slingshot effect of her hand on the stanchion carried her into a *mae-tobigeri*, the flying front thrust-kick, one of the most deadly and effective of all attack techniques.

The ball of her right foot smashed into the Sikh's face in a devastating *koshi* strike, pinning his head against the door frame. She flexed her knee to absorb the impact, feeling his skull cave in under her foot, and spun out of the kick to land facing the door to the kitchen, perfectly balanced on all fours. Something flashed through the air in a blur and she heard the unmistakable thud of a knife striking home, followed by a ghastly sound, like the gurgle from an emptying bathtub. The second man hit the floor, the hilt of a knife protruding from his throat.

She glanced back to the stairs, where Jason was leaning around the wall, right arm frozen in follow-through. She rose to her feet, as Jason walked past and bent down to jerk the knife out and wipe it clean on the dead man's shirt.

Suddenly, all the tension her was released. It was a catharsis.

In the crystalline mental clarity that followed, she 'saw' what had been bothering her ever since Pammie's shooting.

It all came together, then, and she gasped in disbelief.

"What's up, Red?" Jason asked urgently.

She could manage no more than a hoarse croak. "Jonathan! It's Jonathan!"

A look of utter confusion crossed Jason's face, but she couldn't bring herself to explain. Instead, she shouted to him in rapid-fire sentences, "Jason! Quick! Wipe everything we might have touched. And fix things to look like they killed each other in a brawl. We have to get out of here before anyone turns up."

"What the hell has gotten into you?" Jason asked angrily as she swung the door open. She was through it almost before the next words left his mouth.

"And where the hell are you going?"

She stopped and turned to face him. Taking a deep breath, she said in a shaky voice, "To find Jonathan. He's in their car."

PART FOUR

BLOOD TRAIL

CHAPTER 1

There was swirling fog. Through it, he felt like a jackhammer was pounding in his head, incessant and agonizing.

Arms lifted him up like a rag doll, and a flash of light exploded through the fog.

A voice murmured, like distant music, washing over him, carrying him away.

The fog closed in again.

* * * * * * * * * * *

A hand stroked his forehead. Caressing him, soft like velvet. Malcolm? No! Not Malcolm! Malcolm was dead.

He cried out again, feeling grief stab his heart like a knife.

The voice was there again, like a healing balm. Warm. Comforting.

Loving?

There was wonder in his soul. Then darkness rose and reclaimed him.

* * * * * * * * * * *

He felt hands on him. This time, he knew it was her.

A shudder of revulsion went through him—his crippled body. The ugly, puckered scars. The surgically-created openings. The bags of excrement. She couldn't see him like this!

He tried to fight her, to push her away, but her voice was like a wave rolling up a beach, gentle and unstoppable.

"Hush, now! It's okay. Go back to sleep. I'm here."

He wanted to wake up and tell her it wasn't right, but he was helpless against her voice. He drifted away on the rolling waves.

His last thought was that her hands were so much softer than Malcolm's.

* * * * * * * * * *

Jason's hands were trembling as he splashed a generous shot of bourbon into a glass and gulped it down.

In the rush to get Jonathan home, figure out why he was unconscious, and what to do about it, his mind was in overdrive. So, he had no time to absorb the shock of finding Jonathan comatose in the Land Rover. The delayed reaction finally hit him when Jonathan sank into sleep and Alexis said it looked like he would be okay.

He refilled his glass, feeling the bourbon burn a trail down his throat. As he hitched his butt up onto the bar stool, he felt the edge of the leather travel folder cut into his thigh. He reached into his pocket and pulled it out, conscious of a pulse of excitement.

It had a couple of airline flight itineraries and an Indian passport in the name of Naresh Gupta, with a photograph corresponding to the Uzi–wielding hit man in the Siddhu killing. According to Sol Steinberg, his real name was Randhawa, a henchman of a shadowy international criminal named Kalidas.

There couldn't be a link between the Siddhu killing and Jonathan's abduction, could there? It made no sense! Why would Kalidas send his henchman to kidnap one of the richest men on the planet and also help a fringe group of Sikh fanatics trying to bring recalcitrant 'donors' like Siddhu into line? Randhawa had to be freelancing, like Steinberg said, to help an old friend. That snippet of conversation they overheard about increased "donations" did suggest that money was the motive for the Sikh group.

But not for Kalidas. Why take Jonathan across the Pacific to the other side of the world if ransom was his motive? Revenge was more plausible, because Jonathan helped the Indians persecute Kalidas, but that made even less sense!

Why now? It was no secret that Jonathan never used security, so Kalidas could have grabbed Jonathan at any time over the years.

Jason sighed. No matter where he looked, all he reached was a dead end, with more questions and no answers.

He put down the passport and turned his attention to the airline itineraries. Both were in Gupta's name, one for a Bangkok-Vancouver round-trip, outbound completed a couple of weeks ago, return open, and the other a so-called 'open-jaw' itinerary, outbound from Dhaka in Bangladesh to Bangkok, timed to connect to the Bangkok-Vancouver outbound leg, and an open return from Bangkok to Yangon in Myanmar, not Dhaka.

Why the difference?

He visualized the map of that area. Bangladesh and Myanmar were in close proximity, separated only by the isolated part of India called the "Northeast", a geographic anomaly connected to the larger Indian land mass by a narrow corridor between Bangladesh to the south and China to the north. It comprised several troubled states with ongoing insurgencies. Nagaland was one of them.

Now it started to make sense! Reddy and Grewal had talked about "Naga whores"! So, if Kalidas's camp was in that geographic area, Dhaka and Yangon made sense as outlets to the world.

Which was very interesting, but didn't explain why Kalidas—!

The sound of the bedroom door being closed interrupted his train of thought, and he swiveled around to see Alexis walk in.

"He's resting peacefully now," she said. "The worst is over. He took quite a knock on the back of the head, and there's a puncture mark on his forearm showing they gave him something to keep him sedated. We'll see how he is when he wakes up, but I don't think there's any serious damage from the concussion. We can decide after he wakes up if he needs a C.T."

Jason trusted her judgment. She wouldn't risk keeping him here if there was the slightest chance of something serious.

"If we take him to hospital," Jason said, "there'll be questions about how he got the injury. The last thing I want is for it to be traced to that house."

"I'm sure that's the last thing Jonathan will want, too, but let's put it to him when wakes up. Then, if he agrees, he can say he fell out of the wheelchair and bumped his head."

"That should cover it," Jason said, relieved.

Alexis sat down, and looked at the printed itineraries. "So, they *were* headed for Kolkata!"

Jason went over what little he'd figured out, ending with, "So, kidnapping Jonathan was Randhawa's mission on behalf of Kalidas, and Siddhu's killing was Randhawa freelancing, like Sol thought. I don't think there's a connection."

"Yes there is, Jay. I didn't see it until after we tangled with those goons back there in the house."

Jason's interest was piqued. "So, what was it you 'saw'?"

"You're not going to believe this."

"Try me."

Alexis took a deep breath. "Siddhu wasn't the target. I was!"

Jason was speechless from shock.

She rushed to explain. "Do you know why I reacted as fast as I did, when I saw the car with the Uzi sticking out of the window? Because I knew, without any doubt or hesitation, that I was the target, not Siddhu, even though he was directly in their line of fire."

Her eyes challenged him to scoff, if he dared. Jason knew better. Recognizing an opponent's intent was integral to all high-level combat. What she was implying went far beyond recognition. It was *pre*cognition—*sakki!* An intuitive ability that bordered on the mystical, and found in only the very highest realms of combat, sakki enabled the ultimate combat master to thwart an opponent's intent even before it was conceived. So, if Alexis sensed she, not Siddhu, was the target, despite him being directly in the line of fire, it had to be sakki!

It dawned on Jason that there was so much he didn't know about his twin. But how far did it go? Had she intuited the connection to Kalidas's quest for vengeance?

He asked cautiously, "Any idea why you were targeted, Red?"

"Because of a stuffed elephant."

"What?" Jason gasped.

Alexis related what happened on her flight to New York, and the deadly confrontation in which Ravi saved her life. "You remember I thought the hit man was familiar when I saw his photo? After it all came together back there, I realized he was the Sikh who sat next to me. Customs arrested him, which fits with Steinberg's statement that Randhawa was detained at Kennedy on suspicion of drug smuggling. The drugs must have been hidden inside that stuffed elephant, and he was out to avenge whatever punishment he got from his boss for fouling it up."

Jason opened his mouth, but she cut him off. "Siddhu died, taking bullets meant for me. I can never repay that debt. And I'm the reason Pammie could—!" Her voice broke with emotion.

"You're not, Red," Jason interrupted sharply. "Kalidas is."

"What?" Alexis exclaimed, clearly incredulous.

"Why postulate two separate reasons—a stuffed elephant for Randhawa's drive-by revenge, and the dossier for Kalidas's abduction of Jonathan—when one will suffice? Occam's razor and all that! Kalidas is the thread that ties everything together."

"I still don't get it," Alexis said dubiously.

"Think about it, Red. Randhawa was Kalidas's man. He stayed

141

with the lot who grabbed Jonathan. And we heard them say Kalidas got 'half of what he wants'. You were Randhawa's target because you were the other half, not because of a stuffed elephant!"

Alexis shook her head dismissively. "Now that's a real reach, Jay. The timeline just doesn't make any sense. I can see why he waited until now to get me, because no one knew I was his daughter. Why would Kalidas wait four years to get Jonathan? You have to come up with something better than that, Jay-boy!"

She had found the flaw in his logic. "I'm not sure I can..." Jason started to say. Then he remembered another snippet he overheard, and took a wild stab. "How about this? The kidnapping was timed to celebrate whatever they called 'Khoon ka Snaan'."

Alexis scoffed. "That makes even less sense! And it's so sick that I don't want to think of a scenario where anyone would kidnap Jonathan to celebrate a bloodbath."

"All right, I take your point. But Kalidas is the connection between both attacks. It's the only lead we have. We have to follow it. We can't sit around waiting for him to make the next move."

"You're right. So what do we do, Jay?"

"What do you mean, 'we'? This isn't a one-on-one fight, like you're used to, Red. This is my kind of fight. Let me handle it."

"No way, brother mine! For four good reasons. Siddhu. Pammie. Jonathan. And the oldest and best reason of all—you!"

She bowed, clearly teasing him. "I'll make sure not to get under your feet, or mess up your commando operation, Major Wolff."

Jason leaned forward and punched her in the shoulder. "Idiot! But, if that's the way you feel, it's your funeral."

"Not literally, I hope!"

He grinned. "If you get under my feet, it could be." He became serious. "I think it's time one of us got some sleep. I'll take the first shift with Jonathan. In three hours it'll be your turn."

She said, "Okay," and headed for the spare bedroom.

CHAPTER 2

Awareness dawned slowly on Jonathan. His head throbbed. His cheeks and lips were bruised and swollen.

He forced his eyes open and registered the familiar surroundings of his bedroom. A moment of incomprehension followed, as he groped through the fog. How did he get here? Why did his head hurt?

The fog parted and, in one blinding flash, he remembered Malcolm dying to protect him, and the physical pain was nothing compared to how much his heart suddenly hurt.

Tears formed in his eyes, but he brushed them away angrily. There would be time for that later. Right now, he needed to deal with much more important things than his grief.

Like what the hell was going on! How did Jason and Alexis find him? He remembered trying to phone for help. After that, nothing, except a vague memory of Jason carrying him, of Alexis's soothing presence, and the wonder of it resurfaced for a moment, only to be brutally suppressed for later.

He hauled himself into his wheelchair, willing back a wave of dizziness and headed for the aroma of fresh-brewed coffee emanating from the kitchen.

He was halfway down the hall when Alexis saw him and ran up to give him a tight hug. Burying her face in his neck, she murmured, "Thank God, you're okay."

Stunned by her open show of emotion, he sat with arms half raised, uncertain if he should hug her back. Then Jason appeared, and she let go and straightened up. The moment passed.

Thrown off balance, he said stiffly "I can't begin to thank—!"

Alexis interrupted, giving him a playful pat on his cheek, "Shut up, you!" She then bent down again and kissed him there. "Don't be so formal. It's the least we could do for our fa—friend."

Jonathan pretended not to notice the word change. "Thank you, anyway," he repeated. "I need coffee. And we need to talk."

"Coming right up," said Alexis.

When all three had coffee in hand, Jason said, "A lot has happened that you need to know about, Jonathan. But first, can you fill us in on what happened to you last night?"

"There isn't much to tell. Malcolm parked the car in the garage and we rode up in the elevator. They were waiting for us in the foyer. Malcolm went for his gun, but he was not quick enough. One of them shot and killed him."

He paused, feeling pain stab his heart again. "I got through the door of the living room and slammed it shut. I remember grabbing the telephone, then someone inside knocked me out."

Jason was looking down with a frown, muttering to himself, "It doesn't make sense." Then his head snapped up. "You called Malcolm at ten, so everything must've been fine then. Couldn't have been more than twenty minutes before you returned."

"So?" Alexis asked.

Jason's snarled. "So, how did the kidnappers know exactly when to break in? And how did they do it without the guards seeing them, then override the penthouse elevator controls, and get in the penthouse without triggering the security system? All of that in the twenty minutes after Malcolm left and returned with you?"

He picked up the phone and unscrewed the mouthpiece of the receiver. "Just as I thought," he said grimly, holding up a tiny electronic transmitter. "All right! Stay put while I look for the rest."

Jonathan watched Jason go through the apartment, his face become steadily grimmer as he found twelve more. Finally, he checked the security panel, and removed a makeshift chipboard bridging the terminals.

When he was done, he said, "You can't spend another night here, Jonathan. You'd better move in with Alexis. Now that we know now how far this Kalidas is prepared to go, we stay on guard. We can't give Kalidas a third shot at any of us."

Shock made Jonathan stutter, "A th—third sh—shot?" Then realization dawned and said to Alexis in a hushed voice, "You too?"

Alexis nodded. "It's time for you to hear the whole story."

Jason and Alexis recounted the story they had pieced together, dovetailing their narratives as if a single brain was at work. As the details emerged, a strange sensation began a slow crawl across Jonathan's neck. It was terror. Unlike anything he'd felt before.

He knew they were getting personally involved in something deadly. His mind jumped tracks, then, and he thought bitterly of the lost years when he should have been with them.

He tried to be business-like. "Tell me why you're so hell-bent on making this your problem? Nothing—and that includes me!— is worth risking your lives."

Alexis smiled at him. "It's sweet of you to say that, Jonathan. I'm not downplaying how much I value it. But there are some things that are worth risking your life for." Her voice hardened. "Let's forget, for one moment, that you alone are worth it. But I can't forget that a little girl lost her father and lies fighting for life because they took bullets meant for me. I want justice for them."

She paused, then went on. "Now, let's get back to you. Kalidas isn't going to abandon his vendetta just because he's failed twice. If anything, the fact he's come so close twice will make him keep trying. So, none of us is safe until he's destroyed."

"Why can't the Indians handle it?" Jonathan asked. "I'm willing to use all my resources to convince the Indian Prime

Minister to track him down. Kalidas is their problem, not yours. So why do you have to—" He searched for the right metaphor, then blurted, "—to be the Sword of Retribution on their behalf."

Alexis laughed in delight. "The Sword of Retribution? Did I really sound that pompous? Well, to extend your own metaphor, Jonathan, I have no intention of getting involved in a crusade, sword-wielding or otherwise, on India's behalf! But what makes you think the Indians can take care of their 'problem', as you called it, when no one knows where he is now? They couldn't find him, let alone take care of him when he was in India, despite all your help!"

She had zeroed in on the fatal flaw in his argument, but Jonathan wasn't willing to concede. "Just because they can't take care of the problem doesn't mean you have to. I'm even prepared to get security—personal bodyguards, if that's what it takes"

Alexis smiled. "That's very sweet, Jonathan. I know how much you hate security, and don't think I don't appreciate it. I do. But it won't bring Pammie's father back, or heal Pammie's wounds—!"

The phone rang, and she broke off, answering it with brisk, "Hello. Jonathan Wolff's residence." Her face brightened. "Inspector Murphy!" she exclaimed, "Here's Jonathan."

Before Jonathan could bring his wheelchair forward, though, she asked in surprise. "Me?"

There was a pause. "Sorry, but I've been with Jonathan since early this morning. That's why you couldn't reach me at home."

There was a longer pause. Then, all of a sudden, Alexis became very still, and her knuckles turned white as she gripped the phone. "Thanks, Inspector," she said, her voice barely above a whisper.

Alexis replaced the handset, and stood with her head bowed for several seconds. When she straightened up and turned around, the transformation was shocking. Her face was ashen, and twisted with such unimaginable pain that he felt he was watching something very fragile about to break. He wanted with all his heart to take her in his arms and tell her that everything would be all right, but all he could do was sit there and watch her crumble in front of his eyes.

Alexis passed a weary hand across her brow. "Pammie Siddhu just died."

She stood with her head down and shoulders slumped for several seconds, and the silence screamed at Jonathan. But there was nothing he or anyone could say at such a time.

The silence dragged on and on...

Suddenly, her head snapped up, and he saw a feral light flash in her eyes. When she spoke, her voice brought to mind the sound of clashing sabers. "Just before we were interrupted, Jonathan, I said that I wanted to find Kalidas because he is responsible for Siddhu's death. I don't just want to find him now. I want vengeance. That little girl died for me. So don't tell me justice for her isn't my business."

Jonathan felt light-headed. He had never seen that look in her eyes or heard than tone in her voice. He tried to lighten the mood. "Heaven help anyone who tries to stand in your way, my dear. I've done far too much evil in my life to qualify for such celestial protection, so I'm certainly not about to stand in the way when the Sword of Retribution is on a mission of vengeance."

She stared at him for a second, and his heart clenched, thinking he had been too flippant. Then she figured out his convoluted joke, and laughed with delight, and the tightness eased.

Jason spoke up. "I'm going to check Alexis's apartment before we move in. And you have to report Malcolm's disappearance."

"What do you suggest?"

"Just remember that the men who killed Malcolm have paid the price, so Malcolm rests in peace. Call the police in the afternoon, and keep it simple. Say nothing about the kidnapping. Just say he mentioned something about going out to buy groceries in the morning. You woke up late, saw he wasn't there, and thought that was where he'd gone. When he hadn't returned by the afternoon, you got worried and called to report he was missing."

"Okay," Jonathan replied. "I'll call from Alexis's apartment."

He looked at the clock, suddenly feeling very tired. It was just after 10 a.m. "I think I'll go lie down until we're ready to move."

* * * * * * * * * * *

Jason returned after helping Jonathan into bed to find Alexis in the lotus pose, deep in a trance. She had turned inwards to rebuild defenses shattered by the shock of Pammie Siddhu's death.

Satisfied she was in control, he left and drove to her apartment. He searched it thoroughly for bugs, but came up with nothing. Even the locks showed no evidence of being forced. Mystified, he searched again, only to draw another blank.

How did Randhawa know when to strike? Was it really a spur of the moment decision? He found it hard to accept, given the meticulous planning that went into kidnapping Jonathan, but there seemed to be no other explanation.

Satisfied there were no bugs in the apartment, Jason returned to Jonathan's penthouse to find Alexis exactly as he left her. Relieved to see her still in a restorative trance, he went to the kitchen to think things through.

The way to find Kalidas was through his contact with the outer world—"Mukherjee in Kolkata". If they could locate his radio, bug it, and monitor radio traffic between him and Kalidas, they could get a fix on Kalidas's location by triangulation using sophisticated signals equipment.

Surveillance of that kind was impossible in India without official permission. But, with Kalidas likely to have infiltrated every level of the corruption-riddled Indian bureaucracy, that would be tantamount to telling Kalidas himself!

They needed someone who was part of Official India willing to help them unofficially.

Someone they could trust with their lives...

CHAPTER 3

Ravi Iyer prized his anonymity above all else.

No one, other than a handful of senior civil servants, knew his true role in the bureaucratic morass that was the Government of India.

His official designation was Director of the oddly named Division of Information Exchange within the Home Ministry, but the name and ministerial assignment were bureaucratic nonsense. He was answerable only to the prime minister, not the home minister, who had nominal jurisdiction over him, and the "Information Exchange" in which he was involved covered all counterterror-intel in India.

His department superseded all other agencies involved in gathering intelligence on terrorist activities in India. The politics, jealousies and internecine warfare within and between those agencies guaranteed that no single agency had the wide perspective needed to detect patterns, or the deep insight to make connections.

His department was the exception to that otherwise universal rule, and he was the reason it was an exception. No more than two dozen individuals knew he was the "foremost expert on terrorism in India". That mantle sat uncomfortably on his shoulders, and it came at an unimaginable price: his wife and two-year-old daughter killed in a terrorist attack, and a lonely existence dedicated to recognizing specific terrorist threats before they struck. His relentless dedication to that effort, and his success rate in detecting such threats, were why he had survived six transfers of power across the political spectrum, without partisan interference or meddling.

He had the highest security clearance, with unfettered access to the databases of every intelligence agency in the country, civilian or military, including, but not limited to, the Defence Intelligence Agency, the Air, Naval and Signals Intelligence Directorates, the Intelligence Bureau for domestic threats, and the Research and Analysis Wing for external threats.

His staff's clearance, although not as wide-ranging, included every local, state and central police and paramilitary database, including the Central Bureau of Investigation. Their single purpose was to collect and collate every incident report mentioning any of the different insurgent, rebel and terrorist groups operating inside and outside India, and then categorize, analyze, and correlate them. Since they did not gather the information themselves, he and his staff were unknown in terrorist circles as well, which made stringent security unnecessary.

Their anonymity was invaluable, considering the highly sensitive nature of the job. Most of it involved cross-referencing incident reports received each day from every corner of the country, to identify links, trends, or patterns. It was tedious and unrewarding for the most part. Once in a great while, though, an otherwise worthless fact would reveal itself as part of a larger pattern.

Like the appearance of the phrase 'Khoon ka Snaan' in four unconnected reports from widely separated insurgencies. Ravi had a grim foreboding that it represented something very dark and ugly for his country.

First, the Hindi phrase was too unnatural and contrived to be anything but sinister.

Second, its appearance in reports from four widely separated areas in the country—Punjab, Kashmir, Nagaland, and Andhra Pradesh— ruled out coincidence.

Third, all four reports appeared in a four-week period, suggesting momentum might be building to some sort of climax.

Fourth, and most disturbing of all, the insurgent organizations involved had such vastly different ideologies that any suggestion of cooperation defied logic. How could there be any grounds for cooperation between a fundamentalist Sikh, a fanatic Muslim, a Maoist, and a revolutionary Marxist-Leninist?

Unless Khoon ka Snaan involved all the major insurgencies!

There were at least seven major and a dozen minor areas of insurgency in the country. The most publicized was the so-called 'jihad' in Kashmir. Less well known was the Northeast problem, a festering sore in India's side for decades, with at least two major and four minor pockets of insurgency. The Naxalite movement was less cohesive, but it had widespread support in the tribal regions as an outlet for violent revolt against oppression. The civil war in Punjab in the eighties was now dormant, but easily reignited with a few well-timed 'atrocities'.

It made for a terrifying picture, especially if you threw in many other groups in different corners and pockets, each with their own grievances and demands. If all of them went on the offensive at the same time, it would stretch the resources of the paramilitary forces to breaking point and the turmoil would escalate until India fell apart under the stress of civil war.

Ravi knew he should report this to the PM, but how could he, when he had no evidence of this conspiracy, only a series of obstacles that made it inconceivable?

The planning needed to coordinate such a geographically and ideologically diverse group of insurgencies was staggering. None of them had the communications capabilities for it. Nor would they join forces even with rivals who shared their ideology, let alone those who didn't.

Most importantly, given their inherently paranoid and secretive character, there *couldn't* be anyone in the world who could bring them together.

Could there…?

CHAPTER 4

Karim Chand was basking in Kalidas's praise.

His master was pleased with him for organizing the summit to launch Bloodbath. And closing the one unfinished chapter in his life.

Jonathan Wolff had been kidnapped, Reddy and Grewal were on their way to the US, and the cripple would be on a ship headed for Kolkata in forty-eight hours.

All that remained was to snatch the girl who would star in the temple ritual to celebrate the launch of Bloodbath.

There was a knock on the door and Jarnail and Gurung entered the conference room

When they sat down, Karim Chand passed out copies of the girl's photograph, saying, "This is the girl for the special ceremony to celebrate Bloodbath."

"Who is she?" Gurung asked.

Karim Chand swallowed uneasily. This was the toughest part. "She is an orphan who lives in the jurisdiction of Inspector Ghose in Kolkata."

"One of Mrs. Chakraborthy's wards?"

"Not in the strict sense. She isn't a resident of the hostel, but she studies at the Kolkata College for Women where Mrs. Chakraborthy works."

The Sikh spoke for the first time. "Kalidas has ordered you to never pick anyone from outside your system. How did you dare to disobey him?"

"Because of the importance of this ceremony."

"That doesn't justify the risk!"

"Just hear me out," pleaded Karim Chand. "According to Mrs. Chakraborthy, she's an orphan, with no family, only one brother. And you can easily take care of him."

"Why did Mrs. Chakraborthy pick her if she isn't one of her wards?"

"She hates the girl. She imitates Mrs. Chakraborthy's accent and voice perfectly, which the students, and even some of the younger teachers find very entertaining."

Gurung snickered, holding up the photograph. "I'm not surprised that hag hates her. This one is the best so far."

"Why do you think I saved her for this occasion?" said Karim Chand with pride.

"I think we know very well why you saved her for this occasion!" Gurung sneered.

Karim Chand squirmed at the open contempt in the Gurkha's voice. "That kind of talk can be very dangerous, if the master hears about it!" Karim shot back.

"Oh, don't tell me you can't take a joke, Karim."

Karim Chand's point made, he moved on, confident he was back in command. "With the summit only a week away, the master will not tolerate a slip-up. The two of you will personally collect and transport the subject, and eliminate the brother. Here are the details."

He handed them a list of instructions and a copy of the photograph, and the two men left.

Karim Chand looked at the photograph and felt the longing rise in him yet again. As Gurung said, she was "the best ever".

CHAPTER 5

Eight hours of non-stop work brought Ravi Iyer no closer to solving the riddle of the strange but sinister term, Khoon ka Snaan. He was about to give up and go home when the phone rang.

He was surprised to hear Jason's voice. "Jason! It's been ages since I heard from Alexis or you. What made you call today?"

Jason's response exploded in his head like a grenade. "Something called 'Khoon ka Snaan' being planned by a man named Kalidas."

He was so stunned that the receiver slipped from his grip. He lunged to grab it, knocking the phone sideways, and breaking the transcontinental connection. He replaced the receiver and waited for it to ring again.

By then, he had regained his composure. "Jason, I'm sorry, but I was so stunned by what you said that I dropped the receiver."

"Ravi, I apologize for throwing that out so off-handedly," Jason said. "I was sure you'd scoff. Even I was convinced it was a crazy idea, based on a bunch of wild guesses."

"Your guesses are right on the mark. You've given me the answer to a question that has been plaguing me all day. The coincidence is uncanny!"

"So what do you know about Khoon ka Snaan?"

Iyer took a deep breath. "I believe it's a conspiracy to plunge India into civil war. Until you gave me the answer, I just couldn't figure out who could get so many insurgencies to cooperate with each other. How did you figure it out?"

"I didn't, Ravi! It was pure dumb luck I overheard someone say that a man named Kalidas was planning something called 'Khoon ka Snaan'. I had no idea what it meant. So I called you."

"Dumb luck or not, what you overheard could be a catastrophe for India."

"So, do something about Kalidas. The conspiracy falls apart if you eliminate the broker."

"You're right. All it would take is one surgical strike by the army. Unfortunately, we have no idea where he is."

"Could he be hiding in the Naga Hills?"

Iyer thought for a couple of seconds before answering, "I don't think something as big as Kalidas's base would remain undetected all these years, if he was in India. Someone, a villager or maybe a captured guerrilla, would almost certainly have let something slip by now. What made you think of Nagaland?"

"In the conversation I overheard, one of Kalidas's men complained about the Naga whores on the base. Another had airline tickets outbound from Dhaka, return to Yangon. Those two destinations fit if Kalidas's base is in India's Northeast."

"Hold on!" Iyer exclaimed as an idea struck him. "The Naga Hills and Patkai Hills straddle the border between northeast India and northern Myanmar. Dhaka and Yangon would make even more sense if the base was in northern Myanmar."

"So all you need is a reconnaissance mission and that surgical strike. Problem solved."

"I wish! Unfortunately, the PM cannot authorize an attack on foreign soil without absolute proof that Kalidas is there. Even if we had it, the PM would need full Cabinet approval, and we'd have to inform the Myanmar junta. Secrecy would be blown right there."

"Surely the PM knows that telling the Myanmar junta is tantamount to telling Kalidas himself? If he's been operating out of Myanmar with such impunity, he has to be doing it with their knowledge, if not their protection."

"That's logical, Jason, but international politics isn't logical. A covert military operation would make for a very ugly international incident. Even with absolute proof of Kalidas's presence there, the Myanmar junta would denounce it as an act of war, invoking the specter of Indian imperialism. And the Chinese, who are very cozy with the junta, would mobilize. I couldn't even think of asking the PM based on a conversation overheard by you."

"That leaves us with only one option, doesn't it? We'll have to find this man ourselves."

Ravi couldn't believe his ears. "Are you crazy? Do you have any idea how dangerous this man is? Two of his known associates are deadly assassins—"

Jason interrupted him. "You don't have to tell me how deadly or dangerous he and his associates are. He's tried twice to get back at Jonathan for helping drive him out of India."

"What?"

"Yes! I won't go into details, but the point is that we cannot wait until he tries again."

"It's insane to think of doing this yourself."

"Listen to me, Ravi, and then decide if what I propose is insane. All I want you to do is locate a man called Mukherjee who is Kalidas's agent in Kolkata."

"If he's an associate of Kalidas, we may have a file on him. But what's your plan?"

"To trace Kalidas through Mukherjee and let you take care of the rest. For it to work, though, you have to keep it to yourself. You know what would happen if we let anyone in the Indian bureaucracy hear about this, don't you?"

"All too well, my friend," said Ravi, with feeling.

"So, how long will it take to get the information on Mukherjee?"

"It shouldn't take too long. Most of it would be suspicion and unconfirmed innuendo. No proof. But that doesn't worry you, does it?"

"Of course not! I have all the proof I need."

Ravi hung up. It was almost 6 p.m. and the office staff was gone, but he knew where to look for what Jason needed.

CHAPTER 6

Gill wrinkled his nose at the fetid odor of cigarette smoke and stale Indian food in the office suite.

He saw the remains of the last meal he ate with Khullar just twelve hours earlier, and his grief resurfaced. Then, they were on the threshold of realizing a dream with unlimited promise, with the keys to the door tantalizingly close to hand—the woman's death and the cripple's abduction.

The failure of the drive-by had put their dream in jeopardy. Everything now hinged on the cripple's kidnapping. At least that seemed to have gone off without a hitch—Cheema would've called by now if it hadn't. And they still had a chance to recoup their losses, if they gave Kalidas the monitoring help he needed.

He opened the windows to let in the morning breeze and switched on the monitoring equipment. It was trained on the woman's window, exactly as he left it. With Brar released by Reddy, the two of them would have to work twelve-hour shifts until Cheema got back.

It was 11 a.m., and Cheema must be halfway home after seeing Reddy and Grewal on their way to L.A. The route went through some pretty rough country, where cell service was non-existent, so Gill wasn't worried that he hadn't called. Everything was going according to plan. Kalidas would be pleased.

He put on the headphones and settled into the chair. The apartment was silent. The bitch must be running around trying to figure out what happened to her father.

CHAPTER 7

Jason finally relaxed when the move to Alexis's apartment was completed. It was safe place to plan their next move without fear of surveillance.

Over lunch, Jason filled Jonathan and Alexis in on the gist of his conversation with Ravi Iyer. "If Ravi is right and Kalidas's base is in northern Myanmar, then Kolkata makes sense as the primary route for Kalidas to communicate with his world-wide empire. We know Mukherjee was going to relay news of Jonathan's kidnapping to Kalidas. So if we can locate Mukherjee, we should be able to work backwards from him to Kalidas."

"Good God!" exclaimed Jonathan in disbelief. "You can't just walk up to him and ask him to take you to Kalidas! Mukherjee will be forewarned, and expect something like this. He would see through any ruse or disguise!"

"Not if we do it right. You're right that no disguise will fool someone who's suspicious. The trick is to sound so plausible that there's no reason for suspicion."

"How?"

"By posing as a member of an Iranian resistance group looking for weapons to fight the mullahs. I have no doubt that he's used to being approached by customers like that dozens of times each year. I look the part, so he'll have no reason to suspect I'm not who I say I am."

"But won't he wonder why you're coming to him directly, not through his Iranian drug network?"

"No. Because that would risk betrayal to the religious police. After all, treason carries a much higher price tag than drug dealing."

Bloodbath

"I admit it's plausible," said Jonathan. "But I still think that you're getting into something very dangerous. Promise me that if you find proof he's in Myanmar, you won't do something stupid and try to take him on. Call me, instead, and I'll take it to the Indian PM. With proof, the PM can threaten the junta for harboring Kalidas. They may not hand him over, but that would certainly prevent Kalidas from threatening India—or us, for that matter."

"You have my word, Jonathan. All I want is to generate a lot of radio traffic between Mukherjee and Kalidas, which Ravi can monitor. Then the Indians can go after Kalidas themselves."

Jonathan sighed with relief. "That makes me feel better."

Jason caught Alexis staring at him and quickly looked away. In that one glance, he knew she could tell there was more to it than he was letting on.

Like her role in his plan. He hadn't yet told her what it was.

He knew better than to tell Jonathan.

* * * * * * * * * * *

When Ravi called, Jason switched to speakerphone so Alexis and Jonathan could hear what Ravi had to say about Mukherjee.

It wasn't much. Mukherjee had no criminal record, and there was no proof he was Kalidas's man, but Jason was interested only in Mukherjee's address and phone number.

He thanked Ravi for the information and, knowing it was midnight in Delhi, added, "Get some rest, Ravi. But before we sign off, there's one more thing. Can you help get us some basic gear when we get to India? We can't bring it with us, obviously."

"Send me a list," answered Ravi. "I'll also look into whether Kalidas's base might be in Nagaland. The Inspector General of

161

Police in Kohima is a friend from the Police Training Academy. I'll ask him under the pretext of an informal update on the Naga problem if he's heard rumors of a large rebel camp or base in the area. I'll also review any satellite photos of northern Myanmar on file. Maybe there's something going on in that remote corner of the world and no one's realized it yet. It can't hurt to check."

"That's great, Ravi," said Jason. "Look forward to seeing you again. We'll call you back as soon as we finalize our travel arrangements to Kolkata."

"When do you plan to arrive?"

"I'll e-mail you our itinerary. Can you arrange for us to have a day to relax, out of sight, and recover from jetlag before we head to our meeting with Mukherjee?"

"Sure. I'll take care of it."

CHAPTER 8

J ason remembered Kolkata as a squalid and decaying urban nightmare, home to more than twenty million human beings, many maintaining a tenuous foothold on existence under the most appalling conditions.

Its sights, smells and sounds could assault the senses of even an old India hand like Jason with unimaginable ferocity.

Ferocious was also the best characterization of the bedlam outside the international terminal, with importuning luggage porters—*coolies*—and cab drivers pressing forward without regard for the bottleneck at the gangway. Over the heads of the throng, Jason could see the tall figure of Ravi Iyer standing a few yards off, avoiding the melee at the exit.

Ravi saw them and his face broke into a wide grin. He walked up to them and took Alexis's hand in his own, saying nothing. This was India, where any public exhibition of affection, particularly between an Indian and a white woman, would instantly attract a crowd of onlookers and obscene comments. They couldn't risk that.

After they exchanged greetings, Ravi said, "We have an 11:30 flight to Bagdogra, and a private limo to take us to Darjeeling where I've booked a tourist bungalow for us to relax for a couple of days and discuss your plans without worrying about who's watching or listening."

It made sense to Jason. Two days in Darjeeling would be welcome after the long journey from Vancouver, through London and Dubai. Even though First Class on Emirates was as good as it got, they needed to recover from jetlag before their meeting with Mukherjee in two days.

163

They reached the domestic terminal, where a line of passengers was waiting at the entrance to have their tickets and IDs verified before entry. They joined the line, running another gauntlet of coolies pressing in from either side, pleading to carry their bags.

Ravi ignored their pleas, looking straight ahead to avoid making eye contact with them. Jason took his cue from Ravi and did the same, as did Alexis. It took an effort to stay together with the crowd pressing in on them.

"One more thing," Ravi said, under his breath. "Jason, watch your wallet, and Alexis, your purse. There is no more inviting target for a pickpocket than a firangi in a crowd. Remember that a US passport is prized on the black market!"

Jason laughed. "I didn't spend all those years in India without learning a thing or two, my friend. I keep my passport where no pickpocket can reach it. As for my wallet, if someone is able to nick it, he's welcome to whatever's in it. I'd even salute him as the greatest pickpocket in the world."

"Don't be too smug, Jason," Ravi warned. "And keep your voice down, for heaven's sake! Don't tempt fate."

Alexis rolled her eyes. "Jason thinks he's one of the greatest sleight-of-hand artists you'll ever have the misfortune of meeting. That's why he's so smug."

"An essential commando skill, I suppose," Ravi said, sarcastically.

"Sneer all you want, my friend, but don't lose any sleep over me, okay?"

They showed their IDs and tickets and entered the terminal, heading for the Indian Airlines ticket counter to check in for their flight to Bagdogra.

CHAPTER 9

The young coolie hurried away from the airport, trying to walk as fast as he could without showing he was in a hurry. To anyone watching, he was a simply a man trying to catch the bus home. Inside, though, Mohan Sinha was exulting over his good fortune.

Stupid firangi, he thought to himself. *I taught you the lesson you deserve. You can salute me as the greatest pickpocket in the world!*

There still were ten minutes before his bus arrived, so he ducked into a deserted alleyway and checked the wallet. He caught his breath when he saw it contained five thousand rupees.

Magnificent as it was—over three months' worth of tips!—he was disappointed not to find any dollars. Five thousand rupees was about eighty dollars, and firangis usually travelled with a lot more.

He sighed.

The risk of picking a firangi's pocket was as high as the reward, if the wallet contained dollars. Without dollars, though, the risk wasn't worth the wrath of the man he feared more than any other.

Jagga, the overseer of the coolies, was the boss of all the rackets at the airport, and he ruled with an iron hand, permitting none but a select group of thieves to operate in his territory. The fee for that "permission" was a twenty-five percent cut, and Jagga's goons enforced it with brutal authority.

Mohan was terrified Jagga would discover that an 'unauthorized' pickpocket was operating on his turf. For that reason, he was very careful to stay away from picking the pockets of firangis. But how could he resist, when the idiot firangi chose to challenge him, the greatest pickpocket in the world?

So, showing up the man was reward enough. He would offer a hundred rupees at the temple of his favorite deity Hanuman, the Monkey God, to thank Him for His benevolence. Five thousand rupees would cover next semester's tuition for his sister, Seetha.

His heart swelled with pride at the thought of his brilliant, beautiful Seetha. Three years younger than him, she was the focal point of his universe and his one reason for living.

He could recall no one else who ever meant anything to him, or to whom he meant anything. Even the abusive uncle and aunt who kept them as bonded labor in the remote village of their birth in Bihar were now just faceless figures from a distant past, remembered only for vicious beatings and relentless toil.

He remembered running away with his sister when he was ten, trekking across the fields in the night to the tiny wayside station ten kilometers away. With no money for a ticket, they travelled on the roof of the first train headed east. For the next sixteen hours, he didn't dare to close his eyes. With his sister clutched in the crook of his arm, he was terrified of losing his grip on her if he slept. He also had to stay alert so they could quickly jump off when the train entered a station, to avoid the police looking for ticketless travelers.

That they made it to Kolkata without being separated was a miracle—the first in an endless series of such miracles that convinced Mohan he was under the protection of the god Hanuman, the embodiment of courage and wisdom. The greatest miracle of all was that they escaped the fate of countless other destitute children trying to eke out a miserable existence on the streets of Kolkata.

Some died of starvation or disease. They were the lucky ones.

Most fell prey to the vermin who dealt in the flesh of children. Many were deliberately blinded or maimed to make them more 'marketable' as beggars. Others were terrorized into joining gangs of child thieves, or sold into prostitution—only to be discarded to die when they outlived their usefulness.

Bloodbath

Not him. Nor his sister. They survived.

A big reason was that they had each other to keep fighting against the odds stacked against them. Still, it was an unequal struggle and it would have overwhelmed them, but for Mohan's self-confidence, and his faith in the benevolence of Hanuman.

He perfected his exceptional talent for picking pockets into a survival skill, but had the good sense to keep it a secret from his sister, knowing she would never allow it. Once he was old enough to look the part, he took a job as a coolie at the airport by bribing the overseer. Since the generosity of customers was so erratic, he could always make his income from pickpocketing 'disappear' without raising Seetha's suspicions.

It was how he scraped together the money for her education. His proudest achievement was that, through it all, she hadn't missed a day of school. It was worth it because she was brilliant. In a year, she would be eligible for admission to medical college. Nothing was going to stop her from becoming a doctor. When that happened, his life, as wonderful as it was, would get even better.

Then he remembered the one small shadow marring his otherwise blissful existence. For the last five years, Seetha had taken it upon herself to continue his education.

She insisted he spend one hour each night studying the books he abandoned after the fourth grade. It was no use resisting because she had zeroed in on his one Achilles heel. If he refused to study, she refused to eat!

Once, in the early days, he tried brazen it out, refusing to study. For two days, not a drop of water passed her lips. It ended in his abject surrender on the third morning. He never tried it again.

He had to admit, though, that English literacy was a good skill to have. Without it, he would never have learned computer programming. Or discovered his remarkable aptitude for hacking computers. So remarkable, in fact, that he convinced his "instructors"—a group of identity thieves operating out of the slum—that he was a total idiot who couldn't hack a computer to save his life!

He never put that skill to use. He found hiding in the shadows to steal someone's identity without risk dishonorable, even despicable, compared to the man-to-man risk of pickpocketing. But his computer skills might yet be useful in the future, when he needed a respectable job as "the brother of Dr. Seetha Sinha"!

English literacy had more tangible and immediate benefits, too. He was now quite comfortable conversing with firangis and their funny accents. Impressing them with good English was a huge advantage, because they always gave the best tips.

His bus arrived and he squeezed aboard, taking care to safeguard his prize. He would make sure Seetha didn't find it when she gave him a hug, and to hide it inside one of the mud bricks in the walls of his *jhuggi*, the little hovel that he called home. It threatened to dissolve every time the monsoons arrived, but it was home, and his sister would be waiting for him there.

CHAPTER 10

Alexis propped herself on an elbow to look at Ravi, fast asleep beside her.

His face still had the vulnerability that attracted her when they first met. She knew he would never get over his loss completely, but the lines of pain around his eyes were now gone. She liked to think that she had something to do with their disappearance.

Last night was wonderful, just the way she remembered. Ravi was a tender and caring lover, different in many respects from other men she had known. His gentle lovemaking was unique because his focus was to satisfy her. In that respect, it was a fulfilling rather than draining climax.

She slid out of bed and pulled on a robe. Making as little noise as possible, she left the room and went to the veranda, where she knew she would find Jason.

Jason gave her a broad grin. "Good morning, Red! Did you and Ravi get much sleep last night?"

"Mind your own business, Jason Wolff!" she answered, pretending anger.

He continued to smile at her. "I couldn't have minded it if I'd wanted to. What with all the noise coming from across the corridor, I hardly slept a wink."

Alexis laughed. "Hah! You and I know perfectly well the reason you couldn't sleep. You shot your mouth off and got your come-uppance. How's your pocket today, buddy?"

Jason squirmed. It was a good thing the wallet only had the money he exchanged on arrival, or she might not be laughing.

Thankfully, their passports, the rest of the money, and their credit cards were safe. The wallet was already replaced.

"That's not the point," he protested weakly, "so don't try to change the subject. The point is I've been living the life of a celibate for the last week, just so my sister could indulge her own carnal desires. At this rate, I might as well give up mine and become a hermit."

She punched him in the shoulder and he pretended to cower. "That's rich, coming from you. You, give up your—what did you call them?—carnal desires? Snowflakes have a better chance in hell than that happening. If you ever became a hermit, Jason Wolff, half the women you know will commit suicide. The other half will simply set up shop at your hermitage."

As Jason pretended to shake a fist at her, she marveled at how they could both tease each other. He was comfortable with simply being a friend to her. Uncomplicated. Undemanding. And the best friend she had.

She looked out at the sun rising over the Himalayas. There was nothing in the world to compare with their awesome beauty, peak after majestic snowcapped peak rising twenty-thousand feet and more into the sky. The timeless peace they represented was contagious. She felt a tranquility she hadn't felt since the drive-by shooting.

It was good, this interlude. Pammie's death and Jonathan's narrow escape held dangerous echoes of old psychological traumas. She was glad to be able to recharge her emotional batteries.

She sensed Jason's appraisal without having to look. "I'm back, Jay-boy, all the way."

"I know," he said.

Just two words, but they were all she needed to hear. It was enough.

She continued to stare at the view in silence. It was hard to imagine that such beauty could hide something as ugly and evil as Kalidas.

She felt Jason's hand on her arm and turned. "You're thinking he's hiding somewhere out there, aren't you?" he asked.

She nodded, not surprised that he read her mind.

"I hate to disappoint you, Red, but it doesn't look like he's in northern Myanmar."

Jason opened a folder in front of him and spread out a number of aerial satellite photographs on the table. "Ravi gave me these to look over last night. All I see are a few scattered logging camps and a geological survey mission, all quite open and above board. Ravi's friend in Kohima is also sure that Nagaland is out of the question."

Before Alexis could respond, Ravi appeared in the veranda doorway and interrupted her. "That's right. It means you're going ahead with your suicidal plan, isn't it?" He dropped a kiss on her cheek and clapped a hand on Jason's shoulder before sitting down.

Last night, before they went to bed, he listened without saying anything as Jason sketched out his plan to contact Mukherjee, locate his radio, and bug it to monitor transmissions to Kalidas. At the time, Ravi's expression made clear how he felt about it, but the agreement was to defer any discussions until morning.

Ravi wasted no time getting straight to his point. "Jason, how do you know that Mukherjee hasn't already told Kalidas of your proposition? Your cover may already be blown and you may be walking into a trap."

"I don't think so, Ravi," answered Jason. "After all, why should Mukherjee suspect a perfectly legitimate approach?"

"But after the meeting, won't he become suspicious?"

"We're counting on that happening," Jason responded. "We want him to think there's something phony about me. He will panic and head straight to his radio to call Kalidas for instructions. That's where Red comes in. He's going to lead her to it."

Ravi couldn't believe it. "Good God!" he exclaimed. "Alexis intends to follow him around Kolkata? Do you think a firangi woman can simply stroll through the alleyways without being accosted, if not assaulted? Are you nuts?"

"Give me some credit!" Alexis broke in. "I won't be a firangi woman. I will be a traditional Muslim woman, covered from head to foot in a *burkha*. It is such a common sight in this city that, even if Mukherjee is worried someone might be following him, it won't register. After all, isn't that the point of the burkha?"

"I suppose that's true."

"Once Red locates the radio," Jason added, "we pay a night visit to bug it and listen in on all transmissions to and from Kalidas. Then it will be simple to find the base by triangulation."

Ravi's response was derisive. "Do you expect Kalidas to oblige you by sitting on his hands while we try to locate him? His immediate reaction will be to order your execution."

"You're forgetting one thing, Ravi," Jason answered. "Kalidas won't know who we are until after we meet Mukherjee. It shouldn't take your experts more than a few hours to locate Kalidas's camp, given the volume of radio traffic our meeting will generate. Nobody could pull off a grab or an execution in that time with both of us on our guard."

Alexis knew Ravi had no choice but to agree. Ravi had neither the personnel nor the authority to pull off something like this. There was no one he could trust to do it, either, since there was no way of knowing which departments Kalidas might have penetrated.

Ravi agreed, grudgingly. "Okay! I guess there is no other way. I made a call to the Air Force Chief, under the pretext of getting a fix on a rebel base camp to set up the signals watch. Also, a suitcase full of the gear you requested will be delivered to you in Kolkata.

Some of the items on the list, though—why do I feel you're planning for more than you're letting on?"

"They're purely for defensive purposes," Alexis reassured him.

"Then there should be no reason why you can't promise that you'll first check with me before deviating from the plan."

"That's the whole idea, darling," Alexis said.

She saw him grimace and knew he had exhausted his arguments.

The arrival of the attendants with breakfast halted further discussion. While they ate, Alexis suggested they take a hike in the mountains after breakfast.

Ravi thought it a great idea, but Jason tactfully demurred, saying he wanted to study the files that Ravi brought with him, ostensibly to "familiarize myself with the topography of the region, including northern Myanmar, and identify potential locations for Kalidas's base camp".

With the peaceful surroundings providing a welcome respite, Ravi regained his good humor during the hike.

CHAPTER 11

Mohan's workday was shaping up to be a complete loss. His usually flawless sense of timing seemed to be off. He not only failed to catch the eye of any of the affluent customers that all the coolies coveted, he also failed to snag any of the bread-and-butter folks.

It was not all bleak though. No one reported a stolen wallet the previous day. It was unheard of for a firangi victim, but a real relief to Mohan.

With still a couple of minutes left before his shift ended, though, he was hanging around, hoping for one last chance, when a taxi pulled up at the curb. Out of it stepped a fat man with his wife and five children in tow, almost at his feet, and one look told Mohan all he needed to know. They were rich and not bashful about flaunting it.

Before the fat man could say anything, Mohan was at the trunk of the taxi, unloading the baggage. The suitcases were heavy and there were eight of them, but he carried them without complaint through the baggage screen and to check-in.

The way the day had gone should have prepared him for the last straw. The fat man gave him a measly ten rupees in return for twenty minutes of heavy labor. It was so unfair that he protested angrily, citing the set minimum per item of luggage. The fat man shouted back, threatening to file a police complaint against him.

The threat forced Mohan back down, knowing it would go to Jagga. The last thing he wanted to do was attract his attention. In any case, Jagga's concept of justice was to have any "offending" coolie given a sound beating, as a matter of principle.

Bloodbath

Mohan swallowed his resentment and walked away. He was so upset over what had happened, however, that he ended up doing something he had never done before.

He picked the pocket of a customer he had served.

He snuck up behind the fat man while he was pushing his way to Security. Then, he was gone, just another coolie mingling in the crowds.

He hurried out of the airport. Unlike yesterday's firangi, the fat man would surely throw a fit, and Jagga would turn the airport inside-out to find the light-fingered thief who had dared to intrude into his territory.

Mohan did not take out the wallet to examine it until he ducked into a garbage-filled alley near home. The wallet was fat, so he expected there to be a huge sum. Still, nothing prepared him for what he found.

With trembling hands, he counted twenty-five one thousand rupee notes!

In his wildest dreams, he never imagined holding this much money in his hands. The hole in that mud brick would be bursting today!

It meant he could stop worrying about Seetha's college tuition. And he could buy her an expensive silk sari to mark Raksha Bandhan, the festival in which a brother reaffirmed his love for his sister. First though, he'd buy her the propane gas stove she had always wanted, so she would never again cook on a coal-fired bucket-stove. He needed to be very careful, though, so she did not suspect how much money he had or how he got it.

He began to whistle as he threaded his way through the maze of filthy alleyways in the shantytown.

The whistle died on his lips when he made the last turn and saw a crowd gathered in front of his jhuggi. Knowing Seetha must be in some kind of trouble, he ran forward, not caring who he knocked aside to get to her. When he broke through the crowd, though, he stopped dead, coming face-to-face with his worst fears.

Two men and a woman were waiting for him. The woman he knew. It was Mrs. Chakraborthy, the warden of the hostel affiliated with his sister's college. The two men, though, were so terrifying that Mohan felt his knees buckle just looking at them. One was a Gurkha with a deformed face. The other was a huge Sikh, whose turbaned head had been visible to Mohan from afar, towering above the rest of the crowd.

All this he registered in the split second before they realized who he was. "Your sister has been taken to hospital," the woman told him. "You must come immediately."

Panic made Mohan hysterical. "Has she asked for me!?" he yelled. "Is she going to die? Where is she? Please take me to her, I beg you."

"Calm down!" The Sikh's voice sounded so sinister it sent a shiver though him. "We took your sister to hospital. She is not seriously injured. We have a car waiting to take you to her."

Without waiting for an answer, the Sikh turned around and left. Mohan followed like an automaton, unable to think, let alone ask any questions.

With each step he took, though, his panic began to recede. It was a relief to know that Seetha was not seriously hurt. It could have been much worse! He lived in constant terror that someone might lure her away from the safety of the shantytown. So, he and Seetha agreed on a secret password that would tell her if a message supposedly sent by him was genuine. It had twice saved Seetha from would-be abductors who brought news that Mohan was injured and asking for her.

Seetha, of course, insisted that it should apply both ways. He scoffed at her, saying that no one would want to kidnap him, but she refused to listen. He recalled, with a smile, how she made absolutely sure of it. She made him promise in front of Hanuman to never accept a message supposedly sent by her unless it came with the same password.

The memory wiped the smile from his face.

Why had she forgotten their pact? Maybe she was more seriously hurt than they were letting on and unable to give the password!

He looked over his shoulder at the woman. "Are you sure she is all right? She isn't unconscious, is she?"

The woman snapped, "I spoke to your sister myself after she was taken by these kind men to the hospital near the college. I promised her I would show them where you lived."

Mohan felt his throat constrict. He knew she was lying. Mrs. Chakraborthy was the last person Seetha would contact if she were in trouble. The hostel warden had been particularly vindictive towards Seetha ever since she caught her using her extraordinary gift of mimicry to make fun of the woman's rasping voice and distinctive accent.

Even though he was sure she was lying, Mohan still clung to a vanishing hope. Gulping to steady his voice, he asked, "Did she give you any special message for me?"

"Why are you asking these stupid questions? I told you her message. It was for you to come with these men to the hospital, that's all."

Mohan panicked. No password! But why lure him from the shanty town with this lie about Seetha's accident? Were they trying to kidnap him? Why him and not Seetha?

Then the answer struck him and he confronted his worst nightmare. They were trying to get rid of him because they already had Seetha!

He felt his knees start to buckle, but he somehow managed to keep walking. He realized he was no longer in the shantytown, where someone might respond to a cry for help, but in the bazaar. Here, no one in the impersonal throng of evening shoppers was going to intervene on his behalf. He was on his own.

With that, he felt a sense of total detachment. He registered for the first time that both men were keeping him hemmed in and that the Sikh was maintaining a firm grip on his shoulder.

Then, miraculously, he got his chance. For one split-second, the irresistible ebb and flow of the crowd forced both men away from his side, and Mohan reacted without thinking. He twisted out of the Sikh's grasp and ran, and was swallowed up by the throng.

Ducking his head below shoulder level, he slipped through the crowd, until he stumbled into a small alley and crouched down on his haunches behind a pile of rotting garbage. With his arms crossed and hands tucked into his armpits, he began to rock back and forth on his heels, moaning in fear.

He stayed like that, oblivious of the surroundings, until he saw a car crawl past the mouth of the alley. He glimpsed the Sikh and Gurkha in the front and shrank back in terror, the garbage shielding him from their view.

The car inched away, the irate driver honking at the people crossing the street. It awakened Mohan to reality and his sister's abduction. He had to report it as soon as possible if there was to be any chance of saving her.

Craning his neck past the garbage, he read the license plate of the car, committing it to memory. When it was out of sight, he started running through the side streets to the local police station.

He rounded the last corner, his legs ready to give out, when he saw the same car at the curb in front of the police station, and his blood turned to ice. Inspector Ghose had his head bent down at its open window, nodding at the giant Sikh.

Bloodbath

Mohan sidled closer to listen to what they were saying. He heard the Inspector say in Hindi, "Very well, sir! I will circulate the photograph you found in the girl's purse, naming her brother as the prime suspect in her disappearance. Don't worry, Sir. As soon as the fool shows up to report her disappearance, we will arrest him, and I will take care of it."

The Sikh's hoarse whisper also reached Mohan's ears. "Make sure he is shot trying to escape, Ghose. For your own sake, I hope you have disposed of him by tomorrow."

"Rest assured I will, Sir."

Mohan couldn't believe his ears! Ghose was agreeing to have him arrested and killed. How could he, a penniless coolie, fight a force that was so powerful as to corrupt even the police?

He turned away, tears stinging his eyes. Over the years, despite all the misfortunes he faced, he never once despaired, or doubted that Hanuman was watching over him. He wore that belief like armor in his battle for survival, and it gave him the courage to fight, no matter what happened. Now, for the first time ever, he knew despair. The truth was that there was no good in the world, only evil. He, who always thought Hanuman was on his side, was now alone in his time of need.

He was crying openly now, oblivious of the passersby staring at him. Blinded by tears, he bumped into a fat man who had his back turned to him. The man turned around, grabbed him by the shoulder, and slapped him hard on the cheek, accusing him of trying to pick his pocket. Without letting go, he checked his pockets to confirm nothing was missing. Then, he gave Mohan a shove and told him to get away from him.

Mohan massaged his cheek, watching like a zombie, as the man waddled away, his huge ass swaying from side to side. A hysterical giggle bubbled up inside, as he remembered another fat behind waddling away in the airport, just before he picked his pocket.

Mohan gave a shout of triumph. Hanuman had not forsaken him! He wasn't penniless.

If the evil men had bought the police, he had the money to buy the help of someone to fight on his behalf.

But who? It had to be someone who could match the power of the men who kidnapped Seetha. The local *goondas*—the shantytown thugs—did not have that kind of power. Anyway, they would just steal his money and beat him up in the bargain. He needed someone who not only had power, but also knew him well enough to take his problem seriously...

Someone like Jagga!

The overseer had a gang of twenty thugs who enforced his will. They would be more than a match for the two kidnappers!

Mohan hurried to the nearest bus stop, wanting to get to the airport immediately. Then he remembered the time—Jagga would be long gone from the airport by now. He would not be in before noon tomorrow.

Mohan dragged himself back to his jhuggi. As he crawled into bed, he wept silently, his body racked by sobs. Sometime later, he fell into a sleep of total physical and emotional exhaustion.

CHAPTER 12

Ravi's upbeat mood had evaporated. He looked morose, almost despondent at dinner, refusing to participate in Alexis's playful banter with Jason.

Alexis waited until the attendants left before asking "What's the matter, Ravi? I thought we agreed not worry about the plan. Give us credit for being able to look after ourselves."

"This has nothing to do with your plan, or your abilities. I am worried because neither of you has any idea what you're getting into with Kalidas."

Jason shrugged. "Trust me, we know. Anyway, you are forgetting that we want to find him, not take him on. You are the one who's going to take him on."

"It's the finding that scares me. I worry that he'll find you before we find him."

"We've covered this, Ravi," she said. "We'll be ready for him."

"Ready or not, you don't want to tangle with the two gorillas he has for bodyguards. The Sikh and Gurkha who work for him—or, should I say, kill for him—are very bad news."

Alexis saw Jason freeze. "A Sikh and a Gurkha?" he asked Ravi very softly. "What do you know about them?"

"Enough to be scared! You wouldn't be so cavalier about going up against Kalidas if you knew what I know—"

"So tell me!" Jason interrupted forcefully.

Startled by the snap in Jason's voice, Ravi began to recite from memory. "The Sikh's name is Jarnail Singh. He is a giant, six feet ten inches tall, and a ruthless enforcer whose forte is killing with his bare hands. He isn't the fastest or the most athletic of individuals, nor is he particularly adept at the martial arts, but he has never needed to be. His strength is so immense that it more than makes up for his deficiencies. In a country without a strong martial arts tradition, he is a fearsome weapon in Kalidas's hands."

Ravi paused. "Oh, yes! There is one other thing! He speaks only in a whisper. No one knows why. But the whisper makes him even more terrifying."

She saw Jason nod, his face as if carved out of stone.

Ravi went on. "The Gurkha's name is Nar Bahadur Gurung. He is only five-feet-six, but freakishly proportioned, with a fifty-inch chest, and extremely powerful, reputedly able to bench-press four hundred pounds. He was a *naik*—a corporal— in the Gurkha Brigade, until he was cashiered for killing a sergeant who provoked him into a fight with the kukri."

"That is not in character," said Jason. "The Gurkhas take great pride in their skill with the kukri, but they are not wanton killers. What happened?"

"The facts are indisputable. All the witnesses were Gurkhas themselves and, to a man, they said they had never seen anyone use a kukri the way Gurung did. It was over before the victim could use his own kukri. The sergeant fell to his knees after being disemboweled by the first slash to his belly, and Gurung beheaded him cleanly through the neck with his kukri as he was bent over, much as he would slaughter a goat."

"Beheaded?" Jason sounded incredulous. "You've got to be kidding me! I know they behead goats during their festivals, but it is impossible to behead a man with one stroke of a kukri! It would take superhuman strength."

"Incredible as it may sound, the eye witnesses were unanimous. He was court-martialed, of course, but he spent only two years in prison because the sergeant was the first to draw his kukri. There also was evidence of extreme provocation by the sergeant, who taunted him incessantly about his grotesque body proportions.

"After his release, he disappeared for a while. Details are sketchy, but he resurfaced in Kalidas's employ, having suffered a terrible facial injury that left him hideously deformed. All his front teeth are missing, together with a large portion of his upper lip and jaw. It's almost as if he was mauled by a wild animal."

She saw Jason lean back, his face cracking into a grim smile. "Well! Well! Well! It's a small world, after all!"

Alexis was stunned. "You mean you know these men?"

Jason nodded. "I do! It was after you'd left for Japan, Red. I never told anyone because, as far as I was concerned, I'd had a run-in with a bunch of hoodlums."

He described what happened, but even without full detail, Alexis was in awe of the unorthodox combat move he used to disable the two bodyguards. The way he immobilized the four men, playing on the average Indian's fear of any public display of nudity, left her and Ravi in splits!

Jason was in no mood to share in their laughter. His voice remained grim. "Maybe I should have finished the job when I had the chance."

"That's hindsight, Jay," said Alexis. "You couldn't know this was how it would turn out. At the time, you had nothing to gain by killing them. You were only interested in getting away."

He shrugged. "Some things begin to make sense, though. I could never understand why a simple, everyday graft transaction became an exercise in lethal intimidation. Now that I know it was Kalidas, I can see it fits the picture of a psychopathic killer who terrorizes for pleasure."

"Unfortunately, it gives him another reason to hate the Wolffs," Alexis said.

"Of course! Look at it from his perspective. First, I humiliate him. Then Jonathan foils his assassination plan, driving him out of India. And let's not forget you and Randhawa with that stuffed elephant thing in New York. Put them all together, and it's more than enough for him to get paranoid that the Wolff clan is engaged in a vendetta against him, don't you think?"

Alexis sensed Jason was trying to defuse the now palpable tension in the room. She played along, maintaining a stream of light-hearted conversation that forced Ravi to join in. Soon he was laughing too, his worries shelved even if they weren't forgotten.

CHAPTER 13

Mohan went straight to the office of the Coolies Union in the baggage marshaling area when he got to the airport at noon.

Tarun, one of Jagga's right hand men, was leaning against the wall outside, a cigarette dangling from his lips, cleaning the dirt under his nails with a penknife.

"Tarun, I need to see Jagga *Sahib*, please." Mohan remembered to add the honorific reserved for a superior.

Tarun answered with a sneer. "Why?"

"I am in trouble and only Jagga Sahib can help me."

"That doesn't mean you can see him, son of a dog. Why would he waste time on an asshole like you? Anyway, he isn't yet here." He went into the office and shut the door.

An hour went by, during which Mohan's anxiety rose to near fever pitch. Just when he was about to throw caution to the wind and knock on the door, it opened, and Tarun crooked a finger at him. He got up and went in.

Jagga was sitting with the chair tilted back, his feet on the table, chewing *paan*, the betel leaf and tobacco concoction so common in India. Ignoring Mohan, he spat out a stream of red spittle onto the floor.

One of the other men in the room, a man named Rana, began yelling at Mohan, "Jagga is busy, you son of a whore! Be quick! What do you want?"

"I beg you to help me, Jagga Sahib," Mohan pleaded. "Two goondas have kidnapped my sister."

Tarun laughed. "So! A whore runs away with her pimps and you expect Jagga Sahib to bring her back? What do you take him for, imbecile? Go find your whoring sister yourself!"

"She is not what you say she is," Mohan burst out in anger. Then, remembering his purpose, he controlled himself and appealed to Jagga. "Please believe me, Jagga Sahib! I saw the men who took her. They tried to kidnap me too but I got away. They have the police in their pay and I have nowhere to turn for help. You must believe me! I need your help to find her, please. I will pay you for it."

"What makes you think you can afford Jagga Sahib's help, you penniless wretch?" Rana asked scornfully.

"I have two thousand rupees," replied Mohan, unable to contain his eagerness. He congratulated himself on having the good sense to keep the real amount a secret.

The words were barely out of his mouth when he saw a flash of anger in Jagga's eyes. The overseer sat up immediately. "Where did you get that kind of money, you sister-fucker? Are you the *pocket-maar* who has been operating without my permission in my airport for the last five years? Yesterday a wallet was stolen. I know that none of my boys did it. Was it you, you son of a whore?"

"No!" Mohan burst out. He had made a terrible mistake, trying to convince Jagga to help him. He had to get away before they searched him and found the money. He tried to stall. "I've been saving it for my sister's tuition. I put it in a locker when I got here, so I wouldn't lose it. I will get it for you, if you want."

This answer didn't fool Jagga. He held out his hand "The key, you worthless dog!" he commanded.

Mohan lied again. "I hid it behind a cistern in one of the bathrooms because I was afraid of losing it," he managed to say.

Jagga reached out and squeezed Mohan's chin with such force that it brought tears to his eyes. "All right! Go with Rana and

Tarun and get the money. If you are lying, you will be thrashed so mercilessly that you will wish that it was your ass that those men were screwing instead of your sister's."

He gave Mohan a brutal shove, letting go of his chin and sending him stumbling backwards into Rana's waiting arms. He was hustled out of the room.

He walked up the stairs to the baggage claim area, numb with the realization that he should never have come to Jagga for help. He was trapped. There was no point in calling for help or trying to run. Nobody would dare risk Jagga's wrath by helping him. He would never leave the airport alive if he ran. Tarun and Rana knew it. That was why neither was bothering to hold on to him.

They entered the baggage claim area and Mohan noted from force of habit that the Bagdogra flight had landed, and that passengers were collecting their bags from the carousel. Even with his mind clouded by panic, he recognized the firangi whose wallet he stole two days ago, and his woman companion.

They had just picked up their bags and would reach the exit almost at the same time as him.

CHAPTER 14

Alexis was a few feet from the exit when she saw three coolies bearing down on them from the right. Before she could call out a warning to Jason, the young coolie in the lead stumbled and fell against him.

Jason grabbed the coolie, keeping him from falling down. Instead of offering an apology, the coolie asked, "Coolie, sahib?"

For an instant, his arrogance surprised Alexis. Then she saw the mute desperation in his eyes. Before she could figure out what it meant, though, one of the other two coolies, a man with a heavy beard and a coarse face, struck the young coolie a savage blow in the back and snarled in Hindi, "You impudent dog!"

The young coolie grunted in pain and staggered, but Jason's grip kept him from falling.

The bearded man drew back his hand to hit the young coolie again, when Jason's right index finger embedded itself in his solar plexus. Remembering his cover, Jason mustered a thick Iranian accent, exclaiming, "What is the meaning of this?"

The other man could not reply. His face turned grey and his mouth opened and closed without a sound, like a gaffed fish.

Alexis couldn't believe it. No one but her had seen Jason's *ippon-nukite* strike, so only she knew why the bearded coolie couldn't answer. But things were going to turn ugly very soon unless Jason had something up his sleeve!

The third coolie sensed something was wrong. He stepped forward, pointing to the youth. "So sorry, Sahib! This young dog is disgracing us all with his rudeness behavior. I will make sure he is being punished very badly."

Bloodbath

Alexis saw Jason struggle with his conscience, but better judgment prevailed. He let go of the young coolie.

The third coolie grabbed him and jerked him away with a cruel smirk. His bearded associate, now on his way to recovery, managed an ingratiating smile. Touching his forehead in a deferential gesture, he said, "I beg Sahib and Memsahib to excuse for bothering."

Alexis had seen the hope flare in the coolie's eyes. It died as the other two began to drag him away.

It touched a chord inside her. "But we wanted him to carry our bags. Let him go!" she demanded.

The coolies stopped and turned around.

The bearded man decided to take care of the annoying firangis. "All right, Memsahib," he said, and stepped forward. The flat of Jason's hand met his chest in mid-stride and he stopped as though he had run into a brick wall.

"She said him, not you," said Jason, and gave him sharp push, sending him stumbling backwards into his comrade. Both of them went down, allowing the young coolie to wriggle free.

Before they could untangle themselves, he snatched up their bag and ushered them out of the hall, leading them to the cab-booking counter, the uniquely Indian method of protecting unwary travelers from unscrupulous cab drivers.

While the counter clerk was taking down the details from Jason, Alexis kept a watchful eye on the other two coolies. They were arguing with each other, casting venomous glances at the young coolie, who was being very careful not to leave Jason's side.

All of a sudden, she saw Jason freeze as he reached into his pocket. When it came out, it was empty.

Jason had his pocket picked yet again!

Struggling to keep a straight face, she watched him frown, trying to remember when and how it could have happened.

When he figured it out, he whirled around to face the young coolie, his cover forgotten in the emotion of the moment. "You little bastard, I have half a mind to…"

He stopped in mid-sentence. The young coolie was holding out the brand new wallet Jason just purchased in Darjeeling. "Are you looking for this, Sahib?" he asked.

Jason looked at Alexis. All she could do was shrug to let him know he was on his own on this one. She had no idea what game the young coolie was playing.

Why steal the wallet just to hand it back? Why wait for Jason to discover it was missing before giving it back? It made no sense.

Jason took the wallet and made sure nothing was missing, then turned back to the counter to complete the transaction, keeping one hand firmly on the young coolie.

He took the receipt with their assigned cab number and moved away from the counter. Once they were out of the clerk's earshot, he asked in a quiet voice. "Now, tell me what you're up to."

His question elicited an incoherent mélange of Hindi, English, and Bengali. Taken aback, Jason shook the young coolie's arm. "Slow down. I am not going to hand you over to the police, if that's what you're scared of. Do you understand?"

The coolie nodded. Jason relaxed his grip. "All I want is an explanation. In English, okay? Take your time."

The young coolie took a deep, anxious breath. "Two days ago, I heard the sahib say only the greatest pickpocket in the world could steal his wallet, and that he would reward anyone who could. Instead of a reward, I beg you please, please, to help me escape from here. Those men will kill me if I stay here."

Alexis recalled Jason's exchange with Ravi. "You did say that, Jay-boy. It serves you right for shooting off your mouth."

She said to the coolie, "Did you pick his pocket then too?"

The young man said without any arrogance. "Yes, Memsahib. I am the greatest pickpocket in the world."

"You are. But the sahib may be your easiest mark ever."

Jason scowled at her before turning to the coolie. "A promise is a promise," he told him. "We'll take you with us if you tell us why those two goondas want to kill you."

The young coolie's relief was palpable. "Thank you, sahib! You have saved my life. My name is Mohan Sinha. It is a long story and I will tell it to you, but first, let us go outside and pick up your taxi. I will tell you everything once we get to your hotel."

He led them to the line of taxis outside, and located the cab assigned to their trip. When Jason told the cab driver that Mohan was going with them, he shrugged, as if it was none of his business if the crazy firangis wanted to take a coolie boy with them.

A thought struck Alexis. "If we take him back to the hotel with us, Jay, he can't be dressed like a coolie," she murmured.

Jason grinned. "You're right, Red. We'll stop on the way and get him some clothes."

Alexis found herself wondering about the young man, Mohan Sinha. His exceptional presence of mind in getting out of his predicament, and his fluency in English were unusual for a manual worker in India. She found herself interested in his story.

Not that there was anything they could do about his problems. While it was unlikely that a minor incident involving a couple of foreigners and a coolie would get back to Kalidas, any help Mohan wanted would almost certainly result in major problems.

They couldn't afford that kind of complication. Not when they were going to meet Mukherjee in a few hours.

* * * * * * * * * *

Mohan gave a contented belch and leaned back in his chair. Never in his life did he imagine eating a meal like this, dressed like this, in a place like this, with two people like this.

The firangi sahib and memsahib bought him a set of clothes at a fancy Raymond's showroom and a pair of sneakers at an upmarket Bata shoe store. His protests that he didn't need anything so expensive fell on deaf ears, the sahib reminding him firmly of the challenge he laid down. That anyone who stole his wallet was entitled to everything in it. He had done it not once, but twice!

He told them his story between mouthfuls, including many things he hadn't told anyone before. They listened, without interrupting. Not just with their ears, but with their hearts, like his story actually mattered to them.

They were strange, this pair. They had an intimacy that he could not define. He was sure they were not husband and wife. They could be brother and sister, but there was no competition or rivalry between them, just like his own relationship with Seetha.

Now that he had told them everything, he felt as though a great weight had rolled off his mind. Just to share everything he had been feeling was a relief.

But he hoped it would be more. Maybe they would help him find his sister.

* * * * * * * * * * *

Alexis felt sorry for Mohan Sinha. The loss of his sister had shattered him, and he was desperate for help from Jason, his hero. Better let him down gently now, before he built up his hopes. The most they could do was to ask Ravi if he could help, in which case it would not hurt to have something concrete to pass on.

With that in mind, she asked, "Do you know who kidnapped your sister?"

"Oh, yes, memsahib! Who could forget such a pair? One was a Sikh, a giant of such size that he would make the sahib here look small. His voice will echo in my ears as long as I live. The other was a Gurkha, shorter than me, but as broad as he was tall. He did not speak at all, but his face will haunt my worst nightmares. It was as though he was mauled by a tiger."

Alexis saw Jason start, just as she did, when Mohan began describing the men, and she marveled at the caprice of Destiny. The chance of such a coincidence was virtually impossible to calculate. Yet, once you got past the astronomical odds against their running into Mohan Sinha in a city of over twenty million inhabitants, it was not so surprising that Kalidas should be behind his troubles. He must control the major criminal enterprises in the city, including the prostitution racket. The only puzzling thing about it was why he would use his two most lethal assassins for something as straightforward as the kidnapping of a girl for sale as a prostitute.

She kept her thoughts from showing on her face. "These men you describe—I do not have to tell you that they are very bad. There is a chance that you may never see your sister again."

Mohan was defiant. "Then I must find them."

"They will kill you, if you do."

He thought about it for a few seconds. "I must try even though I know they will kill me."

Alexis felt like applauding. There was simple dignity in his words. No denial. No histrionics. Not even the fatalistic resignation one expected in India. Just calm acceptance.

She saw Jason yawn. It was contagious. She yawned too, feeling unaccountably tired, as if jet-lag just caught up to her.

At that moment, the waiter appeared with three cups of *masaala chai*, the creamy Indian tea flavored with spices. She took a couple of sips of the chai. It was incredibly sweet and strong.

She waited for the waiter to leave before resuming the conversation. "Mohan, we are visiting Kolkata on business and cannot get involved in something like this. I'm sorry but there's nothing we can do to help you or your sister right now."

"Yes, memsahib," he said, but his voice sounded mushy and far away.

He was holding his cup with intense concentration, as if fearful of dropping it. The cup slipped from his grasp anyway.

It seemed to hang suspended in midair. Then it began to tumble downwards...ever...so...slowly.

She watched it land on the table but could only stare, mesmerized, as the brown stain crept across the tablecloth in slow motion. From a great distance, she saw a second cup land on the table and found herself looking at her empty hands.

Gathering the last strands of her consciousness, she tried to stand up. She just about made it to her feet. Then her muscles seemed to turn to jelly and she felt herself toppling over.

The last thing she saw before the darkness closed over her was Jason slumping forwards. The sound of his head hitting the table echoed in her head.

Then there was nothing.

PART FIVE

BLOOD LUST

CHAPTER 1

Consciousness returned to Alexis like a shroud unraveling in slow motion. As it unraveled, her sensory perception expanded, bringing with it a growing awareness of her surroundings. So, the first time someone tried to rouse her, she heard but didn't feel the slaps. The next time, she felt them, but didn't react, staying limp and unresponsive.

Afterwards, she floated away to a place of peaceful silence, until the sedative wore off completely. She opened her eyes, in full control of her faculties, and took stock of her surroundings.

She was in a windowless room, with walls of concrete block and a steel door at each end. It was bare except for a camp cot, table and chair, and privy and sink in the corner. Light came from a naked bulb, dangling overhead from a short length of flex wire.

She was lying spread-eagled, shackled by her wrists and ankles to four steel rings, with primitive locks that could be easily picked. They might as well be welded shut, for all the good it did her.

Encircling her midriff was a broad metal band, hinged on her left flank and held together with a padlock on the right. She had no idea why it was on her, or what its purpose was, only that it did not prevent her from lifting her hips off the floor.

Both her shoulders felt sore, so she must have been given at least two shots of a sedative. Something like phenobarbital would last about six or eight hours, so she was probably out for at least fifteen hours, maybe longer.

It was obvious, in hindsight, that Kalidas knew they were coming. How he did was beside the point. They never suspected he knew, so they walked into his trap with their guard down, never anticipating the food might be spiked. With the spices to mask the taste, a sedative like Valium in the food would go undetected. Then, a fast-acting hypnotic like chloral hydrate in the masaala chai would act as an instantaneous knockout drop.

The rattle of a key in the door interrupted her thoughts.

The door opened and sunlight flooded the room. Squinting against the glare, she saw a small, dapper man with snow-white hair walk in, and knew, with frightening certainty, that this was Kalidas.

With him were five others. Two were armed guards who took up positions on either side, staying out of each other's line of fire. Two others she recognized from Ravi's descriptions as Jarnail Singh, the giant Sikh, and Gurung, the grotesquely proportioned Gurkha with a hideous face. The fifth was a sparrow of a man with steel-rimmed spectacles, and a digital camera around his neck.

She saw Kalidas looking at her with his hands clasped behind his back, and had to suppress a shudder of revulsion, as if she was in the presence of carrion. She managed to keep it from showing.

Kalidas bowed to her. "Ah! Miss Wolff!" he said. "We meet at last. I am Kalidas. I am sure you recognize my name. Your family has made it its business to intrude forcibly into my affairs with a repetitiousness that I find quite tiresome. Now it is my privilege to return the favor, but with a finality that will preclude further meddling on your part. I greatly appreciate your willingness to come to me. It has saved me a great deal of effort and time."

She didn't show any hint of surprise at his impeccable if bombastic English, letting her gaze drift to the bespectacled man, who now had his eye glued to the viewfinder of his camera.

Kalidas followed her gaze. "Karim Chand is keeping a pictorial record of my achievements for posterity. And, given the many unpleasant contributions your family has made to it, you will appreciate the importance I attach to this moment."

She did not respond, so he went on. "I see you are not of a mood to engage in idle chit-chat. So..."

He brought his hands out from behind his back. "What do you think of this little toy of mine?" he asked.

Clenched in his right fist was some kind of electronic device with a short telescopic antenna and a pistol-grip trigger, which he was squeezing. A steady green light glowed at its base with an intensity she found strangely mesmerizing.

Kalidas's voice continued to bore into her brain. "When my men remove your chains, Miss Wolff, I urge you not to yield to any impetuous desire to take matters into your hands. You must trust me when I say I hold the life of your brother, the estimable Mr. Jason Wolff, in my hands. Quite literally!"

He pointed with his other hand to the device.

"You see, Miss Wolff, as long as I squeeze this trigger, the light glows green, and his body stays intact. However, if you do anything I deem even remotely threatening when you are freed, I will be compelled to release the trigger. Then, to my great regret, and yours too, no doubt, Mr. Wolff will meet a rather gruesome end."

Alexis kept a blank expression on her face, but inside, she was delighted to hear that Jason was still alive. Kalidas misinterpreted her silence for disbelief.

"Please do not underestimate the seriousness of my purpose," he insisted. "I beg you to suspend your skepticism for just a few more minutes. If, at the end of that time, you are of a mind that I have indulged in hyperbole then I will be the first to concede you freedom of action. So please be patient."

She nodded, keeping her expression blank. Kalidas signaled to the guards and they removed her shackles. After they handcuffed her, he turned and walked out of the prison, holding the trigger device. She followed him outside and took in the surroundings as they walked.

She was in a clearing, about three hundred yards square, surrounded by a ring of tree-covered hills in the distance. Behind her, a stone bluff rose five hundred feet from the edge of the clearing. An ornate stone stairway zigzagged up its side to the summit, where a massive temple stood, glowering down on the camp.

Her prison was in the shadow of the bluff at the northwest corner of the camp. An identical building stood next to it, separated by some distance from a row of small cottages extending down the western perimeter of the rectangle. A windowless structure of solid concrete was sunk halfway into the ground on the northern edge, and a large barracks-like building occupied the east side of the rectangle. Diagonally across from her prison, at the southeast corner, was the generator building, its smokestack belching smoke. The only other structure on the south side of the rectangle was a sprawling bungalow with a flat concrete roof.

Her gaze was suddenly arrested by a figure in the foreground, and her heart gave a lurch. Jason! He had his back to her, a metal belt similar to hers around his midriff, with his upraised arms shackled to the crossbar of a goal in the middle of the clearing.

Kalidas led them to the goalpost on Jason's right and called out, "Mr. Wolff! Miss Wolff! Please direct your attention to the other end of the soccer field."

He pointed to a man chained like Jason to the crossbar of the far goal. "There stands Tenga, whose tenure in my employ came to an abrupt end yesterday. Dissatisfied with the generous heroin allowance, he thought he could steal what he wanted, and get away with it. The penalty for such stupidity of course is summary execution, but he made such a piteous plea for clemency that I granted him a stay of execution.

"In exchange for his reprieve, he volunteered for a little demonstration that will be of compelling interest to both of you. Observe around his waist a belt identical in every way to your own."

Bloodbath

Kalidas handed Jason's transmitter to Gurung, taking care not to release the trigger, and took a second from his pocket.

"I beseech you, please, not to let your attention wander from Tenga for the next few seconds. He may be a volunteer, but even his generosity has its limits. He will not grant you a second chance to witness this little demonstration."

Kalidas twisted a dial at the base of the device while holding the trigger shut, and a green light begin to glow on its face. Alexis scalp crawled from anticipated horror.

"The device is now activated," intoned Kalidas. "As long as I hold the trigger closed, nothing happens. But when I release it..."

He opened his fingers and the light turned red.

The instant Alexis saw the light change, there was a puff of smoke and a dark spray spurted from the figure, followed immediately by the muffled thump of an explosion.

Alexis flinched and stumbled backwards.

The air was rent by a blood-curdling scream, cut-off before it crescendoed, and the lower half of the body fell away, leaving the mangled remnant dangling from the crossbar jerking spasmodically.

The echoes of the explosion rolled across the valley. Alexis flinched with each volley. From far away, she heard the cawing and fluttering of crows wheeling across the sky in frenzied alarm. Then, everything faded into silence, and all she could do was stand, frozen in horror, staring at what was left of a human being twitching and swaying in the distance.

"It is always good to see Grewal's toys in action," Kalidas said. Alexis heard Kalidas speak, but she could not tear her eyes away from the legless torso performing its midair dance.

An eternity passed before it became still.

Alexis knew that the purpose of Kalidas's 'demonstration' was to break her will, and that any sign of torment from her would only embolden him. But knowing it and hiding it were two different things. She was helpless to stop it from showing.

He saw her anguish and said, with a smile of satisfaction, "I hope, Ms. Wolff, that you now understand what I meant when I said I held your brother's life in my hands. As you have just seen, each of your belts has an explosive charge powerful enough to literally blow your guts through your back."

Kalidas took the trigger for Jason's belt back from Gurung, saying, "The metal belt directs the blast inwards, so it poses no threat to anyone who is not in intimate contact with you. Grewal assures me that the device will work from as far away as two thousand meters and through concrete walls."

He laughed. "Not that those facts are relevant to your circumstances. You will never leave this camp, so you will never be outside your transmitter's range. Also, a guard with the activated trigger device for the other's belt will accompany you at all times."

He brandished the device at her. "Since both of you will never be free at the same time, any display of aggression will mean instant death for the other. So you will each be the guarantor of the other's good behavior. Do I make myself clear?"

Alexis was too shaken to answer. She groped desperately for some way to restore her mental and emotional defenses, before Kalidas could undermine her will and destroy all hope.

Then she heard Jason shout, "Hey, you! Second from the corner! I'm in chains and by myself, and I need my nose picked, but can't do anything about it. I need you to scratch the south side to reach the goober."

Alexis heard him and, for one hysterical moment, she wondered if Jason's mind had become unhinged even before hers. Then she realized his purpose and burst out laughing. Her fear evaporated. "That goes for me too," she chimed in.

Kalidas looked from her to Jason, with and expression of

shocked disbelief. He took one quick step forward and slapped her with his open palm, sending her staggering.

"I don't know what game the two of you are playing," he snarled, "but you will find little to amuse you in the next two days. Jarnail and Gurung are eager for their revenge, so it would behoove you to curb your insolence. When I ask you a question, you will answer immediately. Do you understand?"

He hit her again backhanded across the mouth, splitting her lip, and she tasted blood. This time, though, she kept her balance.

"If you believe we are helpless and in your power," Jason shouted, "you're an even bigger fool than we imagined. You don't think we'd allow you to take us so easily without a reason?"

"Pah!" spat Kalidas. "You had no idea you were walking into my trap. And you had no clue where my camp is located!"

He stabbed a finger at Jason. "I know everything about your pathetic plan to get to me through Mukherjee, posing as revolutionaries from Iran. All I had to do was to wait for you to walk into my arms at the Shalimar."

"It just shows how little you know!" Jason retorted. "We knew you were hiding like a jackal in the Patkai Hills. This camp is listed as a geological survey operation. Its exact location is twenty-six degrees, five minutes north and ninety-five degrees, twelve minutes east. All we needed was conclusive proof that it was your camp."

Alexis saw Kalidas start. Jason's inspired guess had hit home! It was based on Ravi's satellite photos. There was no evidence of any logging, so that left only the geological survey operation. The map coordinates must have stuck in Jason's memory.

Jason pressed on. "To get that proof, we set ourselves up as bait, knowing you were waiting for your chance to grab us."

"You are bluffing," shouted Kalidas, his confidence shaken.

Jason snorted. "Dream on! Even now, a satellite may be

taking pictures of us. That will be all the proof the Indians need to mount a raid with their Black Cat commando squadron."

Jason's bluff astounded Alexis. If it panicked Kalidas, he might leave them an opening. Provided, of course, he didn't execute them first. But Jason was relying on the Sikh and Gurkha wanting not just revenge, but to regain their honor for their humiliation. That might be just enough to keep them alive, bluff or no bluff.

She saw Kalidas take a half-step towards Jason. Then he controlled himself. "You lie!" he hissed. "Why haven't we seen even one reconnaissance flight here since you disappeared?"

Jason shrugged and looked away, showing no concern.

Taking her cue, Alexis added, "Do you know that Reddy and Grewal, who you sent to kidnap Jonathan Wolff, are dead?"

She saw Kalidas start again and turned away to walk back towards her prison. "Stop, bitch!" Kalidas screamed. "Or your brother dies." Alexis turned back.

"I thought your little demonstration was over," she said.

"You will leave only when I tell you to!" he shrieked back.

"If you insist."

Kalidas snarled. "Reddy and Grewal don't matter. As for the deluded eunuch who thinks he is your father, do you really think he will escape? My vengeance now will be far more satisfying than anything I originally planned. You see, it has always puzzled me that he should forget his sliced-off genitals when he claims he impregnated the whore who gave birth to you. Maybe I can jog his memory with pictures of your bodies with your genitals sliced off."

He paused, clearly expecting some response, but when he got none from either of them, he had no choice but to go on. "We'll see who has the last laugh. The Black Cat Commandos you are expecting will get a surprise if they stick their noses in here."

He turned to the Sikh. "Jarnail! I want a total blackout of the camp every night. Place the Stinger platoon on alert twenty-four hours a day until the Bloodbath summit is over."

The Sikh nodded without speaking.

Kalidas had his confidence back. "The woman will accompany me to learn what is in store for her. Her brother stays here to guarantee her good behavior. Then get our other two guests. We must not keep them in the dark regarding my plans for them."

He looked at Gurung. "Tell Bansal to get rid of Tenga's body, then gather his belongings and bring them to me later. I will decide what to do with them."

He walked off, heading for the bungalow in the distance. Alexis fell in behind him after exchanging a smile with Jason. His defiance of Kalidas had not only steadied her nerve, his exchange with Kalidas told her where and how he was imprisoned. That could be important in the event that either was able to get free.

Jason had also won them one important advantage. The blackout would be invaluable if they had to move around at night.

CHAPTER 2

Mohan could hear a voice calling to him. It was very familiar, but he wished it would stop. He wanted to go back to sleep.

Another vice, no more than a whisper, ordered him to get up. He felt the sting of a slap and tasted something metallic and salty.

Someone was sobbing, pleading with them not to hit him, and he thought, *Good old Seetha! Always looking out for her older brother.*

Then, nausea overwhelmed him and he vomited. When it subsided, he struggled to sit up, conscious of the sour odor of vomit, and the slimy mess on his chin and chest.

His eyes opened and he saw Seetha. She was sobbing, struggling to escape the grip of a heavy-set woman. A wordless scream broke from Mohan's lips and he tried to stand, but his legs gave out and he fell.

Pain exploded in his side. He curled into a fetal position, struggling to understand. The last thing he remembered was drinking masaala chai with the firangi sahib and memsahib. Then everything became clear. They had to be members of the gang that kidnapped Seetha!

He tasted rage in the back of his throat, bitter and every bit as real as the metallic taste of blood in his mouth. It gave him strength. He rolled over and got to his hands and knees, only to have a kick crash into his side. It lifted him clear off the ground and he felt as if a red-hot poker just skewered him. He made it back up to his hands and knees again, bracing for another kick.

It did not come. He heard laughter, then rough hands lifted him up by the collar and dragged him away. He caught just a glimpse of the giant Sikh holding him before he was forced to his knees, and a stream of ice-cold water came cascading over his head and shoulders. He gasped and spluttered, but the Sikh's iron grip held him there.

At last, the cobwebs fell away and he opened his eyes, only to be pulled up almost immediately by the Sikh and toweled off with rough force. Then he was hustled towards a long bungalow-like building, where he saw Seetha disappear through the doorway.

* * * * * * * * * * *

Alexis was surprised to see Mohan, but her surprise was nothing compared to the shock on his face when he saw her. She almost burst out laughing, seeing him stare at her, as Jarnail Singh forced him into a chair.

Kalidas rapped his knuckles on the table. "Welcome, Mr. Sinha," he said to Mohan. "My name is Kalidas. Miss Wolff, of course, needs no introduction, and you know my associates, Jarnail Singh and Gurung. But I must introduce you to two other members of my staff who will be of particular interest to you."

He pointed first to the powerfully built woman gripping the elbow of a slim and very attractive sari-clad girl.

"Please meet Bijli, the lady in charge of your sister, Seetha…" Kalidas pointed to the man wearing glasses standing beside him. "…and my secretary, Karim Chand, who has been seeing to the welfare of your sister during her stay with us."

Alexis heard the girl gasp. Kalidas continued.

"Now where was I, Miss Wolff? Ah, yes! As I just started to say, I have waited for years, with great forbearance, to settle accounts with your family. I use the term 'family' loosely, you understand, when it comes to one key member who is missing."

He sneered at her. "The impotent cripple who lives in a fantasy world of miraculous conceptions, where both of you sprang from his withered loins."

She heard Karim Chand snicker.

"I hear he is now very attached to both of you and you to him. He will spend his days wondering whether the agony of his living or the violence of your dying was the worse fate!

"Just in case you are contemplating escape, I want to assure that I am fully aware of your abilities. Your brother is a highly skilled commando and you, dear lady, once had an international reputation as a martial arts athlete of distinction, even before you spent several years in a ninja monastery. That is why you will have neither the time nor the opportunity to formulate any plan of escape. You will be kept apart at all times until both of you are dispatched in a manner that satisfies my associates."

He waved his hand at Jarnail Singh and Gurung.

"Gurung won the coin toss with Jarnail for the privilege of killing your brother, so Jarnail has the less challenging task of dispatching you. As sporting men, they feel they cannot regain their honor if you and your brother are in anything but peak condition. So, we will wait until both of you fully recover from the effects of prolonged sedation."

Alexis felt an explosion of relief. They weren't going to be summarily executed! Kalidas was giving them the one thing they needed more than any other to escape. Time.

How much, though?

Kalidas told her in his next breath.

"I have planned a great feast for the day after tomorrow to celebrate the launch of Bloodbath, the most magnificent endeavor of my life. Early that morning, Gurung will slaughter goats for the night's feast. That always triggers his killing lust, which puts me in quite a predicament, you understand. If I don't slake it with blood, he won't be on even keel for the crucial events later that day. Killing your brother should do the trick."

Alexis was thrilled. Two whole days were an eternity for anyone as resourceful as Jason! He would find a way to escape in that time. Even if he did not, she would bet on him against any opponent, in any form of mortal combat.

Kalidas now switched his attention to Mohan.

"So we come to you, Mr. Sinha. It was through Miss Wolff that we chanced on you, and through such chance encounters are great events sometimes born. You must thank my men for having the foresight to call me when they found you in Miss Wolff's company. Because of it, you now have the opportunity to meet your sister before both of you pass on to greater things."

Mohan's voice quavered. "Why are you doing this to me and my sister?" he asked. "What have we done to you?"

"Nothing, I'm happy to say! I just described the happy coincidence that brings you here. But we have Miss Chakraborthy to thank for your sister's presence here."

"That woman!" Mohan exclaimed.

"Yes, indeed! 'That woman', as you put it so pithily, is sadly lacking in humor, if you must know. And that, I'm afraid, is the source of your sister's problem.

"You see, Miss Chakraborthy, bless her gentle heart, did not share in the general mirth generated by your sister's uncanny mimicry of her rather distinctive voice and accent."

"For that she had Seetha kidnapped and killed?" Mohan cried.

"Oh no! You misunderstand the dear lady's motives. She desires that your sister be sold into prostitution. Just between you and me, I think it is because your sister possesses in such abundance the physical charms she herself so sadly lacks. So, please do not judge her too harshly. She does not know the real reason I desired your sister. And lest you worry about that, let me assure you it is something chaste and pure beyond all question."

Suddenly, Kalidas's cold, toneless voice turned manic. It made Alexis's skin crawl.

"Do you know why all of you stand helpless before me? It is because I am Kalidas, the greatest servant of Kali! She is my mother, and she has delivered you to me, just as she always delivers everything I want for the furtherance of her cause and her glory. Her benevolence makes it incumbent on me to express my gratitude in a manner that is worthy of her."

Foam flecked the corners of his mouth. His voice became shrill. "The night after the Bloodbath summit, on the darkest night of the month, I will do something befitting such a great occasion. I will give her the blood for which she thirsts in double measure."

He lifted both arms, looked to the heavens like some demonic messiah, and screamed in ecstasy, "The blood of brother and sister, virginal and pure, will pour over my hands and mingle at her feet, in a bloodbath of purification that will cleanse me as it honors her!"

Alexis stood motionless, staring in disbelief, as the extent of Kalidas's depravity dawned on her. She heard Seetha moan, saw the look of utter despair on Mohan's face, and her hatred of Kalidas almost made her lose it. Before she could do something stupid, there was a knock on the door, and she came to her senses.

Kalidas's eyes were on her, anticipating her breakdown with sadistic glee. He saw her regain control and pounded his fist on the table in anger.

"Who is it?" he shouted.

A man in olive green fatigues entered the room carrying a duffel bag and an AKM assault rifle. He dumped both on the table, saying in Hindi, "These are Tenga's things, Huzoor. Gurung told me to bring them to you."

Kalidas's face contorted with fury. "Imbecile!" he hissed. I said to bring them later, not when I am in a meeting!"

Bansal bent over, hands folded in supplication. "Please forgive me, Huzoor. I thought—"

Kalidas interrupted him. "It is not your job to think, you fool. It is to obey."

"I made a big mistake, Huzoor. I will come back later."

"No! Take this filth away from my office and distribute it between the men to take what they want. Leave only the rifle. Jarnail will return it to the armory after we are done here. Now get out, Bansal, and if you or anyone else interrupts me again, they will meet the same fate as Tenga. Do you understand?"

Bansal face turned pasty-white. He nodded and hurried out with the duffel bag.

When the door closed, Kalidas spoke to Karim Chand in Hindi. "Give Jarnail the new code for the armory."

The Sikh looked surprised. "Why was the code changed?"

The secretary answered without looking up as he scribbled on his pad, "You and Gurung were in Kolkata when the last stocks of weapons for Bloodbath were delivered, and Bansal had to supervise their storage in the armory. I gave him the old code and re-programmed the lock, as Huzoor's security rules require." He tore off the sheet on his pad and held it out to the Sikh.

Jarnail Singh took it and stared at it intently for several seconds. Then he handed it back to Karim Chand without saying a word.

The secretary waved him off, saying, "Keep it until you get used to it."

The Sikh put the paper in his pocket and picked up the AKM.

Kalidas continued in Hindi. "Good! Jarnail, you take the boy and girl with you and lock them up. I am sure they would like to spend their last days in the world together. With the brother as the chaperone, you can assign a man to guard him and his sister."

He turned to Bijli. "Bijli, you will guard the Wolff woman from now on. Take her back to her prison, and lock her up. Remember that she is very dangerous."

He turned, at last to the Gurkha. "Go and bring the Wolff bastard here. I will tell him our plans and the role he will play in them. Do not release him until Bijli confirms his sister is shackled in her prison. "

Kalidas switched back to English to address Alexis. His voice showed no trace of manic intensity. "Miss Wolff! Bijli will escort you back to your personal living quarters. Please do not give her any trouble. I am sure you would not want your brother to lose the opportunity of hearing what lies ahead."

Alexis nodded, saying nothing.

He bowed to her. "Until the day after tomorrow, Miss Wolff."

CHAPTER 3

"**J**ason and Alexis have been snatched by Kalidas."

Jonathan Wolff heard Ravi, and his mind went blank. His worst fears had come true. He managed to say, "How can you be so sure, Mr. Iyer?"

"I called the Shalimar Hotel to ask to speak to them," Iyer replied. "The manager said they got food poisoning shortly after arriving, and had to spend a day in a local hospital. They checked out next day, leaving no forwarding address. Proof enough they've been snatched by Kalidas, don't you agree, Mr. Wolff?"

"It's Jonathan please, Ravi. Cut the formality and tell me what you're doing about it."

"All right, Jonathan. The truth is that I cannot help them, because of the deep-seated official paranoia about the 'foreign hand' attempting to destabilize India. I would be accused of aiding foreign agents, and subject to summary arrest for treason."

"Why not do it under the pretext of getting Kalidas?"

"I can't, because I would have to document my sources when the situation is so fraught with international implications, which brings us right back to the 'foreign hand' problem."

Jonathan digested what Iyer said. "You're clearly powerless to help them, Ravi. And so am I. I do not have the clout to get Washington to take up a private cause on my behalf."

"It would be very counterproductive, anyway," Ravi replied. "The U.S. has virtually no diplomatic leverage in Myanmar. The only way is for you to do something about it yourself."

"Unfortunately, I have neither the organization nor the manpower to carry out an armed incursion into hostile territory.

With time and meticulous planning, I'm sure Jack Russell could get a group of mercenaries together to do it, but time is something we don't have—presuming Jason and Alexis are still alive, of course."

"I've been trying not to think about that," Iyer said.

"There isn't any point in hiding from it."

Ravi said nothing. In that momentary lull, a thought struck Jonathan, "Do you think it would be useful for me to call the PM and ask for help?"

"To do what?" Ravi shot back. "You can't expect him to authorize a military operation with international ramifications just to save your son and daughter?"

"So! I can't ask him to intervene, because he'll suspect a paternal motive involving Jason and Alexis, and you can't because telling him the proof involves Jason and Alexis will land you in serious trouble. Stalemate. And checkmate for Jason and Alexis."

"Wait a minute!" Ravi exclaimed. "The way you said it just gave me an idea how to break the stalemate without involving Jason and Alexis. If you supply me with the proof of Kalidas's presence in Myanmar, I can use it to get action."

Jonathan saw what he was driving at, and his excitement spilled into his voice. "You're a genius, Ravi! In fifteen minutes, you will receive an official communication signed by Sol Steinberg and Jack Russell stating that Lone Wolf has learned from impeccable sources of an imminent terrorist plot to undermine India's stability named Bloodbath. It will include every detail we deduced about Bloodbath as if it is fact, including that the international fugitive, Kalidas, is behind it, and that he has his base in northern Myanmar."

Ravi's response was enthusiastic. "That's as good as it gets! The PM will know their names in connection with the attempted assassination of his predecessor. It should convince him that the threat is real and that northern Myanmar warrants a closer look. He might then authorize a reconnaissance flight over the area, or at least to a listening watch, in case Alexis and Jason manage to get a message out."

"The message will include two other things, Ravi. One is that two of our agents are already in northern Myanmar investigating the business, and the other that the listening watch should be tuned to a specific frequency, which happens to be the one set aside for my personal use."

"Fantastic! As soon as I brief the PM, I will fly to Dibrugarh in Assam, which isn't far from the Myanmar border, to supervise the listening watch."

"Can you get permission for me to join you?"

"The area is restricted but I think the PM will be prepared to bend the rules for your sake. Let me see what I can do." Ravi sounded hopeful.

Jonathan felt his spirits lift. "I'll be in Kolkata by tomorrow, no matter what."

CHAPTER 4

Despair. Alexis feared it more than any mortal foe.

For the past two days, she had been waging a rearguard action to keep her mounting despair at bay. She hadn't come close to conquering it, and her defenses were starting to fray in the face of its relentless onslaught.

It had nothing to do with her treatment. She hadn't been abused physically. The food was nutritious and plentiful, if somewhat monotonous: lentil *daal*, curried vegetables, rice, and even a generous side-portion of powdered red chilli peppers, in case she found the food too bland! And she was allowed to exercise four times a day for half an hour.

There were discomforts, of course, but the cold nights and hard stone floor were minor pinpricks compared to the hardships she had to endure during ninja training. And isolation and sensory deprivation were integral to the inner state of perfect physical, emotional and mental harmony called *zazen*.

Despair was something else altogether. None of her mystical techniques worked against it if there no hope. And, after two long days, she had to confront grim reality. There was no hope of escape. Kalidas's security was foolproof.

It wasn't just that the doors at either end of her prison *always* remained locked from the inside, or that Bijli, her guard, was *always* with her, or that the trigger for Jason's belt was *always* at hand. It was the *"nevers"*, not the *"always"* in Kalidas's airtight security rules that destroyed all hope of escape.

Bijli *never* opened the doors to admit anyone, not even Karim Chand, without first confirming the visitor's identity over her two-way radio. Bijli *never* left the room without first summoning a patrolling guard to take her place, however briefly. And Bijli *never* removed her shackles unless the patrolling guard was there, holding the activated trigger for Jason's belt far out of her reach—even when she wanted to use the toilet, modesty be damned.

From what she overheard on Bijli's radio, she knew that a single patrolling guard provided the back-up for both prisons. It was another example of the detail that went into making the arrangements foolproof. With only one patrolling guard to backup both prison guards, Jason and she could *never* be free at the same time, even by mistake.

She had learned two things about the patrolling guard. One was that shift changes occurred at 7 a.m., 2:30 p.m., 10 p.m., and 2 a.m. The other was that the patrolling guard slept outside the wall at her head at night.

Knowing those minor details did not change the fact that escape was out of the question. Nor did those details have any bearing on what the morning would bring.

She knew it was going to be a fight to the death. And there was no one in the world she would rather have on her side than Jason in a fight to the death.

The thought comforted her, fending off despair—for now.

She slept.

CHAPTER 5

Kalidas decided enough was enough. It was 2 a.m. and he was no closer to sleep after three hours of tossing and turning.

He got out of bed, wrapped a light shawl around himself and went into the hallway. He hesitated for a moment, looking at the door at the far end of the corridor, then decided it was not the answer, and went to the elevator instead. He placed his hand on the scanner and the door opened with a beep of approval.

The elevator whisked him to the surface. He stepped into the hallway of the bungalow and disarmed the security system before going out into the veranda. The night air was cold. He closed his eyes to breathe it in, trying to settle his nerves.

This feeling was foreign to him, but it was understandable. He was experiencing anxiety like he never felt before, because tonight was a night like no other. And dawn would bring a day unlike any in his life—or the history of the world! The launch of Bloodbath would change the destiny of the world.

His ears caught the faint sound of snoring from Gurung's suite at the far end of the bungalow, and he shook his head in wonder. In six hours, Gurung would fight Jason Wolff to the death, the man who inflicted the only defeat of his life, and he was sleeping like a baby! It exemplified Gurung's approach to life.

The Gurkha lusted for only two things in like. To kill, and to copulate—both in as brutal a manner as possible. Given either, he was like a baby given its pacifier. And Kalidas saw to it that he got them as often as he wanted, so the Gurkha was his to command, literally to the death.

Bloodbath

It wasn't difficult for Kalidas to satisfy Gurung's sadistic blood lust. Gurung was his appointed executioner.

It was Gurung's sexual lust that was the problem. During their time in India, Gurung would find any unsuspecting whore to screw and brutalize. But that created a trail of unremitting horror that dwarfed any by even the most celebrated serial killers in history. It took all of Kalidas's power to ensure the trail led nowhere.

The problem became even more acute after coming to Myanmar. The very first visit by the Gurkha to the brothel at the camp at Shan caused the women to mutiny, forcing Kalidas to prohibit Gurung from visiting it. So Gurung was left to indulge his lust while on a mission. Worried that it was becoming a dangerous distraction, Kalidas prayed to Kali for guidance.

She answered his prayers almost at once—as she always did.

It dovetailed perfectly with Karim Chand's ingenious scheme to maintain a continuous stream of worthy offerings. It needed a very special woman not just to guard them, but also protect them from the rapacious men in Kalidas's army. Kali brought him Bijli, the one woman who could terrify any man in his camp. She killed her husband during sex, right at the exact moment of orgasm (to fulfill a teenage fantasy she could not resist).

Within days of her arrival, she proved to be the one woman in the world whose strength and sadistic tastes in sex matched Gurung's. Four weeks after their arrival, Bijli and Gurung took up residence as man and wife in the vacant suite in his bungalow. Since then, there were many nights when screams of passion and pain reverberated through the camp.

With Bijli assigned to guard Seetha Sinha first, then Alexis Wolff, Gurung's snores were the only sounds emanating from their suite the past several nights.

That would change tomorrow. After Gurung killed Jason Wolff, and Jarnail dispatched his sister, Bijli would return to

Gurung's bed. And the screams of passion and pain emanating from the suite would be louder than ever.

The thought made Kalidas smile, and his anxiety evaporated. He went back inside to sleep.

CHAPTER 6

Tendrils of fog still clung to the treetops, like wisps of smoke rising from an almost-dead fire, when Jason emerged.

He inhaled the crisp mountain air, reveling in his freedom from that damn explosive belt for the first time in two days. Any "freedom" was purely illusory, of course, with four accompanying guards, and Bhandari, his personal jailer, holding the activated trigger for Alexis's belt, green light glowing.

They were heading diagonally across the soccer field towards the generator building in the southeastern corner, its metal smokestack belching smoke.

At the far end of the soccer field, he could see the figure of Alexis, chained to the goal like Tenga was two days earlier, but facing the other away.

Jason had not seen her since then. He wished he could make eye contact with her just once, to reassure himself she was all right, but their path was taking them behind her.

To his left was the barracks-like building that housed Kalidas's personal army. Its doors were wide open and inside he could see one of the men stoking the grate of a mammoth wood-burning stove, using a ten-foot long poker. Clearly, Kalidas did not believe in wasting electricity on his men when the surroundings provided an unlimited supply of fuel for the stove.

A large oil drum stood outside the door, flames emerging from its mouth. A few men huddled around it, trying to ward off the morning chill. They jeered when they saw Jason. He ignored them.

They reached the southeastern corner, where a group of men was clustered around a raised concrete plinth, watching Gurung gut the carcass of a goat with his kukri. On the ground next to him, laid out in a neat row, were four carcasses, already gutted, and a pile of severed heads and entrails.

Gurung put the skinned carcass down with the others and stood up, sheathing the kukri. He saw Jason and turned away, his disfigured mouth twisting into a grotesque smile, as a sixth goat was dragged onto the plinth, bleating in terror, The Gurkha stood absolutely still as it slid forward on the blood slick concrete, its neck extended and front legs splayed out to resist the pull of the rope.

What happened next was so fast that even Jason's trained eye found it almost impossible to follow.

The Gurkha's right hand blurred to his sheathed kukri. He drew it, lifted it over his head and swung it downwards in a single, explosive movement. As it descended, he dropped into a squat with a wordless scream, magnifying the power driving it. The kukri's blade sliced effortlessly through the goat's neck in one smooth stroke.

The decapitated animal's forelegs buckled and its headless body toppled over, blood gushing from the severed neck.

Gurung remained frozen, head bent, right arm extended, holding the kukri over the twitching carcass, left arm upraised, clenched fist thrusting at the sky. Then, he rose to his feet and lifted the dripping kukri to his forehead in a salute to his audience.

Cheers erupted as Gurung wiped the blade on a blood-stained rag. He turned away to squat down at a large whetstone and start honing the kukri's edge with slow, caressing strokes.

Jason knew the purpose of the demonstration was to intimidate him—to gain that psychological edge that made all the difference in combat. Knowing it and resisting it were two very different things, however. His confidence had just taken a hammer blow. He could feel it in his sweaty palms and the pounding in his chest.

Bloodbath

Everything Ravi said about Gurung was true. He was, without question, a master of the kukri. If their duel was fought with that weapon, there could be only one outcome. Jason had never used it in hand-to-hand combat. No knife he ever saw or held bore even the remotest resemblance to it.

He remembered the kukri he had taken from Gurung years ago. Part machete, part knife, ideal for cutting and slashing but not suited to stabbing. The blade was about fifteen inches long and emerged from the hilt in conventional fashion. After the first four inches, however, there was almost nothing conventional about it. Its blade was neither straight nor curved, but angled at approximately thirty degrees after that point. The blade itself was asymmetric, widening to a width of about four inches before it tapered abruptly to a point. Unlike any other knife-like weapon, its sharp edge was on the inside of the angle, so it was perfect for the kind of cutting stroke he had just witnessed.

As unwieldy and unbalanced as it was, however, it was a fearsome weapon in the hands of even the average Gurkha warrior, and a major reason for the Gurkhas' legendary skill in hand-to-hand combat. Jason knew he stood no chance in a kukri duel with Gurung.

A murmur arose from the crowd, signaling Kalidas's arrival with Jarnail Singh, and Karim Chand, camera dangling from his neck. Behind them were Seetha and Mohan with their guard.

Kalidas halted in front of the goal where Alexis stood, and the rest formed a ragged semicircle around him.

Jason followed his guards into the semicircle and stood with his back to Alexis. The murmuring died down.

The tension in the air was so palpable that Jason could almost smell the blood and sweat of mortal combat in the air.

Then brutal reality took over. Jarnail Singh was handing Kalidas his Bowie knife.

CHAPTER 7

Alexis had never felt so helpless in her life. All she could do was watch and wait for whatever was about to happen.

Jason stood shirtless, with his back to her, thumbs hooked over his belt, appearing nonchalant, but Alexis knew it was a façade. His shoulder and back muscles were visibly corded with tension.

Kalidas raised his hand. An expectant hush descended on the crowd. "Good morning, Mr. Wolff. I trust you slept well?" Kalidas said in English.

"Pretty well," Jason replied in perfect Hindi. "Although the sanitary facilities left a lot to be desired. But then, that is only to be expected when the host is used to taking a crap in the fields each morning, squatting with his ass bared for the world to see."

The color drained from Kalidas's face. "Your warped sense of humor will be short-lived," he said. "Jarnail and Gurung have been living for this moment. Gurung won a coin-toss to determine who would face you. He challenges you to a duel. His kukri against your knife."

Alexis saw the corded muscles on Jason's back suddenly relax, as if something Kalidas said released a spring.

Kalidas removed the Bowie knife from its sheath and pretended to examine it with great care. Then he looked up with a malicious smile. "There is one tiny restriction that I must impose, however. This knife can be thrown, and I have no doubt that you, as a trained commando, have mastered that skill."

He pointed to Gurung with the knife. "Gurung, however, has never has a desire to join that select band of Gurkhas who are adept at throwing the kukri, believing such long-distance killing to be cowardly, even unmanly."

Dropping his voice to a conspiratorial whisper, Kalidas added, "Between you and me, Mr. Wolff, I believe it's because he finds the orgiastic pleasure of his kukri slicing through human flesh too enjoyable to relinquish it."

Kalidas chuckled, and waited for Jason to respond. When Jason said nothing, Kalidas shrugged and continued. "Be that as it may, it forces me to level the playing field, as the English like to say so quaintly. You are forbidden from throwing your knife during the duel."

Sneering visibly now, Kalidas added, "There is the possibility, of course, that the temptation to do so in the heat of battle may be too strong to resist. And then, too, you might transgress with deliberate intent if you find yourself at a disadvantage against Gurung, knowing full well that the consequences can be no worse than the fate you face by not throwing it!"

He paused for dramatic effect.

"So I now provide you with an irresistible incentive to ward off that temptation. If your knife parts company with your hand by deliberate intent, Miss Wolff will find that her chest has parted company with her lower body, in a manner similar to the unfortunate Tenga."

He held up the remote detonator for Alexis's belt.

"I will enforce this rule of engagement myself. It will also discourage you from throwing your knife at me. Even if you do manage to kill me, the result will be the same. Do you understand?"

Jason nodded, saying nothing. He stood quite still, watching Gurung remove his shirt and cast it aside, revealing massive slabs of muscles that rippled in the sunlight.

Gurung took the Bowie knife from Kalidas and walked into the semicircle. Tossing it at Jason's feet, he gestured to Jason to pick it up and drew his kukri from its sheath.

Jason picked up the knife without taking his eyes off the Gurkha, and straightened up. He then dropped into a slight crouch with his knife hand extended, narrowing his focus to his opponent.

Alexis felt sick, watching them. Gurung outweighed Jason by at least thirty pounds, all of it muscle!

Kalidas called out again. "Mr. Wolff! I almost forgot to tell you about another little constraint that I must place on you to make this contest more intriguing. Observe."

Jarnail Singh held up a mechanical clock timer and twisted the dial to start it.

Kalidas shook his head with an expression of feigned regret. "You see, there is a limit to the stamina of my poor fingers. So five minutes are all I can allow for this contest. If you have not disposed of Gurung in that time, my fingers will no longer be able to take the strain of squeezing this trigger. Then, sadly, I will be forced to let go, bringing Miss Wolff's corporeal integrity to a premature end."

Alexis's mind recoiled in horror, but Jason wasn't wasting any time. He began circling warily, holding his knife in his right fist, cutting edge down. Gurung moved with him, the kukri held in his cocked wrist, so the angled blade was parallel to the ground, its longer blade neutralizing Jason's reach advantage.

Jason made a couple of desultory feints, but Gurung refused to be drawn by them, seemingly content to let the time dribble away.

Then Jason made his move.

His knife hand dropped and he stepped forward, as if to thrust the knife at Gurung's groin. It was a feint that Alexis had seen him practice often enough on her, to set up a strike with the other hand.

Gurung's reaction, however, was different from anything she or Jason anticipated. Instead of trying to parry, thereby leaving himself open to the strike from Jason's free hand, Gurung moved into the thrust!

Bloodbath

The concave edge of the kukri swept down to meet the upper edge of Jason's knife, and deflected Jason's thrust, jerking Jason's knife hand across his body and twisting him off balance. In the same fluid motion, the Gurkha pivoted on his right foot and delivered a shuto strike with the blade of his left hand to Jason's now-exposed flank.

Jason twisted desperately, riding the pull of the kukri, and brought his right elbow up and forward to strike the Gurkha in the chest. He was off-balance when he carried out the *hiji-uke* elbow strike, but it was still powerful enough to elicit a grunt of pain from the Gurkha, upsetting his timing. The disabling strike aimed for Jason's kidney landed on the thick muscle pad of his back instead.

She saw Jason grimace in pain. He brought his knife hand up to force the Gurkha's blade away, and reached with the other for his opponent's right wrist, but the Gurkha jumped out of reach, rubbing his chest.

Alexis realized then that the Gurkha was Jason's equal in skill, maybe even better. The full import of Kalidas's time constraint now became apparent. To beat Gurung in the allotted time, Jason would have to take appalling risks.

Another minute passed, during which Jason made a few exploratory thrusts. Alexis knew he was probing for tendencies, so she watched carefully to see what he was trying to set up.

Then, all of a sudden, she saw it! Jason had shuffled forward three times to make a halfhearted thrust at the right side of the Gurkha's neck. Each time, the move was interspersed with a number of cuts and thrusts, and he never committed himself to it, withdrawing without making any contact. She would never have seen the pattern had she not been watching for it. She noticed, too, that each time Jason thrust high and up, the Gurkha reacted instinctively by bringing up his left forearm to deflect Jason's thrust.

Jason moved in again, shuffling forward in a series of quick steps as the Gurkha retreated before him. Then disaster struck.

One of Jason's feet caught on the uneven ground and he stumbled, falling forward with his hand braced on ground.

The Gurkha saw the exposed back of his opponent, and jumped in with his kukri raised. At that instant, Jason snapped erect and thrust his knife up towards the Gurkha's face.

It caught Gurung by surprise. He jerked his head away and brought his left forearm upward and outward to deflect the thrust. As he did so, he left the front of his body exposed.

Jason took a half step towards Gurung and rammed his left hand towards the Gurkha's solar plexus, palm and fingers locked into a blunt spearhead.

Had the *nukite* spear-hand strike landed, the fight would have ended. It did not. Gurung reacted at almost the same instant Jason made his move. He slashed at Jason's exposed left flank with a flick of his wrist, forcing Jason to abort the strike and drop his left forearm in a defensive *ude-uke* parry to the Gurkha's right wrist. It delayed the slashing blade just long enough for him to twist clear.

Fear overwhelmed Alexis as the combatants resumed their wary circling. Jason, who she had always thought invincible, was beaten. Even more frightening was the fact that he knew it. The onlookers knew it too, because there was pin-drop silence, except for the soft electronic whirr from Karim Chand's video camera.

With only sixty seconds left now, Gurung refused to engage Jason, let alone take any risks. Whenever Jason lunged, he leapt back, parrying the blade with his own and staying clear.

Then she saw Jason shuffle forward two steps and lunge off his back foot, aiming an overhand thrust at the Gurkha's throat. It was a move of utter desperation—and he telegraphed it.

Seeing Jason was desperate to end the fight before Kalidas released the trigger, Gurung did not retreat as he did before. He moved forward, his left forearm rising to deflect the thrusting arm outward, aiming a horizontal slash with the kukri at Jason's side.

Bloodbath

Jason seemed not to anticipate Gurung's move. He launched a *tetsui-uchi* hammer-fist strike at Gurung's solar plexus.

At the last moment, he awoke to the kukri arcing towards his flank and dropped his left forearm to block Gurung's knife hand as he tried to twist away. The fractional delay was all it took. Instead of his forearm catching Gurung's wrist, it hit the crook of the Gurkha's elbow. The Gurkha flicked his forearm and wrist and the tip of the kukri's blade sliced into Jason's left flank.

Jason staggered backwards with an inarticulate cry, dropping his knife and pawing like a wounded animal at the blood pouring from his side. He took a step towards Alexis, reaching out with his right arm in an agonizing plea for help. Then his legs buckled and he sank to his knees, doubling over.

The Gurkha had leapt back out of reach the instant his slash struck home. Suspecting a trick, he did not move in for the kill, watching from a safe distance. When he saw Jason collapse, though, he bounded forward with an exultant yell

Alexis realized the dreadful truth of what was coming: Gurung intended to end the fight by beheading Jason.

Then time ground to a halt, and everything and everyone in front of her froze, like a tableau.

There was the Gurkha, standing to Jason's left, with his legs splayed, holding the kukri high above his head in a two-handed grip.

There was Jason on his knees, doubled over, with both hands pressed against his left side.

There was blood on the ground, coalescing in iridescent globules that glittered like rubies in the sunlight.

There was the circle of watchers, holding their collective breath, waiting for the duel to come to its end.

And there was Karim Chand, face pressed to the viewfinder of his camera, mouth open and drooling in anticipation.

An eternity went by.

Then the deadly blade began its descent.

Suddenly, Alexis saw a forearm flash upwards between the Gurkha's legs, to deliver a clenched-fist *kakuto* strike that pulverized Gurung's testicles, smashing them against his pubic bone.

As the strike landed, Jason twisted over to land on his right shoulder, and his right hand fastened onto Gurung's left ankle and jerked it backwards. Then, he pivoted into a body roll, his left hand gripping the Gurkha's crotch as he pitched forward with a scream of agony, the kukri flying from his grasp.

Jason continued his roll 180 degrees onto first his back, then his left side, sending Gurung arcing headfirst through the air on a two-point hoist by the crotch and left ankle. The Gurkha's face hit the ground with Jason's hand in the crotch acting like a pile driver. There was a soggy thump, followed by an ugly cracking sound, as Jason flipped Gurung over on his back, snapping his neck.

From a great distance, Alexis heard the cawing and fluttering of the crows rising from the trees in panic from Gurung's scream.

Jason had won! But at what cost?

He was rising unsteadily to his feet, hands pressed to his left side, with blood pulsing through his fingers. The wound had to be serious to fool a knife-fighter of Gurung's experience and ability.

The onlookers stood in stunned silence. Karim Chand's camera hung from his neck, forgotten. And Kalidas's face was slack, his jaw sagging.

Only Jarnail Singh was unfazed. He stepped forward and removed his shirt and trousers. Then, bare-chested and clad only in boxer shorts, he stood, arms akimbo, like some menacing apparition bent on destruction, watching Jason stagger to his feet.

Under any other circumstances, he would have cut an almost clownish figure, his red-and-blue-striped boxer shorts in garish contrast with the brilliant green patka outlining the topknot on his head—!

In a dazzling revelation, Alexis saw the opportunity for which she had been waiting since their capture. A way to break out of captivity.

The odds were impossible—a one-in-a-million longshot—but it boiled down to one simple detail.

She had to kill Jarnail Singh.

CHAPTER 8

Grey darkness swirled around Jason.

His left thigh was a warm, sticky mess, and he could feel a rhythmic pulsation in his left flank.

Alexis's voice cut through the fog and he thought irritably. *Why can't she keep her damn mouth shut? She should know not to butt in now.*

Suddenly, he realized she was speaking in Hindi to Jarnail Singh, and the shock was so sharp that it parted the fog. And he saw the Sikh looming in front of him like some Goliath.

Alexis was saying, "Only a coward spawned from the womb of a jackal could think his honor is restored by killing a man so badly wounded he can barely stand. I spit on you."

She spat at the Sikh. "Like a jackal that slinks up to kill the mortally wounded tiger, you will howl proudly and proclaim your victory. But, just like a jackal, you will run with your tail between your legs if you had to fight anyone who was not helpless."

He couldn't believe his ears! Why in hell was she picking a fight with Jarnail?

Jarnail seemed bent on ignoring her, but she was remorseless. "Did anyone witness your so-called coin-toss with Gurung? Or did you generously give him the first chance to challenge my brother?"

The Sikh started as if stung, and a murmur went up from the crowd, suggesting that Alexis might have scored with the onlookers.

"I don't believe there was any coin-toss," Alexis sneered. "You were delighted to give Gurung the chance to go first, hoping that Gurung would kill Jason Wolff if you were lucky, or at least hurt him enough to make things easy for you."

Bloodbath

Alexis turned her head to address the crowd.

"Can't you see how full of confidence he is? He was counting on this happening. Gurung is dead, but at least he died with honor. He wounded the tiger mortally, so now the jackal has nothing to worry about, does he?"

There was another murmur from the crowd and some heads were beginning to shake knowingly. Alexis turned back to the Sikh. "Have you stopped trembling with terror now that you can see that Jason Wolff is hurt? Or do your bowels still quiver at the thought that he might hurt you because he isn't dead? Why, I don't think you'd dare to fight even a woman like me, unless I was helpless or hurt. You are a filthy stain on the honor of the Sikh lion!"

Jason couldn't believe his ears! Had Alexis gone insane that she would challenge the Sikh to mortal combat after provoking him? What kind of game was she playing?

Whatever her reason, she achieved her object. The Sikh sprang forward and stuck his face inches from hers. "You slut! I will break your neck with my bare hands and feed you to the jackals myself after I have killed your brother."

"Why after? Why not now? Are you hoping to pretend you are hurt so you can then have an excuse to back out of fighting me? Hah! If you had any courage, you wouldn't be afraid to fight a woman half your size, you coward."

She spat straight into his face. The Sikh recoiled, as if she had slapped him. He wiped the spittle from his cheek and turned to Kalidas. "Now! Now!" he wheezed. "Free her. I want her now. I will kill her first. I will kill him later."

Kalidas was momentarily taken aback, but he nodded.

The guards replaced Jason's belt and he exchanged places with Alexis. When he raised his arms up to be shackled, pain from the wound in his side lanced through his body like a rapier. His legs buckled and he almost blacked out.

Almost. Somehow, he managed to yank himself back in time.

When his vision cleared, he saw Alexis standing about ten feet away, with both hands in the pockets of her slacks, and shoulders hitched up in a pose of calculated insolence.

"I spit on you, Kalidas!" she sneered, and spat at him. Then she turned towards the temple and spat again. "And I spit on that *chudail*—the she devil who is an obscene mockery of Mother Kali, Destroyer of Evildoers like you and that demon *raakshasi*, who feed on the blood of innocents. Today, Jarnail goes to Hell to join Gurung in the chudail's unholy embrace. You are next."

Kalidas was speechless with rage, unable to even find his voice. When he was finally able to speak, he couldn't articulate coherently.

He stuttered, "B-b-blasphemer! F-f-filthy ch-chudail! You dare to mock the g-greatest force on earth? Pay with your life, you whore! Jarnail! Destroy her! Finish her! Break every bone. Now!"

The maniacal rant, so utterly foreign to Kalidas, left everyone gaping in astonishment. Including Jarnail.

Not Alexis. With the Sikh distracted, she sprang forward. Planting her left foot, she drew her clenched right fist back, telegraphing her intent to launch an *oi-zuki* lunging front punch.

If she was counting on surprising him, though, she miscalculated badly. The Sikh saw her out of the corner of his eye. He took a bounce-step backwards that put him out of her reach, and dropped into a fighting stance, with his clenched right fist drawn back for a tetsui-uchi hammer-fist strike, and upraised left hand poised to deflect her oi-zuki strike.

His movements seemed ponderous—almost clumsy compared to hers. Not that it mattered. With his overwhelming weight and reach advantage, it would be over when he got his hands on her.

Seemingly oblivious of the deadly danger she now faced, Alexis launched her punch.

But she had misjudged terribly how far she was from the Sikh. *The punch would never reach its target!*

Something else did, though. Her fist opened in midair and a fistful of dirt flew straight at Jarnail Singh's face.

It was clearly a ruse—a childishly desperate attempt to make the Sikh flinch. He treated it with the disdain it warranted, letting it hit him in the face without even blinking, and launched his hammer-fist strike at her chest.

What happened next was so incredible—so inconceivable!—that Jason thought he was hallucinating.

A strangled gasp tore from Jarnail's larynx. The erstwhile hammer-fist stopped as if it hit a brick wall and shot up to tear at his throat with fingers like talons, while his left hand began clawing frantically at his eyes.

Alexis did not hesitate. Pivoting on her planted left foot, she leapt into the air and landed on the Sikh's right leg below his kneecap in a two-footed side-thrust kick delivered with her full weight behind it.

The Sikh's leg, still locked in extension buckled sickeningly backwards at the knee. The bones splintered, their jagged ends shearing through the skin behind the knee.

Jarnail screamed, his voice shrill with the agony of broken bones and shredded tendons. He staggered, folding over sideways at the waist as his leg gave way. He did not fall, though, somehow managing to stay upright on his one good leg, still clawing helplessly at his face.

Alexis wasn't waiting for him to fall. Pivoting again, this time on her right foot, she thrust her left hip up against the giant's abdomen, no longer worried about the reach of his hands. Her left foot snaked around his good leg to sweep it off the ground, and she upended his bent torso over her hip in the classic hip throw from judo, called *harai-goshi*.

The Sikh went sprawling face down on the ground.

She whirled around and leapt high into the air to pounce on him from above as he fell, landing on his back with such force that the impact jarred her hair loose. Her right knee smashed into his ribs, driving the air from his chest, while her left knee came down on his left arm just above the elbow.

With Jarnail's elbow pinned under her knee, she seized his left wrist and jerked it backwards, snapping the Sikh's forearm.

He shrieked in mortal agony. Then, driven by a last flickering instinct of self-preservation, he struggled to turn over. But not even his prodigious strength could overcome Alexis's weight on his back with the bones in two limbs and several ribs shattered. All he could do was reach back with his one good hand to claw feebly behind him, trying to get a hold on her somewhere.

She brushed away his hand, and delivered a paralyzing shuto strike to his biceps, rendering it useless too. Then she grabbed his top-knot in her left hand and jerked his head up and back. A savage '*ki-ai*' erupted from her lips, as her right hand, clenched in the *seiken* fist-sword, stabbed forward to smash into the keichu, the killing point at the back of the neck where the spine meets the skull.

The Sikh's vertebral column snapped, crushing his brain stem and severing it from his spinal cord.

Alexis still did not let go of his head. She remained motionless for several second, crouching over the Sikh's lifeless body, her head bowed, red hair cascading down to obscure his head.

The avenging Angel of Death consuming her victim!

Jason could only stare, unable to believe what he witnessed.

Jarnail Singh had moved in for what should have been an easy kill, with his overwhelming superiority in weight and strength. Only to collapse without Alexis laying even a finger on him.

It defied rational explanation. Unless...

The dirt! It had to be the dirt she flung at him. But how could dirt have such a devastating effect? Like a spray of Mace—!

Then, in a dazzling revelation, he understood, and his heart sang with the pure joy of it.

It wasn't "dirt"! She had used the powdered red chilli peppers from her food tray to disable the Sikh.

As the enormity of what she achieved began to dawn on him, he felt the grey mists rise up again and had to fight them off. Then his vision cleared. Alexis was on her feet, gathering her hair in a twist, and tying it in a top-knot. She then turned west to face the temple, and shouted a challenge as stirring as the call of a bugler.

"Chudail that Kalidas worships! Today you have witnessed the destruction of two of your minions. You are impotent in the face of my power, my *Shakti*. I do not fear you, raakshasi masquerading as Kali, the Goddess of Life and Death."

Alexis lunged forward and jabbed her right fist upwards in an uppercut, simultaneously slapping her biceps with her left hand in the universal gesture of vulgar contempt. "I challenge you to face me on amaavasya night. Not even on that darkest of nights, when your evil is at its zenith, are you my equal. Bound hand and foot, in your own temple of depravity and in the presence of your most degenerate minion, I will annihilate you as I will him."

Kalidas stared at Alexis in a frenzy of rage, with his face contorted and mouth opening and closing without making a sound.

When he eventually found his voice, he leaned forward, shaking with fury, and shrieked, "How dare you challenge my mother, Kali, you arrogant, blaspheming whore! Tomorrow night, during amaavasya, I will show you who is stronger. I will slit your throat in her presence and wash her feet in your blood."

Jason felt a weight roll off his heart. Alexis's challenge to Kalidas's goddess had changed the parameters of the contest, as far as Kalidas was concerned. By framing it as a test of her power against his goddess, Alexis had ensured he wouldn't execute them on the spot. And by focusing on amaavasya, the moonless night that, according to Hindu tradition, was favored by the dark forces, she had bought them forty hours of life.

What would forty more hours do, though, when the past seventy two had shown that there was no hope of escape?

Kalidas held all the cards, and he knew it. He smiled with all his old menace and arrogance, showing he had rebounded from Jarnail and Gurung's deaths. "Gurung and Jarnail aren't important," he said with a dismissive shrug. "The summit goes on."

Turning to the man next to him, he said, "Bansal, you will take over command of the men until further notice. Karim Chand will explain your duties to you. Now, get rid of the bodies."

"As you command, Huzoor," answered Bansal, then added, uncertainly, "Huzoor?"

"What is it, Bansal?" Kalidas was clearly irritated.

"Do you wish me to attend to the prisoner's wound, Huzoor?"

"Have you taken leave of your senses?" Kalidas shouted. "The whore taunted Kali and you want to save her brother? Let him—"

He stopped in mid-sentence, and a look of unholy glee spread across his face. Then, in a voice quavering with excitement, he continued, "She boasts that her power can annihilate Kali, the greatest power in the universe. So it should be child's play for her to defeat someone as lowly as Yama, who is merely the God of Death, right?"

Kalidas clapped his hands together.

"So, let's make this a contest between the whore's arrogance and Kali's wrath, with her brother's life as the prize. We'll see if she can keep him alive until the time comes for them to face Kali on amaavasya night! So, Bansal, I think you should dress his wound."

He pointed to Alexis. "Bijli! Put the whore's belt back on her."

Kalidas waited until Alexis's belt was in place, then said, with a smile of pure malevolence, "Bhandari! Take off her bastard brother's belt. Bansal will dress his wound with some of the shit from the goat entrails."

Alexis took a step forward but stopped when Kalidas jabbed the trigger at her. "Just try it, firangi whore," he snarled. "You want to see what your brother's disintegrated guts look like?"

Seeing Alexis's face blanch. Kalidas sneered. "What? You don't think you can save his guts with your...what did you call it? Yes! Your 'shakti'! Well, let's see if your shakti can save him from dying before tomorrow night."

Kalidas laughed. Karim Chand and several watchers joined him. Kalidas left without looking back.

Every eye except Jason's was fixed on Kalidas at that moment, and only he saw Alexis's right hand make two quick movements as it hung at her side. Her thumb and index finger curled to form a crescent. Then the first two fingers stabbed downwards.

Jason managed to keep his face impassive as he absorbed the meaning of her gesture. Tonight at two o'clock!

He saw her cast a casual glance in his direction and overcame his disbelief just in time to signal an unmistakable thumbs-up.

Then the mists rose up to claim him.

Ray Rao

PART SIX

BLOODBATH

CHAPTER 1

Jason heard chains rattling somewhere far away and knew he must open his eyes. But they seemed to be glued shut, and he could not summon the will to force them open.

A numbing stupor blanketed his mind, deadening everything but the glacial chill sending needles of icy agony into every bone, joint and muscle in his body.

And he was shaking so hard that his head and his elbows hurt from being pounded on the stony ground.

Reality hit him, then, like a bucket of water to his head.

He was in the grip of a rigor from the infection raging in his bloodstream, and his mind was teetering on the brink of febrile delirium. Fear stabbed at him, bringing a rush of adrenaline that forced his mind back from the brink. He couldn't succumb to delirium. Not with Alexis coming at 2 a.m.!

All of a sudden, he got another fright. Was that a fabrication of his fever-addled brain? Then he remembered her hand signal and his foundering mind seized it like a lifeline to anchor itself in reality once more.

He lifted his head to look at the clock, feeling pain sear his left side. He welcomed it for the clarity it brought to his mind.

It was midnight. Bhandari, his jailer, was fast asleep. And the camp was now silent, Kalidas's celebratory feast for the Bloodbath attendees having wrapped up an hour ago.

The coast was clear for Alexis.

I'd better be ready, or else she'll kill me, he thought, and had an insane desire to laugh. He caught himself in time, sensing his mind was once again edging towards delirium, and closed his eyes. Focusing on the pinpoint of blue light behind them, he brought back an image of the mountains that were his talisman of peace.

His mind steadied itself and he sank into a restorative trance. A part of his consciousness held on to the pain blazing in his side, using it as a brake to stop from sinking even deeper to a place from which there might be no return.

CHAPTER 2

K alidas was ecstatic.

It was past midnight, and the mellow mood of the party was having some surprising effects. The dour, humorless Marxist, Das, was laughing at a joke by the equally fun-loving Maoists! Even hereditary enemies like the fanatic Muslims from Kashmir and the equally fanatic Sikhs from Punjab were hobnobbing with each other. As enjoyable as it was to see, it was time now to get down to business. He clapped his hands twice.

The effect was immediate. The hubbub subsided.

When Kalidas was certain he had everyone's undivided attention, he began to speak in Hindi, the language that all the guests spoke. "Welcome to my home, my friends! I hope you are enjoying yourselves. Now it is time to focus on why we are gathered here. We are about to embark on a journey that will change your future, my future and the future of the world. When you return to your colleagues, you will face opposition and doubt, and you will meet treachery. You will have to conquer all of those.

"Remember only one thing if you feel tempted to abandon our common effort. There are no enemies of Kalidas in this world, only friends."

There was pin-drop silence as Kalidas's words sank in. "I will show you what I mean," he added.

He walked out of the conference room, and headed for the prison buildings. Karim Chand shepherded everyone out behind him.

Outside Alexis Wolff's prison, they were met by the patrolling guard. He identified himself to Bijli and the door swung inward. It

245

was pitch-dark inside, except for the green glow from Alexis Wolff's remote detonator in Bijli's hand.

When everyone was inside, Bijli closed the door and turned on the light to reveal Alexis Wolff, spread-eagled on the ground, shackled hand and foot.

Kalidas waved his hand in a dramatic flourish. "My friends!" he announced in Hindi. "I present for your inspection the daughter of Jonathan Wolff."

He heard gasps of surprise from the crowd. Switching to English, he said to Alexis, "As you can see, Ms. Wolff, your efforts have not affected my plans one whit. Of the nine organizations I invited, eight are here. The ninth will arrive early tomorrow morning. Nothing can stop Bloodbath from becoming a reality."

He paused for effect, then sneered. "For you, alas, reality comes to an end when Bloodbath becomes a reality.

"It grieves me to tell you that your brother is not doing well. I know your shakti is very powerful, but I fear it might fall just a tiny bit short. What a pity it would be if he were unable to fulfil his costarring role in your ill-conceived attempt to challenge the greatest power in the universe. Fear not, however. His death will not be in vain. It will serve to enhance your pain and suffering."

Kalidas could sense from Alexis Wolff's half-closed eyes and numb expression that she was close to collapse. He feigned concern. "Ah! I can see you are greatly fatigued and in no mood for idle chitchat. Just as well! My guests and I have an early start planned and we have a lot of ground to cover before then. But rest assured, you and your brother will not be far from my thoughts."

He reverted to Hindi and addressed his guests. "Next door, you will see her brother. Remember what I said about my enemies? There are no enemies of Kalidas because they all die!

"As for the impotent cripple who is under the delusion that he is their father? He is one of the richest men in the world.

Governments tremble when he speaks. Yet, he is helpless against Kalidas. He will pay, like all my enemies. Not with his life, though. That is mine to take whenever I please. I choose, instead, to give him a life worse than death. He will live with the knowledge that he is responsible for the deaths of those he loves."

Nobody said a word. Kalidas savored the moment, then walked out.

CHAPTER 3

A
exis's eyes opened at five minutes to two—exactly when she had set her internal clock.

She lifted her head and saw Bijli lying diagonally across the cot on her back, eyes closed and mouth open, snoring loudly. Two empty bottles of rum lay on the floor. A third bottle, nearly full, stood upright within reach of her dangling hand.

Bijli started attacking the liquor with single-minded determination the moment the door closed behind Kalidas and his guests. As her blood alcohol rose, her mood descended, starting with grief-stricken calls to the dead Gurung while beating her breast with painful violence, then to maudlin self-pity, and finally to morose contemplation of the bottle in her hand.

By the time she opened the third bottle, contemplation had turned to sullen anger. All of a sudden, she screamed "Firangi chudail!", and tried to get up. Alexis braced herself, knowing that alcohol and grief had erased all of Bijli's restraint.

Fortunately for her, alcohol had also erased Bijli's focus, and it came to Alexis's rescue. Bijli saw the bottle in her hand and took one more swig before falling back onto the cot. She hadn't moved since.

Grateful for her reprieve, Alexis laid her head back and let her mind drift, free of tension until she heard a clink of metal against the wall. The guard outside was stirring.

Through the air vent, she heard the guard groan and stretch and, a few minutes later, the sound of approaching footsteps. There was a low-pitched murmur of conversation, followed by another groan as he hauled himself upright. His footsteps receded into silence, broken only by soft scuffling sounds from the new man trying to get comfortable.

She remained still and patient, waiting for the scuffling to die out. Ten minutes later, she heard his first snore. She let another ten minutes pass before making her move.

Keeping a watchful eye on Bijli, she arched her back to get as much purchase out of the chains as possible and flexed her elbow until her hand brushed the knot of hair on top of her head. Blocking out the pain from the shackles biting into her ankles, she probed the knot of hair with her fingers until she found what she was looking for.

She grasped it delicately between her index and middle fingers and withdrew it, millimeter by millimeter, until she could get a firm grip on it. When, at last, she had it in her fist, she allowed herself a moment of quiet celebration.

She held in her hand a simple metal bobby pin, worth no more than a few *paisas*, but more precious to her than all the riches in the world. It was the reason she made her seemingly suicidal move to challenge the Sikh.

The sight of the Sikh's patka triggered her memory of the patka worn by Pammie's father on the night of his death, and the hairpins holding it in place. She palmed a hairpin as she crouched over the Sikh's dead body with her untied hair streaming down to screen what she was doing, then hid it in her topknot when she re-tied her hair.

That hard-won strip of metal would be her ticket to freedom.

She pulled apart the jaws of the pin into a right angle and gripped it between her thumb and forefinger. Then she inserted her make-shift pick into the keyhole of the shackle on her left wrist. She probed for the tumbler, found it, and twisted the pin. There was a moment of resistance, then the well-oiled mechanism yielded and the metal band around her left wrist snapped opened.

To her, it sounded like a pistol shot, but Bijli did not twitch an eyelid. Alexis went back to work. With one hand free, it was simpler. In seconds, her shackles were off, then the explosive belt.

She spent a few minutes massaging her wrists and ankles to restore feeling and circulation. Then, she stood up and moved towards Bijli, her arm upraised in readiness to strike. Suddenly, Bijli's eyes opened and she looked straight at Alexis.

Alexis froze. Then she realized that Bijli was staring into emptiness, her alcohol-soused brain incapable of processing what her eyes were seeing.

Alexis swept her hand down in a vicious arc to Bijli's exposed throat. She felt the bones and cartilage of the larynx shatter. There was a gurgling sound as Bijli arched her back in a last dying spasm, and then lay still.

After making sure Bijli was dead, Alexis searched Bijli's pockets and found a box of matches, and the keys to her prison. She put them in her own pocket and turned her attentions to Bijli's satchel.

Taking care not to make any noise that might wake the guard outside, she dumped the satchel's contents onto the cot...only to stare in total disbelief at the first thing she saw. Jason's Bowie knife!

She had no idea why it was in Bijli's satchel. Maybe the woman had claimed it as a macabre keepsake for remembering Gurung? It didn't matter. It was enough that it was there. She picked it up and cradled it to her cheek, reaching through the bond to Jason—only to get a terrible shock!

What she got back was...chaos! As if Jason's mind was totally muddled and disorganized. She felt real terror then, but she squashed it ruthlessly, corralling her panic before it derailed her. With her mind back on track, she projected only comfort, reassurance and confidence through the bond, thinking, *Luck's on our side, Jay. Just hang in there for a few more minutes. I'm coming to get you.*

Bloodbath

She combed through the other items, but found nothing else of use—some spare ammunition for the AKM, some Hindi magazines, and a barber's cutthroat razor that Bijli used to shave her legs. In an outside pocket, she also found five clear plastic Baggies containing a white powder—Bijli's accumulated daily heroin ration, three days' worth for guarding Seetha, two for her.

Discarding the satchel, she walked over to pick up the explosive belt and brought it to the table, placing it with its inner surface exposed. With the blade of the Bowie knife, she slit the thick fabric lining and pried out the foam padding inside to expose a sheet of hard plastic held in place with metal clips.

Breathing a silent prayer, she opened the clips, lifted the plastic out, and turned it over. What she saw was deceptively simple. An electronic chipboard with a short ferrite aerial and a baseball-sized lump of PE—plastic explosive—connected to a battery.

Taking a deep breath to steady her shaky nerves, she first disconnected the battery. Not satisfied that the device was harmless, she also extracted the miniature detonator buried inside the PE. Then, and only then, did she relax.

A moment later, delayed shock hit her.

She sat with her heart racing and sweat pouring from her, realizing just how afraid she was of the belt. It was just as well she didn't realize it beforehand, or she may not have been able to do what she just did.

Time to move on.

She didn't bother with Bijli's AKM. It was useless for the deadly work ahead. She drew Jason's knife it from its sheath, put the trigger for Jason's belt in her pocket, and switched off the light. Then she unlocked the door using Bijli's keys and stepped out into the darkness.

The night air was bracing, a welcome change from the stuffy confines of her prison. The mist swirling around her reduced visibility to just a few feet in front of her, but she embraced it. The cloak of invisibility was priceless.

She edged along the wall, using the snores of the sleeping guard to guide her. When she reached him, she saw his head slumped over, exposing the temple. Summoning all the force she could muster, she struck with the hilt of the Bowie knife.

There was the unmistakable crunch of breaking bone, and the guard slumped over, his breathing cut off abruptly in mid-snore.

She knew he was dead, but she made sure, anyway. Then she picked up his two-way radio, turning down the volume to its lowest setting, and headed for the second prison building, drifting through the darkness like a wraith.

She went around to the south side where she knew Jason's head would be, and knelt down to tap the bottom of the wall once with the hilt of the knife. She waited five seconds, before giving it another tap, this time a little harder, and heard the clink and rattle of chains from the other side. Then, using the point of the knife, she made three equally spaced scratches. She knew that Jason would recognize them as the letter 'J' in Morse code.

She heard the clink of chains on the other side, first a short tap and then a long shake for the letter 'A', and blew a silent sigh of relief.

She scratched out GET HIM TO CALL THE GUARD and a second later Jason's voice reached her through the wall, saying in Hindi, "Wake up, Bhandari. I must have some water. I am burning with thirst."

She heard an irritable grunt and a creak from the cot. Footsteps approached and a guttural voice said in Hindi, "Dog of a firangi! This is the last night that you will trouble me. Tomorrow night, you will be dead."

There was a sadistic chuckle, followed by "If you live that long, sister-fucker! How is your side?"

Alexis heard a thump, followed by a gasp of agony from Jason and a harsh laugh. She felt rage explode inside, but controlled it, and moved away from the wall, holding the radio to her ear with its volume turned all the way down.

Seconds later, Bhandari's barely audible voice came over the radio. "Jindal! Wake up, you lazy idiot! The firangi sister-fucker is thirsty. If you aren't here in two minutes, mother-fucker, I'll report you to Kalidas!" Bhandari switched off without waiting for a reply.

She let a minute go by. Then she walked to the door and knocked. She heard footsteps approach, followed by the lifting of the bar. She tensed, knife in hand, ready to cut off his cry of alarm. She need not have bothered. The door swung in and he turned and walked away without waiting to confirm who it was—*and he wasn't carrying the trigger for her belt!*

It just made things easier. She stepped over the threshold and came up from behind, one hand snaking around his throat to choke off any sound, and drove the knife up under his breastbone. Then she kicked the door shut with her heel and let go of his body.

She switched on the light, and her heart jumped into her throat when she saw Jason.

There was a greyish pallor to his skin and an unnatural brightness in his eyes that told her he was critically ill, maybe even fatally so. As she stared at him, his shackled limbs began to flail in a frenzy of clanking.

Alexis grabbed Bhandari's keys from where he had dropped them and leaped to Jason's side. Her hands were shaking so badly, it was a miracle she was even able to insert the key into each shackle, but somehow she managed it. When Jason was free, she lifted his head and shoulders onto her lap, holding him close. Then she unlocked the belt and gently lifted it from his waist.

The appalling stench made her stomach heave. She tasted bile in her throat, but was able to keep it down as she examined the wound on Jason's flank. It was ten inches long, extending up and across the left side of his abdomen almost to his rib cage. She had no way of telling how deep it was, but it gaped at her, overflowing with thick, greenish pus. The surrounding skin was swollen and discolored blue-black.

"I'm sorry, Red," Jason croaked between chattering teeth. "I miscalculated."

She managed a smile. "Not half as badly as the other guy, though," she said, unable to keep the catch from her voice as she spoke.

"I had to let him cut me deep to make it believable. There wasn't any other way to take him. Not the way it was set up. He was just too good and time was running out."

"I know," she soothed him. "The way you tricked Gurung into thinking he could behead you was unbelievable!"

"Your trick with the red chilli powder was even more unbelievable. I wish I'd thought of it myself."

"Then you would've left me with nothing clever to try. Now, no more talking until I make you comfortable. Can you walk over to the cot if I help you?"

He nodded and allowed her to sit him up. His labored breathing told her what an effort it was. She steeled herself to ignore it, draped his arm across her shoulders, and rose up from her haunches. Even though she tried to take most of his weight, the pain must have been unbearable. She saw sweat bead his face, yet he did not utter a sound as she helped him to the cot. After she made him comfortable, she drew the blankets over him and knelt down at his side to wipe his clammy forehead, trying to think.

Jason was dying and she could do nothing about it. The infection had struck with a virulence and speed that she could not have imagined even in her worst nightmare. In retrospect, though, she should have expected it, knowing that Kalidas had ordered the wound to be "dressed" with goat feces, inoculating billions of virulent bacteria directly into the wound, to thrive and multiply in a host left defenseless by severe blood loss.

With Jason in a state of near-total collapse, she could forget her plan to head for the Indian border. Given a head start of four or five hours before the discovery of the dead guards, they might have had a fighting chance of making it. Now, it was unthinkable. She could not carry him, nor could she leave him to go for help. By herself, she would never be able to hack through the dense tropical jungle fast enough to reach the border before the pursuit caught up to her, let alone get back in time to save Jason. He would be dead in a matter of hours, either way.

The inevitability of Jason's death hit her like a sledgehammer. Strangely, though, she had no tears to cry. The pain in her heart was beyond tears.

"You need to get going if you want to fetch the cavalry, Red," Jason insisted. "Just lock me in here and leave me an AKM and some ammo. I'll hold out till you get back."

"Shut up." she chided him. There was no way she was going to leave him.

Alexis focused her mind on their predicament. Her first priority was Jason, nothing else. She had to do something or else he would die.

He might have a fighting chance if she could somehow stop the energy-sapping rigors. She needed drugs for that, and a knife to cut out the putrid flesh that was the source of the poison entering his bloodstream. And an extra pair of hands...

Everything came together then, and she leapt to her feet, reaching down to ruffle the hair on Jason's head. "You won't get rid of me that easily, Jason Wolff!" she teased, but there was grim determination behind it. She softened her tone. "Can you hold on for just a few minutes? I have to leave you for a bit."

He nodded and his eyes drifted shut. Alexis dropped a kiss on his left cheek, switched off the light, and raced out of the room, pausing only to jerk the Bowie knife from Bhandari's body and wipe it clean on his shirt.

Outside, she ran with an unwavering stride to the nearest cottage, where Mohan and his sister were imprisoned. She found the bathroom window and inserted the knife blade between the shutters, forcing the hasp. Then, she hoisted herself over the sill and dropped to the floor.

She saw that the door was half-open and crept to it, taking care to avoid the plastic buckets on the floor. Peering into the bedroom beyond, she saw two forms side-by-side on a double bed. She crept closer, and recognized Mohan and Seetha, sleeping handcuffed to the bedposts.

Without disturbing them, she inched the bedroom door open. A short corridor extended from a small anteroom at the front of the cottage to a kitchen at the back. Across her was an open door to another bedroom, from where she could hear snores.

She made sure that both the anteroom and kitchen were empty before entering the bedroom, where she found a man lying on the bed, dead to the world. The sour smell of alcohol filled the room. Alexis delivered a shuto strike with the blade of her hand to crush the man's larynx. He died without a sound.

She returned to the first bedroom and gently shook Mohan by the shoulder. His eyes registered shock when he saw her, but he did not make a sound. She unlocked his handcuffs using the keys she found on the dead guard. Mohan then shook Seetha awake and pointed to Alexis. Seconds later, she was free too.

"How did you do it, Miss Wolff?" Seetha whispered. "Where is Mr. Wolff?"

Alexis smiled. "The guard is dead so there is no need to whisper, but it is a good idea to keep our voices down. First things first, though. I'm Alexis and he's Jason. I think we can forget formality, under the circumstances." She saw both of them nod and continued. "Do you have soap and running hot water here?"

"Yes," Seetha replied.

"Good!" Alexis said. She then explained her plan. "We have to work quickly. Jason is hurt and I need to clean his wound. I will need your help. Tear the sheets in both bedrooms into strips. Wash them thoroughly with soap and rinse them out. Then soak the strips in the hottest water available. Change the water every three minutes for at least fifteen minutes. Have you got that?"

Both nodded their heads and got up. Alexis squeezed Seetha's hand. "Thank you for understanding. I'll explain everything later."

"You don't have to say thank you, Memsahib—I mean, Alexis! We must thank you for freeing us."

"We can argue later over who should thank whom. Right now, only Jason matters."

Alexis snatched up a glass on the bedside table and ran back to her prison. She tested the cutthroat razor gingerly with her thumb to confirm it was truly 'razor sharp'. Then she put it, and the baggies of heroin into Bijli's satchel, along with the nearly full bottle of rum, and ran back to Jason's prison.

When she turned on the light, Jason did not react, and she panicked, fearing the worst. Then she heard his shallow breathing and incoherent muttering, and her panic subsided.

She filled the glass from the sink and sat down at the desk. She put a couple of granules of the white powder from a baggie on her tongue and grimaced at the bitter taste. Satisfied it was almost pure heroin, she poured the thirty-milligram portion from one baggie on part of a page torn from one of Bhandari's magazines, and knelt down by the cot to shake Jason's shoulder gently.

He groaned and opened his eyes.

They were glazed with pain and high fever, but he managed to smile and nod when she told him what she wanted to do.

Putting her arm under his shoulders, she lifted his head up and tipped the powder into his mouth. Then she handed him the glass of water to wash it down. He swallowed it without complaint.

It was quite a hefty dose of heroin—equivalent to twice that amount of morphine—but when it took effect, it would control the debilitating rigors. More importantly, the stupor that followed would ease the pain of what was coming. At least, she hoped it would.

CHAPTER 4

Alexis switched off the light and returned to the cottage to find Seetha and Mohan hard at work, soaking linen strips in scalding hot water, just as she instructed.

Leaving them to it, Alexis went to the sink, where there was an instant water heater. She ignored it for the moment and washed the razor thoroughly with soap, and left it in the sink. She then proceeded to scrub her arms with soap from the elbows down to her fingertips.

While she scrubbed her arms, she explained to Mohan and Seetha what she expected of them, making each one go over their instructions twice until she was satisfied that they knew their roles. There would not be a second chance to get this right.

After ten minutes of continuous scrubbing, she was satisfied her hands were as clean as she could get them. Using her elbow, she opened the faucet of the instant water heater and let the boiling hot water flow over the razor. She waited a full five minutes for the razor to get sterilized, then picked it up by the hilt and dropped it in a bucket of scalding hot water just collected by Mohan.

They left the cottage, with Seetha leading the way, holding the soap and a bucket filled with linen strips. Alexis followed, hands held up protectively in front of her. Mohan brought up the rear, a bucket of hot water in each hand, one containing the razor, the other more linen strips.

When they got to Jason, his breathing was no longer quite as ragged and shallow as before. The pulse beating in his neck was fast, but seemed strong and regular. He was remote and withdrawn when she told him what she intended to do, but he nodded. She had to be satisfied with that.

Taking a deep breath, she nodded to Seetha, who had the Bowie knife in her hand. Seetha knelt down and began to cut away Jason's blood-caked clothing to expose the wound. The smell and sight were so terrible that it was all Seetha could do to keep from throwing up. To her credit, she did not flinch, even though she was sweating by the time she was done.

The moment was now upon them. They would find out if Jason was beyond all hope, or if what she was about to do might stave off the inevitable for at least a few hours.

Alexis swabbed out the wound with a piece of linen and hot water. When it was free of all loose matter and encrusted blood, she inserted her index finger into the wound and felt for an opening into the abdominal cavity.

She pushed and probed for two of the longest minutes of her life, during which she did not dare to draw a breath. Then a wave of relief flooded over her.

The kukri had not penetrated through the full thickness of the abdominal wall! If it had, the infection would be raging inside his abdomen—a lethal complication called peritonitis—and there would be nothing she could do.

Alexis went to the sink and washed her hands again. When she was ready, she told Mohan to pour rum over them, rinsing several times. Then she reached into the bucket to pick up the razor, oblivious of the scalding heat, and knelt down next to Jason again, with the razor poised to begin.

Holding the wound with her left hand, Alexis began to cut away the gangrenous margins. The razor was unwieldy, making it difficult to control the cutting edge at first, but she got the hang of it soon enough. Still, it took her twenty minutes to work her way around the wound. She did not stop until blood was oozing freely from the healthy flesh around the wound. Then, she scraped away the dead tissue in its depths and swabbed out any last remnants with a piece of linen.

Finally, she wrung out the linen strips and packed them in the wound to staunch the ooze, binding the makeshift dressing in place with two long strips of linen that encircled his midriff.

It wasn't ideal, maybe not even adequate, but it was the best she could do under the circumstances. It was her only consolation.

She got to her feet and went back to the sink to wash her hands, gesturing to Mohan and Seetha to join her.

"I cannot leave him," Alexis said to them, her voice low so that Jason wouldn't hear, "but there is no reason for you to stay. I will point you towards the Indian border and you are welcome to one of the assault rifles, but I cannot do anything beyond that. I wish you luck."

Seetha and Mohan shook their heads in unison. Seetha spoke for both of them. "We will stay, Alexis, if you let us. Without you to guide us, we will die in the jungle anyway. If we have to die, we would rather die here, with honor, than die running away like jackals."

The words had a profound effect on Alexis. Violent death held few terrors for her, but for these two innocents, the obscene evil they were up against must be unimaginable. Yet, in a show of extraordinary courage, they had chosen to stay and confront it.

For a brief moment, she felt her spirits soar.

Then cold reality hit. In four hours, when the shift changed, the relief would discover the dead guard. It would be over. Not only were they immobile, they were overwhelmingly outnumbered and outgunned, with just four AKM's and about two hundred rounds of ammunition to confront Kalidas's army.

She had to tell Mohan and Seetha the brutal truth.

"I applaud your courage," she said. "But I want you to understand exactly what you face by deciding to stay" she said. "When daylight comes, all hell will break loose. We have very little to fight with, so it will not last long. This much I promise you, though, if you stay. I will not let any of us fall into Kalidas's hands alive. Do you understand what that means?"

Seetha shivered visibly and replied in a voice that trembled, "Thank you for that promise, Alexis. We would rather die by your hand a million times than in his clutches."

Mohan nodded vigorously in agreement.

Seetha continued, "I would gladly die if I could only be sure that no one else will ever have to face what I have faced. I don't have to tell you how much Kalidas terrifies me, but I loathe Karim Chand as much, if not more. His voice haunts me at night and the thought of his hands groping me when he said he had to make sure I was a virgin makes my skin crawl."

Mohan threw his arms around his sister. "Stop! Don't think of such things! Alexis has promised he will never violate you again."

He looked at Alexis. "Is there nothing we can do, Alexis?"

Alexis shook her head.

Mohan stared at her for a second. Then a remarkable change came over him. He squared his shoulders, all signs of distress vanishing, and became very animated. "I know! I will put on one of the belts and give myself up. When they take me to Kalidas, you can blow me up. I will gladly sacrifice my life to kill them. That way at least you and Seetha and Jason can be free!"

Alexis smiled. "You are very brave, Mohan. I understand how you feel, but if anyone is going to be a suicide bomber, it will be me. It won't work, though. The first thing they will do is to search whoever they take to Kalidas."

"So we just sit and do nothing until they come to kill us? Can't we sneak up and kill at least some of them while they sleep?"

"Mohan, we need much more than we have here to do something like that. Now if we could only get into the armory..."

Bloodbath

Alexis's voice trailed away. It was a pie-in-the-sky wish, maybe even more impossible than that. There was no way to get past that steel door.

Then, Mohan began to laugh—not just ordinary laughter, but a hysterical cackle—as he fumbled through his pockets. Then, with a whoop of triumph, he thrust a crumpled piece of paper at Alexis.

Alexis stared at him, dumbfounded, thinking he had gone mad. Then, she took the paper from him and smoothed it out.

It was a page torn from a notepad, with six two-digit numbers scribbled on it. She read the numbers twice, unable to make sense of them. Then realization struck.

It was the code for the lock to the armory!

Even before the word, "How?" could form, images flashed through her mind, like a video running in fast-forward. There was Kalidas in the conference room just after his demonstration of the deadly belts, Bansal arriving with Tenga's AKM, Kalidas telling Karim Chand to give Jarnail the combination, and Jarnail departing with Mohan to put the weapon back in the armory.

Mohan must have picked Jarnail's pocket then. It did not matter why he did it. Maybe he needed some tiny measure of triumph over his all-powerful captors just to sustain hope, and he used the one skill he knew would give it to him. It was a seemingly inconsequential act of rebellion, but it might just save their lives!

Alexis slapped Mohan on the back. "Mohan Sinha truly is the greatest pickpocket in the world."

Alexis embraced Mohan, and Seetha joined them in a group hug. Jason heard them laughing and murmured, "Why am I left out of the fun?"

Alexis ran to his side and embraced him gently. "We aren't done yet, Jay! Don't you dare pass out on me now. I'll need all your skill and ingenuity if we're to get out of this alive."

Jason gave her a smile, then drifted back to sleep. The pinpoint pupils told her that there was no need to give him another dose of heroin for some time yet. Motioning to Mohan and Seetha to come and sit by him, she picked up the Bowie knife and hurried out.

The fog was so thick now that she could barely see her hand in front of her face, but her sense of direction, developed under Gabe's tutelage in the Stygian darkness of the African night, took her straight to the armory.

On the wall next to the door was a ten-digit numeric keypad. She punched in the code and the lock disengaged with a soft snick. She nudged it open slightly, and waited, knife at the ready, listening for any sound suggesting the presence of a guard. Hearing nothing, she stepped inside, still not letting her guard down.

It was pitch dark, except for the faint glow of an illuminated wall switch and a lighted keypad. Satisfied there was no one inside, she pushed the door shut and flicked on the lights.

On either side of the central aisle, as far down as she could see, were serried banks of shelves, stacked to the ceiling, bearing placards identifying the class and type of ordnance.

Alexis walked down the central aisle, glancing from side to side for a placard that read "Medical Supplies". She saw assault rifles of every type, sub-machine guns, grenades, grenade launchers, anti-tank missiles, anti-personnel mines, case-upon-case of ammunition of every caliber, and crates of plastic explosives. There were also several man-portable surface-to-air missiles, plugged in and charging along the back wall. Some were American-made Stingers and others had Cyrillic markings, indicating Russian or Soviet-bloc origin.

With her hope steadily diminishing, she arrived at the last row. Then it died. There were no medical supplies in the armory.

She was about to turn back in despair, when something jutting out from the lowest shelf at the far end of the last row caught her eye. It stuck out—literally and figuratively!—in the midst of the neatly stacked shelves. She walked over to it, intrigued, and bent down. And the hope that died a second earlier burst back to life.

It was a collapsible medevac stretcher.

Hope crystallized into concrete action. She grabbed a large canvas backpack from the shelf, scooped twenty AKM clips from the ammunition section into the backpack, and slung it over her shoulder along with an AKM rifle.

Hoisting the stretcher on the other shoulder, she headed for the door, pausing to take one last look at the stacks of ordnance— she would come back later for what she needed—and hurried back to the prison.

Jason was fast asleep, with Mohan and Seetha at his side, just as she left them. Dumping the stretcher and backpack on the floor, she told them her plan. They both nodded, asking no questions.

She was relieved to see that the heroin was working as well as she could have hoped! So well, in fact, that Jason did not awaken when they transferred him to the stretcher.

Alexis covered Jason with blankets from the bed, and buckled the stretcher's straps around his chest and thighs. She slung one AKM over her shoulder and handed the other to Seetha, along with the backpack containing the spare clips, the remaining bags of heroin, and Jason's knife.

Ready at last, she bent down to pick up the stretcher. "On my count, Mohan. One! Two! Three!"

She and Mohan lifted up the stretcher and they headed out, making their way stealthily between the cottages and the outer wall of the camp. This was when the danger of discovery was greatest, when they were within a few feet of terrorists with hair-trigger reactions. Fortunately, they made it to the temple steps without being discovered.

Then they began the climb.

Alexis could never have done it without Mohan's help. His strength and experience as a porter were invaluable. With several stops to rest and with Seetha to massage their muscles, they somehow made it to the top of the steps, where they fell to their knees, having reached the limits of their strength and endurance.

It was several minutes before she was able to turn her attention to the surroundings

CHAPTER 5

They were in the shadow of a great stone archway at the entrance to a courtyard the size of a soccer field.

The silhouette of the temple loomed threateningly in the swirling mist at the far end of the courtyard, projecting such a sinister aura that Alexis couldn't help an involuntary shudder.

Seeing that Mohan and Seetha were even more profoundly affected, she thought, *Best to get where they can't see it.*

They carried the stretcher to the far end of the courtyard, where a giant superstructure without intervening walls rose up on large stone pillars. At the center was a single room, with massive teak doors covered by ornate carving. The sacrificial altar stood a few feet from the doorway. It was a waist-high platform of rough-hewn stone, with a ring at each corner, and an encircling gutter that drained into a channel leading under the teak doors.

Alexis set the stretcher down away from the altar to one side, and headed towards the room, but a cry from Seetha stopped her. She had one hand over her mouth and was shaking the other in a desperate plea for Alexis not to go there.

Alexis nodded to Seetha and turned back with a shrug. It was obvious the room housed the idol and, with Seetha so terrified, there was no point looking inside just to confirm it.

She turned her attention to their surroundings.

A waist-high parapet encircled the perimeter of the courtyard. Beyond it, the impenetrable tropical jungle grew rampant on three sides, except for the slope facing the camp, which had obviously been cleared of all trees, to provide an unobstructed view of the temple from the camp.

She completed a circuit of the courtyard and went to check on Jason. He looked much better than he did earlier. The feverish brightness was gone from his eyes, his pulse was strong, his breathing regular, and her makeshift dressing was doing its job—there was no visible seepage of blood.

Her rudimentary surgical skills seemed to have worked a small miracle!

He read her thoughts. "I don't know that I can ever thank you for what you've done," he said. "I'll save it for later, though. I guess you have a few things on your mind right now."

She replied playfully, feigning anger, "If I didn't have a few things on my mind right now, Jason Wolff, I'd give you a piece of it. If you say another word, I'll dredge up everything you've done for me over the years for which I haven't thanked you. So shut up!"

He pretended to cower. "Okay! Don't get mad. I'll shut up, as ordered." Then he became serious. "What are our options, Red?"

She told him they had access to the armory, thanks to Mohan, and outlined her plan. "We hole up here until the helicopter arrives with the last of Kalidas's guests. I kill the pilot, take over the chopper, and we fly out."

He remained silent, lost in thought. Finally, he said, "Everything depends on the chopper getting here before dawn. In the dark, with surprise on your side, you have a chance of killing the pilot, grabbing it, and flying it up here. The problem is that Kalidas will order his Stinger platoon to shoot us down the second we lift off."

"I've thought of that. When the chopper lands, I wipe out Kalidas and his army by blowing up the barracks and bungalow with the RPG-7's in the armory." With a grim laugh, she added, "Maybe the one sordid chapter from my life in South Africa could have some use. The RPG was front and center in the Self Defense League's plans for urban terror."

"Good thought, but…" Jason hesitated, and Alexis knew, immediately, that he had found some fatal flaw in her plan.

"The cottages are fair game for a rocket-propelled grenade, but Kalidas's command bungalow and the barracks are beyond the RPG's range."

Disappointment burned in Alexis's throat like acid. Jason's encyclopedic knowledge of ordnance was irrefutable. But she wasn't willing to concede they were helpless. "There has to be some way to get Kalidas from here."

"Maybe there's something else in the armory we could use. Tell me what you saw there."

She ran through the weapons in the armory, but he shook his head at each mention, until she came to the shoulder-launched surface-to-air missiles. Then he grabbed her forearm and hissed, "The Russian SAMs! Can you describe the markings to me?"

She took out his Bowie from the satchel and, using its point, lightly scratched a reasonable facsimile of the Cyrillic letters on the launcher casings into the stone floor.

"The Soviet SA-7 Strela!" Jason's eyes sparkled with excitement. "Couldn't have asked for anything better! Can you bring one launcher and a couple of missiles up here? They're really heavy, though. Over ten kilos for the launcher, a little over nine for each missile. That's a lot to carry up that stairway."

"The weight doesn't matter! I'll get them. Just tell me what's cooking in that brain of yours?"

"I'll tell you when you get back. You've got maybe three hours of darkness to make your trip to the armory and get ready for the chopper's arrival."

"It'll have to be two trips. I want to get the RPG's as well. We might as well help Ravi rid India of a bunch of terrorists while we have the chance."

He nodded. "Good idea. Get two launchers and maybe a dozen projectiles. That's another forty kg load."

"I'll take Mohan with me. He should be a great help."

"Don't discount Seetha. I've a feeling she has depths."

"I already know that."

She kissed him on the forehead and began to get up, but Jason stopped her. "Wait a minute! Did you say you saw Semtek there? We could booby-trap the armory."

"Forget it, Jay-boy. I don't have your skill to improvise a booby-trap. I'd end up blowing myself to bits. As for time-delayed or remote detonation, I wouldn't even know where to begin. "

"You don't have to, Red! Someone's already set it up for you!"

She frowned, mystified by what he was driving at. Then he pointed to her belly, and she slapped her thigh in delight. "My God! How could I forget? Jay, you're a genius!"

CHAPTER 6

The shift change was just minutes away.

When the dead guards were found, the alarm would be raised and that would be it. The chopper wouldn't land, and Jason would die.

Just before daybreak, Jason's recovery had come to an abrupt end. His condition had deteriorated, despite another dose of heroin. Although he was still lucid when he was aroused from sleep, febrile coma and septic shock would not be long in coming.

Alexis's anguish and grief were now locked away inside her heart. Whether or not she would live to confront her loss was moot. If that was the way it was to be, then so be it. At least she would extract vengeance in full measure.

Thanks to Jason, she had the means to annihilate the enemy. He had taken her rudimentary idea and transformed it into a strategic masterpiece.

She looked around, for the hundredth time, to make sure everything was ready.

The SA-7 missile launcher lay on the ground next to her. Mohan knelt a few feet away, holding the remote triggering device for one of two charges of Semtek that she had wired (under Jason's direction) to the electronic chipboards from the explosive belts.

A pair of RPG-7V anti-tank rocket launchers lay between her and Mohan. A favorite of terrorists around the world, firing it was simplicity itself. You just mounted the rocket on the launcher after removing the nose cap, cleared the safety pin, sighted, and squeezed the trigger. That was it! When the time came, it would be Mohan's job to reload and hand her the launchers alternately.

In her hands was her ace-in-the-hole, a Dragunov SVD sniper rifle.

She found it propped against the wall in the far corner of the armory, its canvas carrying-case coated with dust. There were twenty-six rounds of ammunition, and it was well-oiled and perfectly functional. The battery for the image intensifier on the telescopic sight was dead, but she never expected to use it in the darkness, anyway.

Why it was even there was a mystery. There was nothing else like it in the armory. Nor was there any spare ammunition for it among the vast stocks. Although it took a 7.62 caliber round and was a semiautomatic weapon, the cartridge was not interchangeable with those for the AKM and AK-47, of which she found several thousand cases.

Still, it was a priceless find. It gave her an excellent chance of killing the chopper pilot and driving everyone else under cover.

Alexis cuddled the Dragunov against her shoulder. Resting her right cheek against the pad at the top of the stock, she squinted down the optical sight. The men at the entrance to the barracks seemed so close that she felt she could reach out and touch them.

All of a sudden, she felt uneasy, remembering Jason's warning about trigger fright. He said that most people, were incapable of killing in such a cold-blooded and dispassionate way. Even he, a skilled commando with combat experience, and accustomed to death at close quarters, would have trouble killing at long distance, unless driven by a powerful motivating emotion, like hate or fear.

She had brushed him off, saying she wouldn't get trigger fright, because her hatred of Kalidas would be more than enough to pull the trigger if anyone associated with him was in her crosshairs.

Now she wasn't so sure.

The sun broke through the fog right then, and everything in the camp took on an ethereal luster so hauntingly beautiful that, for one brief moment, Alexis forgot the rank evil hiding behind the façade. A split-second later it appeared in all its ugliness, bringing her to her senses like a slap in the face.

She saw Karim Chand emerge from the command bungalow and head for the first of the cottages. He disappeared behind it, only to reappear after a few minutes and go to the next in line.

She watched him move from cottage to cottage, and finally take up a position facing the cottages, photographing the summit participants as they came out, one by one, to join him.

Movement in the background caught her attention.

The relief guard!

He was heading for her prison, AKM slung on his shoulder. In minutes, he would discover the guard's body and raise the alarm.

Alexis panicked.

Her plan was in shreds! The two things she was counting on were the arrival of the chopper before dawn, and the element of surprise. The first was lost. In a few seconds, she would lose the second, too. Then she would lose Jason.

She needed Jason, now, more than ever—!

The contradiction—needing Jason to save Jason—was so ludicrous that it freed her of doubt. And she knew what to do.

Six participants were gathered around Karim Chand. Two others were steps away from joining them, and the last had just emerged from his cottage.

She applied her right eye to the sniper-scope, bringing Karim Chand's chest into focus. She made a slight correction to the elevation adjustment knob to compensate for bullet drop and began to take up the slack in the trigger.

In that instant, she froze, unable to squeeze the trigger—she had trigger fright!

Her aim wavered, and the scope drifted down, bringing the camera on Karim Chand's chest into view. Suddenly, she remembered it as she last saw it, pressed against the secretary's face, his mouth open, drooling in anticipation of Jason's beheading.

It triggered a firestorm of hatred that incinerated any inhibition. She squeezed the trigger.

Alexis had never fired a Dragunov before. She knew only that the rimmed cartridge of the SVD carried twice the propellant charge of the standard Russian 7.62mm round, and that the distance between her and her target was well within the range of the rifle.

Even so, she was unprepared for its awesome stopping power. The bullet slammed into Karim Chand's chest, hurling him backwards as if hit by a sledgehammer.

Working the bolt action with easy flicks of her wrist, she put five more shots into the group milling around Karim Chand.

The three remaining participants ran towards the cottages, dodging this way and that like rabbits. She picked them off one by one. The ninth, who had been watching the carnage, as if paralyzed, woke to his mortal danger and whirled around to take cover inside. She snapped off a shot just before he vanished from view.

The relief guard stood rooted to the ground, trying to figure out where the shots were coming from amidst the echoes rolling across the valley. Alexis swiveled the gun barrel to bring him into her sight, adjusted the focus, and shot him. He staggered and fell.

Discarding the Dragunov, she reached for the SA-7 and said sharply, "Mohan! Now!"

Mohan released the pistol-grip trigger and Alexis saw the green light turn red. There was a muted thunderclap and a small puff of smoke appeared behind the command bungalow. Then…nothing!

No explosion of walls. No roof blown off. Not even a slow crumble!

Bloodbath

She waited for something—anything!—while the seconds ticked away. When nothing happened, she knew Jason had misjudged the size of the charge she should have used. She was about to turn away, when the roof of the command bungalow fell in before her eyes.

The charge had blown out the rear wall and the weight of the concrete roof did the rest. The slab buckled and pancaked down, leaving only a small section of the bungalow abutting the generator building still standing. No one inside could be alive. How could she have doubted Jason?

Alexis now hoisted the SA-7 launcher to her shoulder. Even with Kalidas dead in his bungalow, the outcome was still in doubt as long as his army was intact. It would organize and retaliate in strength unless she annihilated it.

Jason's improvisation had given her the means to do just that.

He had the brilliant idea of blowing up the barracks with the Russian SA-7 Strela, an infrared-guided, heat-seeking, surface-to-air missile! Unlike the more sophisticated American-made Stinger, the Strela's detector was susceptible to infrared from ordinary fires.

Resting the launcher on the parapet to keep it steady, she squinted down the open sight at the blazing embers in the grate of the metal stove and went through Jason's methodical instructions.

She squeezed the trigger to the first stop, listening for the electronic whine of the thermal battery powering up. A red light came on.

She waited, holding the target in the sight, and...the red light turned green—the missile's heat seeker had locked onto the fire, just as Jason predicted!

She squeezed the trigger fully. The launcher on her shoulder juddered as the booster charge fired. There was a hushed roar and she felt heat against her cheek. Then the missile was gone.

The sustainer motor ignited and the missile visibly accelerated away. Two seconds later, just as it was about to enter the barracks at close to Mach speed, it grazed the oil drum.

The drum just may have happened to be in the missile's flight path, or maybe, the faint IR from the hot metal drum decoyed the missile. It made no difference to the outcome. The failsafe grazing fuse fired, detonating the warhead as it entered the barracks.

The walls and roof of the building blew outwards with a deafening explosion, and the barracks disintegrated, disappearing in a cloud of dust, smoke, and flame.

Alexis had the launcher back on her shoulder with another missile fitted before the echoes subsided, and pointed it at the generator building. She zeroed in on the metal smokestack at its base, where the heat from the exhaust gases was greatest, and went through the firing sequence again. Seconds later, the generator building and the little that was left of the command bungalow were turned into rubble. The diesel fuel ignited and flames leaped skyward through plumes of thick, oily smoke.

She allowed herself a moment of grim satisfaction before laying down the missile launcher, then turned her attention to her mission of annihilating the enemy out of existence. Picking up the RPG-7V grenade launcher, she aimed it at the cottage closest to the command bungalow and fired. There was virtually no cross-wind to speak of and the large, slow-moving projectile flew true to her aim. The cottage exploded.

She handed the grenade launcher to Mohan and picked up the second one, aiming it at the next cottage, and destroyed it too. Firing the two RPG launchers alternately, she destroyed all twelve cottages and both prison buildings as well, just for the satisfaction it gave her.

After she was done, she surveyed the scene through a pair of binoculars, paying careful attention to the barracks. The camp was in ruins, except for the armory and water tower, and there were no signs of life in the smoking rubble, only shattered body parts—all that remained of Kalidas's army.

Her victory over the enemy was complete. But she was defeated, too. Nothing could save Jason now.

She walked back to where he lay on the stretcher. He opened his eyes as she knelt down by his side. His skin was clammy and his pulse weak. Within the next couple of hours, shock would supervene, followed by terminal collapse. Then it would be over. A part of her would die with him and she would never be whole again.

"It worked, eh, Red?" His voice was a whispering croak.

"Like a charm, Jay." She tried to make her voice sound light, but she couldn't help it breaking when she said his name.

He seemed oblivious of her distress. "The Soviets were experts at making inferior weapons. But they worked if you knew how to use them."

His eyes drifted shut for an instant. "We're home free, now."

Her heart was breaking, yet she kept her face devoid of emotion. "Yes, Jay," she whispered. "We're home free."

She looked up at Mohan and Seetha, standing on the other side of the stretcher. Seetha was crying soundlessly and Mohan's face was twisted in grief. Both knew how critical the early arrival of the helicopter was to Jason's survival.

She had no tears, no emotion left. Feeling utterly defeated, she bowed her head in hopeless surrender.

CHAPTER 7

"**B**laspheming firangi whore!"

Alexis spun around, flabbergasted, when she heard the profane scream. She saw Kalidas in the open doorway of the temple wearing a bullet-proof vest, with an Uzi submachine gun pointed straight at her.

Shock gave way to vitriolic self-contempt for not considering that Kalidas would have secret access to his precious idol. How he survived the collapse of his command bungalow was irrelevant. He had survived, and his eyes showed the terrible madness of an unhinged mind teetering on the edge of full-blown insanity.

Kalidas screamed, "Get up very slowly and walk to the temple door. I want Mother Kali to see you die."

Glancing with savage regret at the AKM rifles she left at the parapet, Alexis got to her feet and walked to the door of the sanctum with Mohan and Seetha on either side. Kalidas circled around the altar as they approached, keeping it between them.

Seetha gasped when she saw the idol, but Alexis's eyes never left Kalidas, as she searched frantically for an opening to exploit.

"You thought I was dead, firangi bitch! I was saved by the grace of Kali, because I was in my bunker when the bungalow collapsed. You dared to challenge Kali, blaspheming she-devil! Now I will cleanse her honor by bathing her feet in your blood."

Kalidas glanced at Jason lying on the stretcher and cackled maniacally. "As for your brother, I will enjoy seeing him die inch by inch, with the help of the chilli powder you used on Jarnail."

His next words proved he was no longer teetering on the edge of full-blown insanity. He had tipped over the edge.

278

Bloodbath

He shrieked, "When she feasts on your blood, with his shrieks of agony for music, she will reward me by returning everything you've tried to destroy. She will bring Jarnail, Gurung, and Karim back to life, and I will rule again! Now die, chudail!"

Alexis saw Kalidas's trigger finger whiten, and readied to make a dive for the altar. If the muzzle rode up, there was a chance she could vault over it to reach him before bullets tore into her.

At that moment, something came whirring through the air from her right to slash across Kalidas's exposed throat, sending blood spurting out in a great gush. Alexis thrust her arms out instinctively, sending Seetha and Mohan sprawling to the ground, and dove behind the altar, anticipating Kalidas's final mortal spasm.

Alexis heard the Uzi sing its murderous song in counterpoint to the metallic clink of spent shells on concrete. After what seemed like an eternity, the deadly symphony of death played its last note and there was nothing left except the ringing in her ears.

Still she could not move.

She lay on the ground, her cheek hugging the rough stone.

She was alive! Jason had done the impossible! Awakened by Kalidas's maniacal screams, he found the knife she dropped earlier near his stretcher. Lying flat on his back, he threw it backhanded with deadly accuracy at the only visible target—Kalidas's throat!

To her dying day, she would never fathom how he pulled it off.

Still dazed, she got up and walked over to him. He was propped on his elbow, his gaunt face split ear to ear by a grin.

"Not bad, eh, Red?" he said.

She shook her head in disbelief. "Not bad? That was beyond unbelievable! But... I don't deserve it."

He shook his head. "Don't blame yourself. Who would've thought he'd have a secret hidey-hole to play with his obsession?"

"I should have known he'd want exclusive all-day, all-weather access to his beloved goddess."

"He has it now, which must make him very happy," he answered flippantly, with a nod at the altar. "He even gave that thing exactly what he wanted."

Alexis looked at Kalidas's body, kneeling with arms spread-eagled and forehead resting in supplication on the sacrificial altar. Blood dripping from the neck into the gutter had formed a dark crimson rivulet that was snaking its way into the sanctum.

She turned to Jason and said quietly, "He can enjoy worshipping it now, wherever he's gone."

Jason's eyes drifted shut, and Alexis got to her feet, energized by resolve. Jason was not going to die. Not today. The weapons she needed to fight for his life were at hand.

She ran to the parapet to grab the AKMs, and called Mohan and Seetha to her. They were shaken and scared by their brush with near-certain death but had regained their composure.

Handing each an AKM, she showed them how to remove the safety catch and hold the weapon while squeezing the trigger to fire it over the parapet. She left Mohan on guard at the stairway, and Seetha at the parapet, overlooking the camp.

She then picked up Kalidas's Uzi and two spare clips from his pockets, and entered the sanctum. The hail of bullets had destroyed the idol, and left deep gashes in the rock wall behind it.

The extent of damage was startling, but the spent shells on the floor explained why. They weren't the standard Uzi's 9mm Parabellum rounds. They were 0.45 caliber rounds. No wonder the soft marble statue disintegrated! All that remained was a pair of shattered legs standing in a puddle of congealed blood.

The macabre irony of Kalidas's last mortal act wasn't lost on Alexis—he fulfilled his desire to bathe his demon's feet in blood!

Bloodbath

She shrugged, ready to move on, and made her way behind the idol to an open trap door above a circular shaft with a spiral staircase. She descended stairs, alert for the slightest whisper of danger, to the bottom, where she saw the mouth of a tunnel that must lead to the 'bunker' Kalidas mentioned in his ravings.

Alexis took off down the tunnel, not breaking stride until she reached the far end. Guessing she was now under the collapsed bungalow, she stopped to listen for any sounds of life. Hearing only static from a radio, she pushed the door open.

She was looking down a lighted passageway with three doors on each side, and the mangled remains of an elevator at the far end. On the left were two bedrooms and a filing room lined with shelves stacked with hundreds of CDs, and a solitary filing cabinet

The first room on the right was the communications room. A compact field radio on the desk was emitting the static she heard. The second had a bank of batteries for backup power to the bunker.

Refusing to give up hope, Alexis reached the last room on the right. When she opened the door, the lights came on automatically…And she knew she had finally hit the jackpot.

It was a miniature hospital operating room, with an operating table. *And a refrigerator in the corner!*

Inside it she saw boxes of antibiotics labeled 'Zosyn' and 'Garamycin', and her heart sang. She had found the weapons she needed to fight for Jason's life!

She grabbed a fully-stocked emergency kit off the shelf and stuffed in several vials of each antibiotic and a vial of tetanus vaccine. She added disposable syringes, needles, infusion sets, and four bags of saline, then slung the kit on her shoulder. She left at a dead run, her singular focus on getting to Jason as fast as she could.

She came skidding to a halt, the crackle of radio static forcing her to think beyond the immediate need.

Antibiotics and saline alone were not enough to save Jason. He needed intensive care ASAP to survive. She had to get him out before the smoke caught the attention of the Myanmar military.

Surrendering didn't guarantee their survival, either. The junta could decide that summary execution and steadfast denial was the safest and least messy exit strategy. But if they knew she had radioed the Indians to tell them Kalidas received sanctuary in Myanmar these past years, it might be just enough to deter the junta. So Kalidas's radio could be a valuable insurance policy.

She slung the field radio over her other shoulder and turned to leave, when her eye fell on a memo pad with a message neatly written in a cramped hand. It read, "2330: Y from PWG arr. 0700. Padda requesting approval daytime transfer. Lynx. Dep 0800. ETA 1000". A simple "OK" was scrawled haphazardly beside it.

On the next line, in the same cramped handwriting, were the words, "2345: Approved. Padda to confirm ETA en route 0930."

Karim Chand's arrangements for the arrival of the tenth participant in Bloodbath by chopper. Too bad! Forget about the chopper coming now—!

All of a sudden, she felt something jog her memory. She recalled Seetha's gift of mimicry. Her abhorrence for Karim Chand. Then it all came together

She glanced up at the clock. It was 7:45 a.m., just ninety minutes since she fired her first shot with the Dragunov!

Slipping an inkpad and blank notebook into her pocket, she left at a dead run, oblivious of the radio and emergency kit bludgeoning her hips. When she got to Jason, she went quickly to work, not even waiting to catch her breath.

She placed an infusion catheter in his forearm, started the saline flowing wide-open, hooking the bag on an ornate projection from a nearby pillar, and injected the antibiotics into the flowing saline. Then she turned her attention to the wound. She removed her make-shift dressing and flushed the wound several times with saline. After squirting in some Garamycin, she applied a large sterile surgical dressing. Finally, she administered a dose of tetanus vaccine and sat back, feeling nothing but overwhelming relief.

Then, the dam burst. The tears she could not cry when she thought he was dying began to flow.

Two minutes later, it was over. She wiped her eyes on a wad of gauze and blew her nose, ready to move on.

She called Seetha to her and showed her how to disconnect and replace the saline when the bag was empty. Then, telling Mohan to stand guard at the parapet with an AKM, she went bounding down the stairway, the Uzi cocked and ready.

Alexis picked her way through the rubble of the camp to the cluster of bodies. Karim Chand lay on his back, a bullet-hole visible over his heart, but his digital camera was undamaged.

She used it to take close-up photographs of his face and body, including the exit wound, to leave no doubt he was dead. Then she repeated the process methodically with the nine other terrorists, using the inkpad to fingerprint them in the same sequence.

Finally, she dragged Karim Chand's body to hide it from view under an uprooted bush. She took one last look around to make sure she had missed nothing, and made her way back to the temple.

First, she replaced Jason's saline bag. Then she collected all the weapons and dumped them inside the sanctum, keeping only the Uzi. Finally, she photographed and fingerprinted Kalidas, dragged his body into the sanctum, and shut the doors.

It was an act performed without thinking, but the instant the doors closed, the symbolism hit her. It represented closure!

All that remained was escape.

She switched on the radio, noting the frequency to which it was set. She then tuned it to the frequency monitored around the clock by Jonathan's communication network, and said, "Bush Lady calling Wolf's Lair. Come in Wolf's Lair. How copy?"

She knew Jonathan would be standing by, so she wasn't surprised to hear his voice burst from the speaker. "Bush Lady! Mister Wheels receiving you loud and clear. What's your status?"

Just to be safe, she used tangential references. "We are conducting geological surveys at the site we discussed. We are in good shape, but our hosts could drop in. We must visit our neighbors in Dibrugarh, before our hosts arrive, though. Our problem is telling them we are coming. If we drop in unannounced, we may not be welcome. Do you copy?"

There was a second of silence. Then, Ravi's voice came over, taking her by surprise, "Bush Lady! This is Otokodate. I hear and understand. I guarantee the neighbors' welcome will be friendly."

Ravi's reference to their first meeting made her laugh. "I read you loud and clear, Otokodate! That's a relief. Please arrange for us to be met by someone who can fix a Jay-specimen that is critically damaged. The highest level of proficiency in specimen repair is mandatory."

Jonathan's voice was sharp with anxiety. "Bush Lady. Rest assured that the world's most proficient mechanic will be available for consultation with the team on your arrival."

She felt the last weight lift from her shoulders.

"Thank you, Mr. Wheels. The Jay-specimen is paramount."

Ravi cut in. "Otokodate here. I promise that the best we have will be on hand to repair the Jay-specimen on arrival. Do you need transport from the survey site?"

"Negative, Otokodate. I am arranging transportation. I cannot wait for you to get it invoiced and approved. By then, the Jay-specimen will be lost. Stand by for further transmission when I secure it. Over and out."

Bloodbath

She cut off without waiting for a reply, and twirled the dial back to the original frequency. Her part was over. It was time to explain her plan to her two baffled young friends.

"Seetha, this is where you come in. A helicopter is on its way here with the last of Kalidas's guests. That's our ride out of here."

She glanced at her watch. It was 9:15 AM.

"The pilot will call on the radio in fifteen minutes, expecting to talk to Karim Chand. If he doesn't hear his voice, he will turn back. Even if he doesn't, the minute he lays eyes on the devastation in the camp, he'll turn back without landing. Whatever happens, we have to convince him to land, because that chopper is our ride out of here. Understand?"

Seetha nodded, so Alexis continued, "Okay. So, we must convince him of three things to ensure he doesn't turn back. That he's speaking to Karim Chand. That the devastation is no threat to him. And that he has to land, no matter what."

She saw comprehension dawn in the girl's large, dark eyes. "I know what you mean, Alexis," she said. "Tell me what to do."

Alexis reached out and squeezed the girl's hand. "Good girl! I thought you'd understand. Now, here's what I want you to do..."

* * * * * * * * * * *

Yelliah was asleep, which was just as well. Padda preferred to fly without having to talk to a humorless Maoist.

It was 9:30 AM. Time to give Karim Chand his ETA.

He switched on his radio headset. "Eagle Three, calling House of the Mother. Are you there?"

He waited, knowing it could take a while before the secretary got to the Communications Room in the bunker. After a minute

285

or so, he repeated his call sign, but nothing but silence echoed in his headset. He was beginning to get annoyed.

He clicked his tongue in irritation, and repeated his call sign a third time. What in the name of the devil was wrong with Karim Chand? Why was it taking him so long to answer?

Suddenly, a hysterical screech assaulted his ears. "Padda! Padda! Thank God. Are you there?"

Padda was aghast at Karim Chand's breach of on-air security. "You fool! No names! Remember the rules! Scrambler first!"

"Damn the scrambler and the rules! It's a complete disaster."

"What the hell are you talking about?" Padda shouted back.

"The Muslims and Sikhs got into a fight, and blew up the camp. Everything is destroyed!"

"Where is the master? Is he all right?"

"He was hit by a bullet and badly injured. I got him down to the bunker just before the bungalow collapsed. We can still save him if you land in the temple courtyard and help me carry him out through the tunnel."

Padda was furious. "No way!" he shouted. "I will return to base and come back with Dr. Pramod and reinforcements!"

There was another high-pitched shriek. "Traitor! We cannot wait that long. The master will be dead long before you return, you worthless dog. You know what will happen if he dies. You will have no one to protect you!"

"I refuse to land while a fight is still going on."

"The fighting is over. They all killed each other. Even the barracks blew up, killing everyone in the master's army. So you have nothing to fear if you land, you cowardly bastard!"

Despite his panic, Padda saw the sense in Karim Chand's argument. "All right. It should be okay if no one else is alive."

"Land in the temple courtyard..." The voice faded and came back. "Come down the tunnel behind Kali...help me carry..."

"Your signal is fading, but I understand you. I will land in the temple courtyard in half an hour."

"...radio was damaged..."

"Okay! Over and out!"

Padda told himself he would take a quick look from the air. If he saw anything threatening, he would not land, no matter what Karim Chand said.

He maintained course, seeing familiar landmarks appear and slip past him. Then, he saw it—a dirty grey layer was spilling out from behind the row of hills surrounding the camp, and he imagined a nightmarish inferno blazing in the valley.

When he got there, it was nothing like he imagined.

The valley was filled with thick black smoke. The acrid smell of burning diesel was everywhere, stinging Padda's eyes and throat. He pulled down his flight goggles to stop his eyes from tearing up, and held a handkerchief to his mouth, maneuvering the joystick with one hand.

He heard a fit of coughing from his passenger, but paid no attention. Keeping his eyes fixed on the Lynx's altimeter, he took the chopper down through the cloud in a slow, controlled descent.

The chopper broke through the cloud a hundred meters from the ground, and he gasped, holding the chopper in a hover.

Laid out below him was a scene of total devastation. Only the armory was still intact. Everything else was rubble. Smoke rising from the remains of the generator building was merging with the smoke-cloud. It was so thick that the sun was a blur, and a shimmering grey darkness blanketed the camp.

Padda heard Yelliah shout in his ear between fits of coughing, and silenced him with an impatient wave of his hand, concentrating

287

on examining the ground. All he saw was concrete debris, and a scattering of body parts from men blown to bits. A cluster of intact bodies lay near the rubble of the cottages. Nothing moved.

He took the chopper on a slow circuit from one end of the camp to the other to confirm there was no one left alive. Then he pulled up to climb out of the smoke-cloud and headed for the bluff, where the temple stood clear of the cloud, unscathed.

Padda landed in the stone courtyard and cut the engine. When the whine of the rotor died away, he quickly explained to Yelliah what happened and why they landed at the temple. Giving him no chance to ask questions, he got out of the cockpit and set off for the sanctum, AKM in hand, as soon as Yelliah joined him.

Near the altar, his nostrils were assailed by the unpleasant odor of blood, and he saw the blood pooled around it. A fearful suspicion began to take hold in Padda's mind.

A woman's voice knifed through the air, saying in Hindi, "Throw down your guns!"

Padda froze, seeing a woman appear from behind the sanctum, Uzi in hand. Not Yelliah. He dove for the altar, twisting in midair in an effort to get behind it.

He wasn't quick enough. A single shot rang out, and a soft-nosed bullet blew a dinner plate-sized hole through the back of his chest. He was dead before he landed face-first on the ground.

"I said drop your weapon! Now!"

Padda obeyed, placing his AKM on the floor, as the woman walked over. She was unkempt and bedraggled, with bruises on her face and blood stains on her shirt.

"Too many are dead and I am tired of killing," she said, in a voice that sounded at the point of utter exhaustion. "I will not kill you without reason, so you can choose to live or die. If you decide you want to live, I will give you fifteen minutes to run as far as you can from here and take your chances in the jungle without any weapons. Or you can stay here and die."

Padda nodded without speaking.

The woman called over her shoulder to someone, taking her eyes off him for an instant, and he seized his chance. His right hand swept under his tunic and closed on the butt of the automatic hidden in the small of his back.

It was as far as he got.

The last thing he saw was a muzzle flash, then something seemed to explode in his chest, and the world dissolved.

CHAPTER 8

A lexis laid the Uzi down and let out a long sigh.

It was finally over. Time to get out of here.

First, she fingerprinted and photographed Padda and Yelliah. Then she climbed into the cockpit of the Lynx. Its controls were very familiar to her, and the gas gauge showed enough fuel for their flight to Dibrugarh. Best of all, the Lynx was custom-fitted as a medevac helicopter to accommodate a stretcher instead of a third row of seats!

With Mohan's help, she lifted Jason into the chopper and anchored the stretcher in place. The emergency kit containing extra vials of antibiotics and bags of saline went with him. Finally, they loaded twenty five cases into the cargo hold containing every CD in Kalidas's bunker, and five cases of material from the filing cabinet, with information regarding every innocent—past and future—selected for Kalidas's gruesome ceremonies, and their procurers. It was a veritable treasure trove of information that would allow Ravi to shut down Kalidas's operations, and identify all his underlings, allies and terrorist contacts.

After Seetha and Mohan were also strapped in, she took one last look around and climbed aboard, eager to put the nightmare behind her. She lifted off and headed northwest for the peaks a mile away. Beyond those lay freedom and Jason's survival.

Only one last act of vengeance remained.

After crossing over the first row of hills, she turned the Lynx around to face the camp one last time. Holding the helicopter in a stationary hover, she nodded to Mohan, sitting in the copilot's seat, with the remote trigger for the other explosive belt in his fist. Hers! It was wired to the Semtek in the armory.

Mohan released the trigger.

She saw a blinding flash of light from the camp, and took the chopper two hundred feet straight down behind the mountain. Then she turned to head for Dibrugarh.

The sound of the explosion reached her two seconds later. The chopper rocked from secondary turbulence, but she had no difficulty maintaining control. Had the mountain not protected them from the shockwave, the chopper might well have spiraled out of control.

A series of smaller explosions followed as the other ordnance in the armory ignited. The inferno now blazing in the valley would incinerate any remaining trace of the monstrous evil that was Kalidas.

EPILOGUE

BLOOD CALLS

Jonathan Wolff had never known what it was to engage in affectionate filial by-play. Nor, as a lonely recluse for most of his life, had he witnessed it first-hand. Until now.

Jason lay in bed, face purple with indignation. "What do you mean I can't do anything strenuous for six weeks?" he exclaimed.

Alexis rolled her eyes. "Exactly that! No exertion. No lifting weights. No sex. Especially no sex. "

"It's bad enough being laid up, but at least let me get laid."

"No way, Jay-boy. Girlfriends have to wait until your scar is strong enough to bear the stress and strain of passion."

"Have a heart, Red. In six weeks I won't have any girlfriends left! How can you do this to me?"

"Quite easily!" Alexis said.

"At least let me wear my own clothes," he pleaded.

"No chance, buddy."

Jason turned to Jonathan. "Do you know the state to which this so-called loving sister of mine has reduced me? All she's given me to wear is one of her silk pajamas."

"With good reason!" she said. "Anything less feminine and you'd either be out of here or you'd ask one of your lady friends over to comfort you as soon as my back was turned."

"Well, I refuse to wear them," he said. "The day that I wear a pair of flamingo pink pajamas is the day I renounce the world."

293

"Suit yourself," she said, with smug satisfaction.

"Celibacy is the hallmark of divinity, I will have you know, and I have been living the life of a celibate ever since we left for Myanmar."

The mention of Myanmar revived Jonathan's mortal dread from seeing the Lynx landing at Dibrugarh Air Force Base, with Jason in a coma, his life hanging by the slenderest of threads, and Alexis staggering out of the cockpit, utterly spent, with her hands trembling and face haggard and bruised.

He was reduced to helpless dithering for the first time in his life, leaving Ravi to take charge, mobilizing every available medical resource. Jason was whisked into surgery right from the airfield. There followed a week of intensive care and another week convalescing in the Base Hospital, during which Alexis helped claw Jason back from the brink of death.

With Alexis refusing to talk to him or anyone else about what happened, he would never have known about their horrific ordeal, or how close they came to death, but for Mohan and Seetha.

They were a pair of terrified orphans in desperate need of someone to care for them in a world seemingly gone mad. And he was a terrified father whose own progeny didn't need him, in desperate need of someone to lean on to restore his floundering sense of purpose.

So he took on the role of a protective father figure. To keep them from going mad. And keep him from losing his mind.

It couldn't have worked out better for him. Just by helping them, he got his mojo back. So, even if they gave him nothing else, he would be indebted to them forever. What they gave him, over and above that, was priceless.

It all came about because Alexis insisted all credit for the deaths of eleven major terrorists, and the most wanted criminal in India belonged to Mohan and Seetha. The bounty totaled twenty-five million rupees, a third of it for Kalidas alone. It made Mohan and Seetha rich beyond their wildest dreams.

It also made them targets for an array of supercilious analysts, all intent on proving they should share in the bounty for helping break up Kalidas's network. Overwhelmed by their bullying, Mohan and Seetha turned to Jonathan, and he 'adopted' them.

Or was it the other way around?

He took charge as only he could, assuming the roles of protector, negotiator, and financial advisor, all rolled into one. As their protector, he became the steel wall between them and every ambitious bureaucrat with delusions about his self-inflated importance, preventing each successive inquisitor from making them relive their horrors again and again. As the master negotiator, he ran rings around the hapless government bureaucrats in charge of arranging the bounty payment, so they got the largest payout for the smallest tax penalty. And last of all, he showed them how to invest their money to get the most out of it.

What he did for them he could have done in his sleep, it was that easy for him! What he got in return was something beyond value: their trust and affection.

Without that, Jonathan could never have come to terms with the diabolical horror concocted by Kalidas. Or made it through the ordeal with his sanity intact.

With his mojo back, he commissioned a medevac jet as soon as Jason was well enough to fly back to New York, and arranged for his convalescence in an exclusive intermediate care facility. After three weeks, he was finally deemed well enough for discharge just this morning.

"Hello! Earth to Mr. Wheels. Anybody there?"

He came back to the present with a start. Alexis was kneeling next to his wheelchair, her hand on his forearm. "Sorry," he said. "I drifted away for a moment there."

"For more than a moment," she said, concern evident in her face and voice. "You looked terrible, as though someone just walked over your grave."

"I only wish it was mine! Please promise me you won't ever do anything like this again. I don't think I could survive another experience like it."

"You? Ole Jaws?" scoffed Jason. "Nah! Everyone knows you're indestructible. Hard as nails and tough as old leather."

He was flustered, so he tried to cover it up with flippancy. "Hardware and rawhide do not apply when it comes to..." He stopped himself in time. He knew she wasn't ready for that kind of open expression of affection.

"You don't have to say it, Jonathan," Alexis's voice was very soft. "The feeling is mutual."

"You still haven't promised," he grumbled.

"I can't promise something I can't control. Remember, we didn't pick the fight. The fight picked us when Kalidas came after you. We were incredibly lucky to be there to intervene."

"Speaking of that intervention," Jason said, "The bodies must have been found by now."

"Yes, thanks to the odor of putrefaction, in what the press dubbed 'The House of Mayhem and Death', aka the MAD House."

"Trust the press to be properly ghoulish about such things," said Jason. "No hint of our involvement, I assume?"

"None whatsoever. The police arrested a fundamentalist Sikh named Gill who signed the rental agreement, and he spilled the beans about Kalidas's plan execute you, Alexis, and abduct me."

"Good Lord!" Jason exclaimed. "Did they question you?"

"I was in India, so they couldn't question me until I got back. I denied I was snatched, of course. And they found no evidence of the high-tech surveillance Gill said they'd find in the penthouse. Gill told them the last he knew, they were waiting for Kalidas's go-ahead. His theory—which the police accept—is that Kalidas aborted the abduction after the drive-by failed, so they removed the devices and left, only to get into a fight over who was to blame."

"So, they bought our set-up!" Alexis exclaimed.

"Lock, stock, and barrel! And why not? Three dead men, one with a broken neck, a second with a busted skull, and the third stabbed with a traditional Sikh dagger, with no other fingerprints but theirs, and all the surveillance equipment in their Land Rover."

"Not one, but two strokes of genius!" Alexis said, grinning. "The Jason touch."

Jason shrugged. "The Alexis touch was the real stroke of genius, to wipe off our fingerprints and set it up as a brawl. All I did was stab the *kirpan* on the guy from the bathroom into the knife wound. And, when I saw the monitoring equipment in the Land Rover, I remembered that stuff was still in my car, so I put it there."

"Anything more about the drive-by?" Alexis asked.

"Some! Gill led them to a vacant office in a downtown high-rise building directly behind yours, Alexis, which had a high-tech laser listening device trained on the windows of your apartment. That's how they knew when to attack."

"And how Kalidas discovered our plans," exclaimed Jason, looking utterly disgusted. "Some expert I turned out to be! I should've known it was the obvious option for a tech savvy group, if they couldn't bug the apartment."

"It wasn't just tech savvy, Jason. It was old-fashioned, brutal intimidation. They terrified a poor Sikh janitor into giving them access to the apartment while I was away, allowing them to override all the so-called 'fail-safe' security, and monitor the penthouse from a yacht in the marina close by. Gill said it was setup by an electronic wizard named Grewal."

Jonathan was looking at Alexis, and he saw something stir in her eyes—something so dark and ugly that he recoiled. Before he could fathom its meaning, she turned to look at Jason.

Jonathan saw him smile and give her a reassuring nod. When she turned back her eyes were calm and tranquil again.

It threw Jonathan off balance. "Did I just miss something?" he asked her uncertainly.

Jason jumped in before Alexis could answer. "Of course not! I'm just amazed how far Kalidas went. What about the janitor?"

"He confessed to helping them. But I won't press charges."

"Why?" Jason and Alexis exclaimed together.

Jonathan gave them a crooked smile. "I cannot bring myself to do that. A year ago, even a month ago, maybe I might have. Now, I'm not sure I'd have the courage, if my family were threatened. I'm realizing for the first time in my selfish life that abstract notions of right and wrong aren't absolute. Who am I to question his courage?"

Alexis squeezed his hand in an affectionate gesture of understanding and stood up.

"Can you do something for me?" she asked.

"Anything you want," Jonathan replied. "You know you only have to ask."

"I know." She looked at him and smiled, her face glowing. "I want Seetha to get her chance at college and medical school in the States. She'll qualify easily. But you can bet Mohan won't, and she'll never agree to go without him. Can you do something about that?"

Jonathan was dubious. "Alexis, they won't even look at him. Pick-pocketing isn't an employable skill!"

"Do you mean to say the head of Lone Wolf can't find one little job for a young man who saved Jason's life and mine?"

He tried to reason with her. "I couldn't justify it, Alexis."

"Can't you do just this one little thing for me?" she pleaded. "Please?"

Jonathan sighed with resignation. "When you look at me like that with those marvelous green eyes, I can't think of refusing. How come your stepfather didn't spoil you rotten, giving you everything you ever asked for?"

She was startled speechless and he knew he had invoked the very thing she was resisting in their relationship. But there was a light in her eyes he had never seen before, and something magical hanging in the air. Then Jason broke the silence.

"The only reason she wasn't spoiled," he said, "was because she had a virtuous brother to keep her on the straight and narrow."

Alexis hurled a cushion at Jason. Then she turned back to Jonathan. "I'd love to be spoiled rotten again, Jonathan."

He knew it might be as close as she ever came to acknowledging in words that he was her father. These were still early days. He had to give it time. He became business-like again.

"I'll see if there's a place for an enterprising young thief in our security set-up."

"Thank you so much, but there's no rush."

Alexis gave him a hug and a kiss. Mumbling something about having work to do, he said goodbye to Jason and wheeled himself out. Alexis waved goodbye and blew a kiss to him as the elevator doors closed.

While he waited for the valet to summon his driver, Jonathan felt strangely euphoric. He noticed several people giving him amused looks, but he had no idea why.

At his office, too, several employees, his secretary included, had peculiar expressions on their faces as he went past. Only after his office door closed did he realize he was whistling.

He laughed with delight. Then he got to work.

He would call Jack Russell later to find a job for Mohan. There was going to be lots of unpleasantness with INS, but he'd given his word to Alexis. Let the legal department deal with it. Nothing was going to spoil his mood.

* * * * * * * * * * *

Jason was already fast asleep when Alexis returned from seeing Jonathan out.

It would take a few weeks for him to fully recover, but he was well on his way. Still, the deep lines of pain and fatigue in his face spoke of how close he came to dying—"Teeth-marks from the jaws of Death!" was his flippant response when a girl-friend commented on it.

Using humor to deflect emotion—that was his gift.

Witness his intervention a few minutes ago, just in time to bail her out of something she wasn't yet ready for—an outspoken commitment to Jonathan.

For now, that was best left unsaid. Like the "Thank you" Jason promised her at the temple. She knew he'd never say it, because it would bring back a memory too painful to relive.

As she turned to leave, Jason groaned, and she was at his side in an instant to comfort him. But he settled down.

It was only because she was next him that she heard him mumble something. The words were slurred, but she caught one distinct syllable.

"...sis..."

Thinking she heard the last syllable in her name, and that he was calling to her, Alexis leaned closer, her ear inches from his lips.

Bloodbath

She heard him whisper, "Thanks, sis, I owe you," and reared back as if stung, staring at him in shocked silence. The thought came that he might be playing one of his jokes, but his eyelids didn't twitch, and his breathing remained slow and deep.

He was mumbling in his sleep! His subconscious had dredged up some childhood memory involving her that was buried deep in his psyche—he hadn't called her 'sis' since their pre-teen years!

All of a sudden, she had a vision of a ten year-old boy with a tear-stained face, leaning against her as she cradled his broken arm, saying, "Thank you, sis, I owe you," as they walked home.

For as long as she could remember, she was the one who did all the leaning, always counting on him to be the big brother, twin and gender equality be damned. Except for that one time!

The realization that, for the first time since that distant childhood day, he was leaning on her released something inside. Something that had been building since that moment when she kind of, sort of accepted Jonathan as the father figure in her life.

With that, the dam burst. All the anguish, the hurt, the fear bottled up inside her since the day she returned to the slaughterhouse that had been her home broke free, and tears of joy began to flow, washing her soul clean.

She left Jason's side and went to her bedroom. In the closet there was a battered old briefcase she hadn't opened since leaving South Africa. From it, she removed a photo frame wrapped in muslin and sat down on her bed to stare at the picture of a tall, rangy man with a shock of white hair with his arm around a slim, attractive woman In front of them was a little bushman, his eyes screwed shut and chest puffed out like a cockerel.

Papa. Mama. And Gabe. The last time she saw them together.

She had buried that photograph in the briefcase for all these years, never to be seen. And with it, her memory of that fateful morning before she left on that trip into the bush with Gabe.

Until today!

"You can rest in peace now, Papa, Mama," she murmured. "I am letting go at last. I love you."

She set the frame down on her bedside table.

Only Jason would know what it meant.

He wouldn't say anything, though. It would be enough for him to know she would never again go to sleep in dread of those horrifying night terrors.